LOVE LIES BLEEDING

LOVE LIES BLEEDING

Jeremy Simpson

The Book Guild Ltd
Sussex, England

First published in Great Britain in 2004 by
The Book Guild Ltd
25 High Street
Lewes, East Sussex
BN7 2LU

Typesetting in Baskerville by
Keyboard Services, Luton, Bedfordshire

Printed in Great Britain by
CPI, Bath

A catalogue record for this book is available from
The British Library

ISBN 1 85776 826 4

Chaper One

Disaster has a habit of striking when life is at its sweetest. This meanest of life's rules made itself manifest to Luke Howard on a serene summer's day as he tried to make sense of a letter which appeared to destroy his future.

As second master and senior chaplain of Melbury College he had a room in the main building. From its large sash windows the view was beautiful. Outside, the ground sloped away to freshly cut lawns, lime trees in full bloom and manicured cricket pitches. On one of these the first eleven were playing a two-day match against Malvern, and winning. He could hear clearly the satisfactory distant sound of bat striking ball. Beyond the cricket fields the city of Melbury shimmered in an early summer heatwave.

Pevsner, in his Wessex volume, had rated the medieval cathedral of St Michael and All Angels higher than its nearest neighbours, Salisbury and Wells. He had also devoted two pages to the buildings of Melbury College, extolling its fifteenth-century inner courtyard, containing exquisite cloisters out of which access was made on one side to the house for the forty Royal Scholars, originally funded by the founder of the school, Henry VII. On the opposite side of the courtyard stretched the chapel, completed in the reign of Henry VIII. It was fan-vaulted and bore many similarities to Bath Abbey, save that it had no tower.

Pevsner was less flattering about the Victorian buildings, which housed most of the classrooms and administration offices and in which Luke had his second master's room adjoining that of the headmaster. Fortunately, Pevsner did not live to see the new science block, theatre, gymnasium and swimming pool, all built in the Eighties. These had been funded by an old boy who had made a fortune out of cut-price supermarkets and

1

insisted on his donation being spent on buildings bearing a close resemblance to his own Bavarian-style grocer's shops.

'Needs must, the Devil drives,' was the comment of the headmaster, Canon John Frobisher, when it became a question of no money at all if the donor's wishes were not followed.

However, all Luke could see from his window were the school's original buildings and its setting. As he gazed at it he was aware of a gentle breeze wafting into his room the mingled perfume of cut grass and lime blossom. It only heightened his sense of impending loss. He stood remembering how at the beginning of term everything in his life had been wonderful.

The term had begun with the headmaster's party. It followed their traditional masters' meeting at which the headmaster, Canon John Frobisher, made the same speech to his staff that he had made at the beginning of thirty preceding terms. He drew attention to the college's ancient foundation by Henry VII.

Canon Frobisher then dwelt on the significance of their founder, insisting that not only academic excellence be a mark of their school, but also development of the boys' characters and indeed their spiritual awareness was to be a mark of Michaeleans, as members of the college were called.

As the headmaster elaborated on this theme with increasing enthusiasm, old members of staff could be seen studying their new timetables or looking out of the window. Unfortunately, on this occasion Mr figgis, the head of biology, had belched, trying to turn the noise into a cough and burying his face in a large handkerchief. The headmaster had glared at him and lost the thread of his speech and brought to an abrupt and embarrassed end his customary reminder that they must preserve the Anglo-Catholic traditions in such disturbed ecclesiastical times; troubled by Evangelical growth inside the Anglican church and Roman triumphalism outside.

At the head's cocktail party the staff were given further encouragement to tackle the tasks of the coming term and mingle with members of the college council. At that party the head had led Luke to talk to the provost, General Sir James Phillipson. After exchanging polite conversation about minor school matters, the head said the provost had requested that he should have a word with him in private.

2

The head had led the way from the Great Hall in the Scholars' House, where the party was always held, to his room on the first floor of the Victorian buildings. They had sat down around a large desk in the middle of the room. The Tompion bracket clock chimed seven o'clock, and when it finished the provost smiled and looked at the head.

'Shall I start?' Without waiting for an answer he had turned to Luke. 'I hope this will be good news for you.' He had paused.

Luke tried to look relaxed but his heart lifted. Was Canon Frobisher going to retire early? Two years before, when he had been made second head, the provost had told him that the college council regarded him as a man with headmaster qualities, and had asked him to wait for Canon Frobisher to retire five years later. Luke had replied to the provost's opening question.

'I shall try and see it as good whatever it is.' As soon as he had spoken he realised he must have sounded unctuous.

'Quite so,' the provost cut him short. 'Canon Frobisher tells me your churchmanship is sound – not great myself in all details of Anglo-Catholicism, but I'm one by instinct. When I smell incense I know there's worship, when I small cordite I know there's a battle and when I smell scent I know there's a woman around – at least, that was until pansies came out in clouds of perfume! Anyway, we have an important task for you. Your senior chaplain duties have been carried out in exemplary fashion. By the way, wonderful your getting the college's Michaelmas Founder's Day Mass on BBC TV – jolly good PR. With your sound theological ideas we think you're the man to mastermind the college's quincentenary celebrations next year. These, as you know, are planned to culminate in a visit from the Queen in December for our Founder's Day. There will be a service of thanksgiving in the cathedral. And to mark this occasion it has been suggested we get the journal of our old boy, first Anglican Bishop of Melbury, edited and published in a finely printed run of one thousand copies, with an extra-finely bound copy to be presented to Her Majesty. With your additional background as head of the history department, you are the obvious choice to edit the journal, and with your proven organisational abilities, the man to be in charge of the celebrations; though, of course, within the

3

guidelines laid down by the college council. What do you say? You'll have a sabbatical from your teaching, though we do expect you to continue your duties as second master and senior chaplain.'

Luke realised these were interesting tasks and, though disappointed to learn that Canon Frobisher was not retiring early, he saw acceptance as strengthening his position for the future.

'I'm very flattered to be asked. Of course, I hope I'll live up to your expectations.'

This meeting was very much in his mind as he read the letter from the provost. It had taken place only five weeks earlier and made the contents of the letter seem like outrageous treachery to Luke. His hand shook as he read it for the third time.

Dear Senior Chaplain, I am writing to inform you before any other of our staff that, sadly, Canon Frobisher is retiring early to become master of our sister college, Michaelhouse, Cambridge. Naturally we are proud that he is receiving this academic accolade, but it has upset our plans for his succession which we expected would occur in three years' time. I realise you had been given expectations in this matter, but because of the current economic pressures on the college, the council has decided to appoint a man maturer in age and with business experience. I am pleased to tell you that the recently retired head of Sedgebury Business School has agreed to be our new headmaster for a period of ten years. I should like to say at the end of that time span you will only be forty-nine, so the council hope you will continue as second master and senior chaplain. We shall need you to help the new head settle in; he has accepted your sabbatical to organise our quincentenary celebrations. You have our support. Good luck. Yours sincerely, General James Phillipson.

As Luke stood reading the letter he saw the curtains billow briefly in a gentle breeze that wafted into the room with the mingled scents of the well-ordered grounds outside. He sighed and moved back into his room to sit behind his desk. He was not versed in employment law, but he saw the letter as notice to quit in a year's time, and the tasks given him for the

4

quincentenary a means of justifying a year's salary. The provost and council knew he was ambitious and would probably leave, but now he was trapped for a year. He buried his face in his hands and fumed with rage and frustration. He recalled how he had endured the bumbling administration of the eccentric Canon Frobisher, while privately planning how he would revitalise the college when the time came. How he had revelled in his vocation as chaplain, as head of history; and with his Cambridge blue cricket background he had successfully coached the first eleven to a season of victories. Now he lifted his head, his hands damp with tears. He looked towards the windows and decided he would make them regret their decision and their trickery in offering him the quincentenary tasks when they must have known of Canon Frobisher's imminent retirement. He would perform superbly and seek a headmastership elsewhere at the end of the celebrations, but heaven help the provost and council if they had made a bad appointment. He would make sure the world would know.

Luke's reverie was interrupted by a knock on his door. Without waiting for an answer, Mr Tom Parker, the school clockmaker, entered. Each Friday Mr Parker, occupying the post of horologist extraordinary to the school, visited to wind and adjust each clock. He fussed over them like a surgeon determined to find a reason for a major operation. He carried a large wooden box containing every conceivable item that might bring instant healing to his charges, a box he always put on Luke's desk, regardless of any papers that might be trapped underneath.

'Excuse me, Father. Don't let me disturb you.' Like the opening phrase of every monastic hour, Parker had greeted him thus every Friday for the last five years. Luke replied now, as he always did.

'Please carry on, Tom. No problem.' He continued to look out of the window; he did not wish to talk.

Parker gazed sympathetically at the broad back and the curly, brown-haired head facing resolutely away from him. He had grown fond of the second master over the years, liking his quiet sense of humour and kindness, reflected in a face lined in keeping with these characteristics and made softer still by smiling brown eyes. Parker concluded to himself that he was a generous-minded man of genuine spirituality. To break the silence the horologist started tut-tutting. He was examining a Georgian bracket clock on the mantelpiece.

'Dear me, seven and a half minutes slow!' Parker looked to see if Luke would turn round and start a conversation. He turned back to the clock, humming constantly to himself as he lifted a flywheel with a pair of tweezers. 'Lovely make. Perigal of Coventry Street. Late George III. Worth £4–£5,000 at least. The school should give it to you.' He tutted again. 'Pity about the chain-fusee movement – its range escarpment needs replacing. I should be able to fix it for about £250. Anyway, Father, I think you will be well out of it – some brigadier barging in as the new head. I gather the council are at least giving you a year off to edit the famous Fr de Witte manuscript. I don't know much about him,' Parker added, 'except that he's considered one of the college's most illustrious old boys, becoming first Anglican bishop.'

Luke was astonished. He tried to speak calmly. 'How the hell do you know all this? I've only learnt about my changed future from a letter delivered by hand half an hour ago. I realise, Tom, your movements about this college make you a repository of all news and gossip – in fact you positively hoover it up as you go about your tasks – but this is a disgrace!'

Parker hung his head but found it hard to hide a satisfied smile. 'I was in the council parlour – you know it has a door into the provost's room – and I just couldn't help hearing General Phillipson and Canon Frobisher. The canon was saying the new head, a Brigadier Henshaw, had been evasive about his churchmanship and theology, and the provost shouted back, "It's not theology we need but solvency!"'

Luke's eyes widened. 'My giddy aunt, you even know the name of the next head. A brigadier. Heavens, what next? Tom, you shouldn't listen at doors, but thanks for the unwelcome news.'

Parker looked sulky. 'I couldn't help hearing – wouldn't dream of listening at doors...' At this Luke started laughing, at which Parker smiled sheepishly.

Luke stood up. Somehow, he felt, facing the facts of his new life would direct him as to how to proceed. first he would watch the cricket match. He looked at Parker.

'Now, how long will you be? I have to go and encourage our cricketers and their parents.'

'Not long now, Father. Can you pass that little oil can? By the way, Mr Tompkins, the librarian, says that towards the end of the de Witte diary there are some pages of different parchment paper or priapus.'

Luke was temporarily stumped for an answer to this phallic reference. 'It's papyrus, not priapus.'

'Whatever! It seems to be, according to Mr Tompkins, a malediction on anyone trying to read the diary. I hope you're not superstitious, Father?'

'Of course not. I'm a Christian.'

Parker grinned. 'I know that, Father. Well, I'm finished now. I hope you return to the school after your sabbatical – you'll be missed. Will you give me your blessing?'

Luke couldn't help laughing. 'You're a gossiping old rogue, Tom Parker.'

'Maybe, Father, but I shall ask you to join me for a drink when you're here. I'm always at the Black Swan on Fridays from about eight o'clock. If you come, then I can keep you up to date with what's happening in the school.'

Somewhat to Luke's surprise, Parker bowed his head. He had no option but to give him a blessing and was touched to see the man sniffing into his handkerchief as he left the room.

Luke picked up his biretta and, garbed in a new cassock, decided he would go to his cricketing tasks, proclaiming his Anglo-Catholic credentials. He would find the headmaster and make an appointment to learn at first hand about his successor.

As he was about to leave his room he paused, turned round and went into a small dressing room leading to a lavatory and shower. He took off his biretta and cassock, put on white trousers and his faded Cambridge cricket blue blazer. Perhaps, he thought, his fervent proclamation of his High Church character had worked against him and had been too extreme for the council to accept him as the next head. So be it if he had been a martyr to his faith, but he would go to the match as a layman in his old Cambridge blue blazer.

He found the head sitting in a deck chair watching the cricket. He was dressed in a frayed beige jacket and wearing a battered straw hat around which a band proclaimed, to those that knew, that he had been at Michaelhouse, Cambridge. A red, silk handkerchief was nearly falling out of the breast pocket of his jacket.

'Ah, Howard, glad to see you here looking like a cricketer – I used to think your priestly garb frightened some of the parents.'

Luke tried to smile. 'Heavens, they knew they were sending their offspring to a proper High Church School. I've never minded witnessing to that. However, having received news of your early retirement in an unexpected letter from the provost and by word of the school clockmaker, I thought I'd slip into something light-hearted to celebrate. Can you find time to enlighten me further – say, tomorrow?'

Frobisher had always felt uncomfortable with Luke, and the fact that Luke had not succeeded him gave him considerable satisfaction. 'Of course, dear boy, ten tomorrow morning.' He turned away to the cricket. 'Well played that man,' he said, thus dismissing Luke.

When they met next morning, Canon Frobisher acted as if the prize of succeeding him had never been thought of as far as Luke was concerned, and was so insensitive to Luke's destroyed hopes as to say he thought the council had been right to find an administrator to succeed him as headmaster, adding that 'fresh blood from outside the college would be a good thing'.

As an academic, Canon Frobisher had been more sensitive about the editing of the journal, and most of that meeting had been taken up with discussing it. Luke told him he had done classics up until the time he had left school to read history at Cambridge, so was fairly confident he could cope with translating the Latin, but otherwise he knew his best friend on the staff, head of the classics VIth, Alastair Galbraith, would help him in this area.

The canon told Luke all he knew about the manuscript and what was known about Fr de Witte. The manuscript itself was bound in grey calfskin and consisted of dated sheets of paper of different sizes and textures. It was known that some of these papers had remained in the hands of the famous old Catholic family Boscannon, at whose manor house in Cornwall de Witte had acted as secret recusant chaplain before becoming an Anglican. As he began telling Luke this, he had stood up

8

and started pacing slowly up and down behind his large partners'
desk. He did not look at Luke as he spoke.

'I think our sympathies are the same. I'm more High Anglican
in the tradition of Jeremy Taylor and Nicholas Ferrer than
you, whereas you are Anglo-Catholic in all its Walsingham
manifestations. But we both are enthusiastic in our vision that
the Anglican Church is the purest form of Catholicism – true
to the traditions of the early councils of the Church and
founded on scripture and the Seven Sacraments.' Luke nodded.
'May I go on to say that we find the Italian mission intrusive,
though obviously some of its manifestations, as in its great
Benedictine schools, we find attractive – positively Anglican in
some respects. However, in spite of ecumenical outpourings,
shared services, pilgrimages and social works, our generation
is secretly at war to preserve our inheritance. Luke, we are
under attack. "Christian, dost thou see them on the holy
ground, how the troops of Midian prowl and prowl around."
You remember that Greek hymn, of course, one of John Mason
Neale's finest translations. Luke, we've got to fight back. Day
after day we are told of large numbers of High Anglicans
wanting to move to Rome because of the women priests issue,
and then we have high-profile conversions such as the ex-Bishop
of London and the Duchess of Kent. Yes, yes, I know we both
are horrified at the developments in the Church of England –
ghastly butch women shouting and demonstrating, and it's
unsettling us, and the increasing numbers of happy clappy
evangelists – but at the end of the day we have decided to be
loyal to our vision of the C of E being the true Catholic
Church for the English, and indeed maybe for the whole world.
The college council want this journal as not only the evidence
of the heroic achievements of an old boy, but also as a witness
to the life of a missionary Catholic priest "seeing the light" in
the sixteenth century and becoming an Anglican.' Here the
Canon paused in his pacing and sat down again. He put his
elbows on his desk and leant forward, resting his chin in his
hands. 'The trouble is, we don't know what the journal's message
is. It could be a Pandora's box of goodies for our cause, with
revelations of Roman ambitions to take over England via the
Spanish Armada and finally de Witte's growing realisation of
the purity of the Anglican vision. Or else it could be for us a

9

can of worms; a story of psychological pressure on a weak man to save his skin by recanting his faith; the story of a man ambitious to advance in the world...' The canon sighed. 'We just don't know, and you have the difficult prospect of working hard to produce a work of history we may not want to use. For that reason the council intend to pay you for this work plus generous expenses, but right of any publication, any statements or indeed the slightest hint contrary to our wishes, are to be controlled by contract.'

Luke raised his eyebrows in surprise. 'Hardly an encouragement for a work of free historical research.'

The canon shook his head. 'It's college property. We have taken legal opinion at the highest level and a contract is being prepared.'

'Supposing I find the Boscannon papers contain bad news for us, is that controlled as well?'

The canon shook his head. 'We are relying on your loyalty, but I have to tell you if you follow our instructions we shall pay you, publication or not. The sum suggested, plus a small royalty on copies sold, is £20,000.'

At that moment Luke realised he disliked his old headmaster. He had always repressed any such feelings, but the journal seemed an exciting piece of historical research and he would publish whatever the financial consequences if the Boscannon papers revealed unpleasant news for the school.

Chapter Two

Three weeks later, Luke's nightmare of a usurping new headmaster turning out to be unpleasant, as well as destroying his future, became a reality. Another party in the Great Hall of the Scholars' House was arranged to introduce him to the staff. Luke heard him before seeing him. There was a gust of laughter at a feeble joke told by the provost. Henshaw had risen in the world by flattering those who could help him.

Henshaw was wearing a brown suit and standing with his back towards Luke. He was a tall man, six feet one inch, so his head was above most of those around him. Instinctively Luke felt an unease at the sight of him that was in no way connected to his own frustrated ambition. There was a threatening appearance in the man's thick neck, which seemed almost a continuation of the back of the head. The head itself was mostly bald, except at the back and sides, and the ginger hair had been closely cropped in an exaggerated army manner more suitable for a military policeman than a retired officer.

Canon Frobisher spotted Luke and came over to him. 'Come and meet my successor before the speeches,' he said, leading him through the crush of people.

Luke heard the introductions but it seemed to him the canon was describing two waxworks with labels, rather than two human beings who instinctively knew they were bound to be incompatible.

'Brigadier Henshaw, may I introduce Fr Luke Howard. You may recall the details from the CVs I gave you of the staff. He's our key man – if I may remind you – second master and senior chaplain. Luke, Arthur Henshaw.'

The response was an exaggerated clicking of the heels that reminded Luke of an SS general in a bad film, followed by 'Pleased to meet ye, Padre', spoken like a musical-comedy squire. He spoke in an affected, clipped, military manner unless, as Luke would discover, he became excited, when he lapsed into his native Yorkshire accent.

Luke put out his right hand to be shaken, but it was not accepted. Brigadier Henshaw was regarding, in an over-interested manner, Luke's cassock with its small cape addition.

'Just come from or going to a Church parade, are you, Padre? Does the school have them at this time?'

'No, it's just my uniform, like an army officer's.'

Brigadier Henshaw shook his head as if not believing what he was hearing and lapsed into his North Country mode.

'We'll have plenty of time to discuss these and other matters when I arrive after half-term. Now, canon, I haven't met General Phillipson's wife. Is she here? I'd like my Angela to make her acquaintance.' He took the canon's elbow as he was led towards his prey: he didn't give Luke another word or look.

Luke took another glass of red wine from a passing waiter. He was deeply depressed. His friend Alastair Galbraith, head of the classics department, joined him.

'You look a bit shaken. I saw you talking to our new Caesar. What's your first impression?'

Luke looked at him over the rim of his glass as he answered, 'Enter the Demon King.'

Brigadier Henshaw moved into the headmaster's house at half-term. A letter was received from the new head by all the staff asking them to be available during the last days of the half-term, so that they could report for meetings as requested. Soon afterwards, it was learnt that the old headmaster's secretary, Margery Brown, was to be replaced by the Brigadier's wife, and that her flat in the school would be needed by an ex-Sergeant Major Carter who was to be the Brigadier's chauffeur as well as taking over the running of the school cadet armoury. Margery Brown had also acted as secretary for Luke. He realised she could continue to help him if she would become his father's housekeeper.

His father lived in the calm of the cathedral close at Melbury, where he had been a canon for twenty years. He lived contentedly in semi-retirement, but, being recently widowed and lacking in domestic skills, was looking for a housekeeper. Luke had contacted Margery Brown and asked if helping his father would appeal to her. It did. She knew and liked the old man. His father was equally enthusiastic and so at least something good came out of the sudden destruction of the old secretary's career.

Luke had just returned from seeing his father and was cooking some baked beans for his supper when the telephone rang. It was Sergeant Major Carter.

'Brigadier Henshaw would like you on parade at 1100 tomorrow in his office. Please be on time, Sah.'

Before Luke could answer, the phone went dead.

The following day Luke put on his best cassock and his biretta. He reckoned the strongest card he could play was in his role as senior chaplain, an appointment made by the council and independent of the headmaster, who was responsible only for housemasters. When he reached the headmaster's study, he noticed the sergeant major standing to attention outside the door in full uniform. Luke went into his own room and sat at his desk for a moment and began to say the angelus quietly. The cathedral clock chimed eleven, followed by the college clock in the tower in the quadrangle.

Behind Luke's desk were two doors. One led to the headmaster's study, the other into a small cloakroom. Backing on to this cloakroom, separated by a thin partition, were similar facilities for the headmaster. Luke had heard the flush being pulled and realised Brigadier Henshaw would be leaving his cloakroom for his desk. Canon Frobisher had suffered from a weak stomach, and when Luke was first appointed he was requested not to use this cloakroom when the canon needed his. The canon explained that he would contact him on his telephone extension by saying he was 'going to Jericho' or just 'Jericho'. This explanation was given with much embarrassment and a mumbled 'You know – Jericho – walls blown down by trumpets!'

The first time this message came through the phone, Luke thought the canon had said 'Cheerio', and thinking he was leaving replied, 'Cheerio'. He knew the canon was going to practise his cricket in the nets that afternoon. The canon had replied with a strangled splutter, 'I'm about to use my cloakroom, please remember Jericho.'

Luke sighed. 'Happy days,' he muttered as he remembered this and, smilingly, went through the door into the headmaster's study, giving it a brief knock as he opened it.

Brigadier Henshaw had just sat down behind his desk and was studying some damp spots on his underpants as he was about to do up his flies. He had to pull his chair rapidly forward to hide this manoeuvre as Luke came into the room. His battle line had been penetrated from an unexpected direction. Sergeant Major Carter was to delay entry and keep everyone waiting when they came for interviews in the study. Carter would announce their arrival and then keep them waiting. They had rehearsed this manoeuvre, as practised by Hitler during his chancellery days, and it was agreed that the sergeant major would then open the door after a few minutes, bark out the name of whoever was waiting outside, click his heels and salute the brigadier, who would give him a royal wave of dismissal while indicating a chair or leaving the visitor to stand, depending on what bullying tactic he had decided to adopt.

Luke's unexpected arrival from the side destroyed his initial plan of confrontation. Luke had seen the undone flies and mentally said to himself, 'fifteen-love', and without awaiting the invitation sat on the chair opposite the brigadier and placed his biretta on the right-hand side of the desk.

For a moment the brigadier fumbled unsuccessfully with his flies, at the same time eyeing the biretta with an expression that would have done credit to Dracula seeing a crucifix held before him by an intended victim.

'Good morning,' Luke said pleasantly.

The brigadier was breathing heavily, trying to control his anger. He had a swagger stick on the desk in front of him and picked it up and began tapping it on his chair.

'I think we had better get some simple drill matters clear if you and I are going to work for this one term together before your sabbatical, let alone on your possible return.' He put heavy emphasis on the word 'possible'. 'In your chapel you no doubt look at home in your God-botherer's garb, but, Padre, our work together as head and second master is strictly secular, so in future keep your papist dressing-up box out of my way.' He looked again at the biretta and his face began to go red again from the neck up. His face was fat and broad like the

14

back of his neck and Luke noticed with distaste a scar on the left side of his lower lip, which remained white and was twitching.

Luke quietly said, 'I don't think your comments are acceptable. This is an ancient school of well-acknowledged Anglo-Catholic sympathies. The chaplains here have dressed as priests since the nineteenth century.'

'Don't interrupt!' The brigadier hit the desk with his swagger stick so hard that the biretta jumped an inch.

Luke raised his eyebrows.

'Just realise, I'm a headmaster of a different cut from your benign old Canon Frobisher. I have been appointed to make the school a success, a financial success. The council have given me carte blanche and anyone who does not share my battle plan will have to go – pronto. So your choice is plain.' Luke said nothing. 'Now, I take your silence as a mute acceptance of my authority, so I'll outline the main objectives.

'At present the school numbers just over five hundred and fifty boys, but we need another one hundred and fifty. Just think, an extra £14,000 a year times one hundred and fifty and the school, instead of breaking even, will increase its turnover by £2,100,000 – make a corking good profit at the end of it.'

Luke looked straight at him. 'How on earth do you intend to do this? It would be a squeeze in all our ten houses to fit an extra five in each. How will you accommodate another hundred and fifty?'

Brigadier Henshaw forgot his open flies and pushed back his chair. 'By intelligent planning and by some entrepreneurial skills. Such skills I find sadly lacking amongst academics.' He laughed unpleasantly, then leant forward, pointing his swagger stick at Luke. 'Plan of battle one. Always find accommodation and food for your army. No doubt you're unaware that the Edward the Confessor Hotel has been losing money since the recession and is for sale. The council has agreed we shall buy it. Accommodation there is fifty bedrooms. I intend to make it into a sixth-form house for those sitting for university places. Plan of battle two. The girls' school on the other side of the town, Lady Edwina's, is in trouble. It once had a hundred girls and now has only sixty-five. We are going to take the girls' school over and build up our numbers of both boys and girls. Most public schools have gone coed ... Rugby, Marlborough, Oundle, Malvern, the list is endless.'

'Every boarding school is fighting for more numbers,' replied Luke. 'How are you going to increase the attraction of Melbury?'

'Padre, you're like all you lot! Lost the virtue of hope, so concerned with your pathetic politics. I have contacts in Eastern Europe, in fact Moscow. My time as head of Sedgebury Management School gave me these. I reckon I shall find forty from there in the next year, which reminds me, it might help if we could offer the facility of an Orthodox chaplain. Know any hereabouts? Also I intend to canvass for day boys – again against your stupid traditions – just because there are a few in the town that can afford it. I'll lay on transport in a twenty-mile radius. Sergeant Major Carter will be in charge – he was in Military Transport during some of his career.

'finally, Padre, we've got to widen the appeal of the school – make it broader in its facilities. The council have agreed to a new business studies department for the less academic. Now, this is where you and your assistant chaplain have got to sharpen up your act. We need a broad-church appeal, so that Methodists, Baptists, etc. will be glad to send their kids here. Get together and give your plan in a report. I want it on my desk at the end of the first week of term. I've already sounded out Mr Jones, the excellent vicar of Emmanuel church on the other side of the town. Good fellow – ex-army padre. Very pally with the Baptists and Methodists and says he can help in a more appealing Sunday service to attract a wider audience.'

Luke was horrified. 'Really that would be totally unacceptable. The man is an out-and-out Protestant.'

The brigadier raised his eyebrows and sneeringly said, 'I believe the thirty-nine articles in the *Book of Common Prayer* make it plain that the Church of England is Protestant, and I seem to remember the Coronation Oath confirms that that's the royal view as well.'

For a moment Luke was stumped, then after a brief hesitation he said, 'The Oxford Movement rediscovered the Anglican Church's Catholic credentials and the school has fostered an Anglo-Catholic spirituality as an established tradition. Having a happy-clappy singalong on a Sunday morning is not in their tradition. I know the provost and council would not consider it. Anyway, Mr Jones would not be welcome here. You may not have met our college episcopal visitor, the retired archbishop from Africa, Dr Humphries. He would not be amused to hear that Mr Jones had set foot in our chapel. Every year the archbishop leads the college pilgrimage to Our Lady's shrine at Walsingham. Last year Mr Jones shouted abuse at him in company with a party of troublemakers from the Protestant Truth Society, and I mean abuse – filthy words. A lot of our boys were very upset by it.'

Henshaw's sneer became more pronounced. 'I should have thought being upset by a few words was not exactly the stuff of martyrs. I always understood that Catholics exalted in a bit of martyrdom. Anyway, I've told the padre from the Emmanuel church to give you a bell to discuss my proposal.'

The Tompion clock chimed the news that half an hour had passed. Brigadier Henshaw looked pointedly at his watch.

'The bursar's due now, thank you, Padre.' He stood up and pointed towards the door.

Luke got up slowly, and with difficulty avoided staring at Henshaw's trousers. 'I think I shall need to speak to the provost and some members of the council first to clarify the position.'

'My God, Padre, don't try tricks like that on me. Get out.' He banged the desk again, narrowly missing Luke's biretta.

Luke picked up the hat and said, 'Thank you, headmaster, a most revealing encounter,' and, as he opened the door, he turned. 'By the way, your flies are undone.'

The sergeant major had been wondering what had happened to the eleven o'clock visitor and jumped to attention, his face a picture of astonishment at Luke's unexpected exit from the headmaster's room.

'Don't bother to salute,' said Luke as he walked away. He resisted looking back.

As soon as Luke got back to his house he telephoned Fr Peter, the junior chaplain, and told him of his meeting.

Any small deviation from normal routine would throw the junior chaplain into a state of nervous excitement. The news from Luke left him speechless for a full minute until finally, like a drowning man breaching the waves for the last time, he gasped, 'Oh, dear me, save us! I shall start a novena to Our Lady of Walsingham and King Charles the Martyr at once.'

Luke knew the boys regarded Fr Peter as an old woman, and such outbursts were usual at times of stress.

'God helps those who help themselves. I suggest that first we contact Archbishop Humphries and get a meeting with the provost and those members of the council on the chapel committee – this is war, Peter – we need guns as well as prayers.'

'Yes, yes, Father, quite agree. Do let me know any developments.' As soon as he put the phone down, he went down on his knees in front of a particularly garish old-master depiction of the martyrdom of a young and virile St Sebastian and sighed. 'St Sebastian, pray for us that this cup may be taken from us.'

In fact his cup had been quickly filled with bitter gall. Next day Fr Peter had come to him in tears. He had had a similar meeting with the head. first he had been questioned as to why he was not married and then laughed at when he said he was a member of the Anglican Guild of Priests, the Confraternity of Gethsemane, who took yearly vows to remain celibate. The head had remarked to him that he had a good idea of the sort of fraternity they got up to, 'no doubt in lace surplices and birettas', and that he would keep a close eye on him. He didn't want to see any fraternal hanky-panky with any of the boys and expected Fr Peter to pass on any information he received in his role as parson.

'Parson, I ask you!' Fr Peter had sobbed.

He was expected to pass directly to the headmaster any moral misdemeanours he heard of – drugs, girls or, most serious of all, fraternal hanky-panky.

Luke's news was received in a more mature manner by the college's episcopal visitor, Archbishop Humphries, a recently retired African Anglican archbishop. He had spent a lifetime fighting ecclesiastical politics and had succeeded in imposing on an African diocese the stamp of extreme Anglo-Catholic customs during his years there. It was said that more incense was burnt there than in the rest of Christendom. Not only was he the college's bishop, visiting them for confirmations and holy days, but also chairman of the chapel committee. Neither the local bishop nor head had authority over the chapel, thanks to rules laid down by its founder. He had regarded the arrival of Brigadier Henshaw as a tiresome disturbance that appeal to higher authority would soon quell. He promised to contact the provost and arrange a meeting as soon as possible. He advised Luke just to listen to 'that *Black Protestant* Jones, as the Irish would call him', and bring his suggestions to the meeting so that they knew what they were fighting.

An hour later, the vicar of Emmanuel rang Luke. 'Hallo, boyo, how are things with you?' The man's cheery Welshness always grated on Luke, adding dislike of the man as well as his churchmanship. He seemed to emphasise his origins when trying to win a point. Luke had heard him in ordinary conversation speaking in a less sing-song manner.

Luke gave a non-committal reply. 'fine, thank you, Father.'

The Welshman chortled back, 'Come on, Mr Howard, you know our Lord's command – call no one Father.'

'Quite so, Father, but that was made in a quite different context. Anyway, I don't recall you reacting adversely to being called "Padre" by our new headmaster – it means the same.'

'Come, come, Mr Howard, let's not fall out over titles. It's about your new head I'm calling. He came to our beginning of term service for Lady Edwina's School and was most enthusiastic, and since then he has asked me to liaise with you to introduce the same service instead of the Communion you have at ten o'clock every Sunday...'

Luke interrupted, 'You mean our High Mass – this is the central point of our week's worship. I don't think our college council will countenance any change to that.'

Mr Jones laughed lightly. 'Your brigadier is very broad-minded. He suggested, look you, a simple said Communion at eight o'clock for those who want it, but the highlight of the week will definitely be our new service. It's a mixture of old and new. We start with the opening prayer of matins, but then, boyo, we let the Spirit move us. Your new head was very taken with our prayer dancing at the end – the girls at St Edwina's do it so beautifully. You must come this Sunday. We are also projecting pictures onto a screen set on the altar table, and very inspiring it is I tell you, Mr Howard, the Spirit is manifesting at Emmanuel.' The vicar's voice rose an octave and his Welsh lilt became more pronounced.

19

Luke interrupted this flow. 'Did you say dancing in your church? I hope you don't expect our boys to start bebopping around in our centuries-old chapel!'

Mr Jones sounded peeved. 'Look, Mr Howard, most of our churches are just sepulchres because no one in the modern world understands a word they hear inside them. We have to awaken their souls with worship they can identify with the modern world.'

Luke laughed. 'Dancing would just dissolve our boys into embarrassment or hysteria. They're quite at home with the mysteries of the Mass, which touches their sense of awe and wonder. Dancing, that's really absurd, and we're having no film screens on our altars – a Cross and six candles are all we require.'

'Don't patronise me,' shouted back Mr Jones. 'Anyway, I remember reading even the idolatrous Roman Church has choirboys dancing in front of the High Altar in Seville Cathedral on Corpus Christi – with castanets, too.'

Luke sighed. 'Not comparable – that's dignified and centuries old.'

'Are you then refusing to discuss my service of worship, which your headmaster has requested?'

'I certainly would rather not, though I believe in following orders when reasonable. I don't think these are, but until I see your order of service I cannot judge properly. Perhaps you could pop a copy in the post and our chapel council will discuss it and incorporate our comments on it in our report to our new headmaster. Thank you, Mr Jones.' Luke put the phone down.

Luke felt in need of a mental distraction from these disturbing events and decided it would be a good idea to see in detail the diary of Fr de Witte. Until now, he had only seen a page displayed in a glass case in the library describing de Witte as the first Bishop of Melbury. He rang the librarian, who said he would be delighted to show it to him and that as he was in the library that afternoon preparing for the new term, any time would suit him.

The librarian, Mr Tompkins, was a small man with a mop of untidy white hair and clear blue eyes. He taught English as well as administering the library. He always moved as if late for an appointment: everything was performed in a great hurry, and he would scurry from bookshelf to bookshelf clasping great numbers of books before popping them into their proper slots. Because of his white hair and air of animated distraction, he was nicknamed the 'White Rabbit'.

However, it was with slow and deliberate care that Mr Tompkins took off the velvet covering over the glass case and revealed the diary underneath. This was done with such reverence that Luke was reminded of a devoted priest removing the cover from the chalice during Mass. Mr Tompkins selected a key from a ring of keys attached to a fob slotted through a buttonhole in a yellow waistcoat that he wore through all seasons of the year under a woolly tweed jacket. It was rumoured that during the heatwave in 1976 he had taken this jacket off, but never the waistcoat.

He opened the case, giving a small sigh as he lifted the single page and, opening the grey calfskin binder, inserted it towards the end in the order of its date. He lifted out the diary and carried it like a delicate piece of china to a small oak table between some of the bookshelves and said, 'There, now, this, we believe, is de Witte's own table. I'll leave you to study the papers undisturbed. What do you know of our illustrious old boy?'

'Very little, I fear,' replied Luke modestly. 'I know he came from the English College in Rome in 1576. His father was Dutch, hence the name, and his mother a devoted Lancashire woman, where of course Roman Catholics were still strong in Elizabethan times. I believe that after a short time in London, where he met some leading Jesuit priests, he spent time in East Anglia; and after that he was dispatched to Cornwall, where he carried out Catholic missionary activities while pretending to be tutor to children of a leading recusancy family there.'

'Correct, well done!' interjected Mr Tompkins. 'The family were called Boscannon and lived in Boscannon Manor on the Helford. Lovely place – I've been there, and it's still in the family. A retired rear admiral of the Boscannon family is there now – a paraplegic, I'm afraid. I understand his injuries stem from being hit by a rogue boom while out sailing. I went there soon after coming to the college some twenty years ago. The rear admiral's father was living there then and I'm afraid going gaga. I went to ask if the college could have the missing part of the diary they have there but got sent away with a flea in my ear. That part dealt with de Witte's time at Boscannon. As far as my knowledge of the diary goes, it seems to me a vitally important part. Here, let me show you.'

Mr Tompkins began to turn the separate dated sheets with great care. He stopped and removed three pieces of parchment somewhat different from those preceding sheets of discoloured paper.

'Your Latin is no doubt better than mine, but the first four pages seem to tell of his duties at the manor, as well as offering some trenchant comments on the bad-tempered character of the Boscannon squire, who was lord of the manor at the time. Then' – Mr Tompkins' voice rose an octave in his enthusiasm – 'just look at this last piece of parchment.' He passed it to Luke, who saw a piece of parchment with only about fifty words on it. Some of them were underlined in red, which had faded to a light brown. The word *Maledictio* began every line. 'Don't you see what this is.' Mr Tompkins took the parchment from him and laid it on the table.

'Well it looks like a warning or a curse of some sort,' said Luke. 'I can't quite make out the letters and my Latin is too rusty – I shall need a good Latin dictionary and the help of my friend Alastair, head of classics.'

'A warning, indeed it is. It's a malediction, a curse with invocations to some rather strong powers – some of them dodgy, spiritually, I should say – but the gist of it is that terrible misfortune will descend on anybody who reads the fifteen pages covering the period from August to November 1589.'

Luke felt a sudden chill, as if a window had been opened behind him in midwinter. It surprised him, as he was not superstitious. He was not given to mind curses put on him by frustrated gypsies when he failed to buy their heather at race meetings, nor those from passing angry motorists.

'Have you read them?'

The librarian shook his head. 'No, they are missing. They are still locked up in Boscannon Manor as far as I can tell. However, I can tell you this. I reckon they must be an important

22

clue as to part of our college hero's life, because the diary continues with him converting to the Anglican Church and his rapid progress to being made bishop, the first Anglican bishop of our cathedral. I think you are going to have an interesting task editing this. I shall be delighted to help all I can, but I suspect some of your sabbatical will involve a trip to Cornwall. I'll leave you to look through the journal and arrange tomorrow for each page to be photocopied so that you can work at it away from here without fear of damage. I'll be in my office if you want me.'

Luke made little progress with the diary, except to conclude it was going to be a long and exacting project. He sat fingering the parchments and tried to picture their writer, a man at some level risking his life for his faith.

On that day, Luke's faith was at a low ebb: he felt that God had deserted him and allowed an evil man to run the school; but worse, was there a God, had Jesus been divine?

Chapter Three

There were still another five days of term to go, and several times Luke and the headmaster passed each other in the school, though the latter refused to make eye contact or else looked straight through him. Such lack of communication was a relief to Luke, though the final days were clouded by his conscious acceptance of the fact that his return as second master was under threat so long as Brigadier Henshaw was in command. He knew he might have to plan a future outside the school after his sabbatical was over. In spite of this he was determined to enjoy the last few days of the term.

The universal anticipation of the long summer holidays ahead was infectious, and his final divinity lessons for the upper sixth forms were always stimulating and fun. He also looked forward every year to the final game of cricket that he usually played with success in the masters' second eleven against the school's second team. In the final divinity lessons it was his custom to get each form member to write down a religious question and put it into a box. These questions would then be drawn and discussed, so it always enabled him to put across some important teachings. Many old boys had referred to those discussions as being significant in their future lives. However, even these usually enjoyable encounters were to be blighted.

The divinity lesson with the combined chemistry and physics upper sixth had gone well until the final question posed by one boy who had always played the part of a cynical unbeliever. The question was, 'During the last year, it was explained to us that one of the arguments for the existence of God was that all creation displays movement and that it must have had an initial outside power to start it going. That power, we were told, was God, the prime mover. If that was so, what moved God in the beginning?'

Luke tried to be patient. The same boy had been disruptive when proof of the existence of God had been studied at the beginning of the year.

'My dear Simpkins, you are raising again the question that we dealt with in January. The existence of God is primarily accepted, with God as the missing part of every intellectual equation that deals with creation and the perfection of the universe. You, as a scientist, recall that recent works reveal that the so-called Big Bang of approximately 15,000 million years ago, which started our universe, had a certain density and a certain velocity of recession to bring forth life. An increase or decrease by one part of a million would have had a totally destructive effect.'

Simpkins interrupted, 'In what way Father?' He was watching Luke with the superior gaze of a cobra spotting a small, vulnerable, furry creature. He knew Luke's speciality was history and theology and suspected his tutor was out of his depth. Luke felt his face colouring. He said a quick prayer. He had been recently reading the religious philosopher Richard Swinburne's book *Is There a God?* He tried to recall the continuation of the argument. His prayer was answered, his colour subsided and he continued smoothly.

'Well, if the chunks of energy matter had receded from each other marginally slower, the universe would have collapsed in on itself. There is incredible fine-tuning in all creation.'

Simpkins was not satisfied. 'Excuse me. Father, I don't think you have answered my question. You imply that God made the Big Bang – OK, but who made God? What was before him!'

Luke tried to stay calm. 'Goodness, not that old chestnut again! I'm afraid you can't have been attending to our earlier discussions. The Aristotelian answer, Simpkins – perhaps you have forgotten it. "The first cause is timeless and spaceless." You see, God is beyond our complete understanding. We can only dimly comprehend that he is beyond time itself. Our language is inadequate. We have to make the leap of faith that God is the missing part of all life's equations. And indeed, only that makes sense.'

'Alleluia, Father,' added Simpkins, and he started a slow handclap.

Luke's anger flared. 'You may be "going down" in four days'

time but it doesn't excuse bad manners. I'm tempted to have you confined to your house till term ends.'

This exchange brought the lesson to a sour end.

The final divinity class with the combined classics and history upper sixth, was equally disappointing. Their end-of-term questions usually concentrated on morality and church doctrines. Several were produced from the box, questioning Anglo-Catholic objections to women priests. By putting up his hand, a boy named Philpot interrupted Luke's explanation that by ordaining women the Anglican Church was cutting itself off from the Catholic and Orthodox Churches; setting itself up as a sect outside the accepted teaching of the early councils and practices of the Universal Church. It undermined the Anglican claim to be the Catholic Church of the English.

Philpot's hand continued to wave.

'Yes?' said Luke, with studied patience.

'Surely, Father, it's because most Orthodox and Catholic priests are female-phobes.'

The class burst out laughing, destroying Luke's points. Someone shouted 'Nice one, Potts!' Luke smiled wanly. 'I think you mean misogynists. Of course that's utter rubbish. You seem to be unaware of the destruction the ordination of women is wreaking in our Church. We are faced with the Anglican Church splitting in two. We have a movement, Forward in Faith, that will lead many members into a new Orthodox Anglican Catholic Foundation, leaving the rest as a Protestant rump.' He tried to continue calmly. 'There is also the fact that God chose to be incarnate in that part of the Trinity that manifested itself as male, and, as you well know, at Mass the priest is taking on Christ's Eucharistic role – a woman cannot do that.'

Philpot interrupted again. 'I think that's unfair. Actors often took on the roles of the other sex in ancient times. Take boys being girls in Shakespeare's time, or girls as principal boys in pantomimes. Everyone understands their role. Anyway, aren't people talking about the Holy Spirit being the female side of God?'

Luke realised the boy was being serious – he had an intense look of anxiety about him.

'Perhaps, but the Mass is not pantomime. However, I agree with your point about the Holy Spirit, but that does not excuse

26

us going out on a limb like all the other Protestant sects.' His voice rose as he said the last sentence.

Philpot looked crushed. 'I can't say I agree with you, Father. My elder sister is about to be ordained in Bristol Cathedral.'

Luke was lost for words and then muttered, 'I see. Well, I understand your concern, I'm sorry.'

An embarrassed silence descended on the class, which Luke broke with an effort. 'Next question is ... Does the Church of England still condemn adultery? If so, can the Prince of Wales be head of the Church when he becomes King?' Mercifully, the bell rang to end the class. 'No doubt we shall know the answer to that in God's good time, if Charles ever takes the throne,' was all Luke could answer.

Again, a keenly anticipated discussion period had ended on a sour note.

There seemed to be a destructive spirit abroad in the school. Luke blamed the new head, who had taken on the teaching of current affairs to the sixth forms for one period every fortnight. He was reputed to be using these classes as a vehicle for propagandising his own views on matters religious.

That afternoon Luke's depression deepened. He had gone to watch the cricket match being played by the first eleven against Winchester. His team lost badly. As the game ended, Alastair cheered him up a little by asking him to dinner after the party that always followed this annual match. The party was in the tuck shop, known as 'the Grub'. It was in fact a converted Georgian orangery, a charming setting for a summer party with the teams drinking on the lawns outside. Luke felt better after his second drink and he found himself talking to the librarian, Mr Tompkins, who had proved a canny left-handed slow bowler in staff matches. His friend Alastair joined them. Behind the buzz of conversation could be heard the clock in the school court, competing with the deeper chimes of the cathedral, telling them it was seven o'clock.

As the chimes faded, the crowd opened in front of the building to allow the arrival of the headmaster's party. It included Mr Jones, who made a beeline towards Luke. He was smiling sanctimoniously.

'So, Mr Howard, I didn't expect to see you here. We all said you would be telling your beads after your team's defeat. Perhaps

27

it was a little godly chastisement to you for spurning my order of service.'

Luke managed to control his temper, but knew his face was flushed with anger.

'Fr Jones, remember, God chastises those he loves, so that pride does not take hold. Let me introduce you to our librarian, Mr Tompkins, and Mr Galbraith, our head of classics. I don't think they attend your singing and dancing club.'

Mr Jones' face took its turn to alter its pasty complexion to a fierce red. He ignored the introductions and, to everyone's amazement, stepped forward and seized the front of Luke's Cambridge blue cricket sweater, pulling it out so that Luke's silhouette looked pregnant. 'Don't patronise me, you poncing crypto-papist. Your problem is that you don't love the Lord Jesus, do you? You're not saved, are you? That's why you're eaten up with the pride of the Pharisees. You say, "Look at me, Lord, I'm not like the ordinary people – I have incense and candles and a fine position," but can you, boyo, say, like me, I love the Lord Jesus?' At this he put his hands together in prayer and looked up to heaven in the direction of the sun, sinking towards its summer horizon.

Luke stepped back. 'Gentlemen, I think drink has been taken, as they say. I bid you goodnight. Father Jones, I can only say I don't discuss my love affairs in public. I shall see you at dinner, Alastair.' He winked at him as he said this and turned away and left the party.

'Crikey,' he said to himself. 'Life is becoming full of stagy exits.'

Mr Tompkins was already at Alastair's house when Luke arrived for dinner. He was regaling Alastair's wife, Charlotte, with the story of Mr Jones' attack on Luke and doing a credible re-enactment of the event, including a particularly good imitation of Mr Jones lifting his prayerful hands in the direction of the setting sun. The merry mood was lifted further by Alastair coming into the room carrying a tray of glasses and a bottle of champagne.

'To toast the summer holidays – thank God they're here!' He opened the bottle and they all drank a toast. 'Charlotte has had a splendid idea,' said Alastair. 'Tell Luke,' he turned to his wife.

She put down her glass on a small table and with her hand brushed her black hair to one side of her head. Luke always remarked to himself what a striking feature of some Scots was their combination of dark hair with blue eyes. Charlotte had both and, with her clear white skin, looked rather doll-like. She was undoubtedly pretty, and bearing three children had not spoilt her looks. Like Alastair she was in her early forties and had a bubbling sense of humour. Having put down her glass, she came over to Luke and took both his hands.

'We want you to do us a favour – come and join us during the holidays in our cottage near the Helford in Cornwall. It will be fun for us to have you.' Both she and Alastair had been worried about Luke. The recent stress was showing. 'We shall be there from the end of this week until the beginning of September – come for at least three weeks.'

Luke was lost for words. He had not had the energy to make plans for the holidays. He accepted gratefully.

Mr Tompkins chipped in. 'You'll be staying very near Boscannon, so you could make an introductory recce.'

Luke nodded. 'Excellent. I'll write to them tomorrow.'

The cathedral chimed eleven just as he left, after a dinner which had been full of merriment, and Luke felt more relaxed than he had been at any time during the last year.

Alastair's house was in the cathedral close, as was that of Luke's father. Both homes were charming, small Georgian houses – open in front but with high walls at the back giving privacy to their gardens. It was one of the lovely features of the close that most of the houses had these private oases. The houses belonged to the cathedral and the tenants were there by favour of the dean and chapter. The rents were reasonable and this had enabled Alastair to buy his holiday cottage in Cornwall.

It was a warm moonlit night and the air was heavy with the scent of roses and night-scented stocks as he walked round the close to the opposite side where his father lived. Luke thought perhaps he should apply for a house in the close. Melbury suited him, though his sense of duty nudged him to consider that if he did not return to the school, perhaps he should seek a parish in a less lush setting. Then he consoled himself by remembering that such a decision could wait until the end of his sabbatical. He was happy for the first time in months when he got into his bed that night, having seen his father sitting watching an art discussion programme on the television and making a running, abusive commentary as each participant made their point. Luke drifted off to sleep just after the cathedral clock chimed midnight. It too would be silent until it struck again, in a civilised manner, at eight o'clock the next morning. Later a single bell would toll on weekdays to tell the world that Mass would start at eight-thirty.

The dean and canons were unashamedly High Church. No Holy Communions or Eucharists appeared on the list of services in the cathedral. There only Low, High or sometimes Solemn Masses. Luke and his father were spiritually at home in the safety of the cathedral and its close. All was right for them in that most English of worlds.

Chapter Four

Luke awoke with the first chimes of the cathedral at eight o'clock, knowing he was on holiday. During term time he took it in turns with Fr Peter to say a simple Low Mass in the school chapel at eight-fifteen on weekdays, which was followed at eight-fifty by the whole school attending morning prayers. Usually those attending the Low Mass, which was voluntary, numbered about thirty, of whom about half a dozen were staff. In vacation time, Luke might stand in for one of the cathedral priests, but always at the start of the holidays he would keep himself free of any commitments.

In the first few days of the holidays he would rise after nine, make himself a cup of coffee and then go back to bed, with his copy of *The Times* and his mail. On this occasion he had been catapulted into the conscious world by the sound of his father cleaning his shoes in the garden below him and coaching his parrot in its increasing repertoire of conversation. The parrot had been christened Magdalene and had been given to his father by an eccentric parishioner who had a collection of ten talking birds – mynahs, parakeets and parrots all gossiping together.

His father had become fascinated in his retirement by the curious vocal ability of this bird, and it lived in a small tool shed at the back of the house. He had recently taught it a variation of the introductory general confession from the *Book of Common Prayer*, substituting lost parrots for lost sheep. 'Almighty and merciful Father, we have erred and strayed from your ways like lost parrots...' The bird was reciting this line as Luke got out of bed. His father had cunningly managed to get it to intone this in an exaggerated, sanctimonious manner.

On this particular morning Luke was horrified to hear his father embarking on a new lesson, each phrase punctuated by

31

the sound of his father vigorously cleaning his shoes. This new parrot lesson was in full flow and obviously close to success.

'Who's farted – not me!' (The 'me' spoken in a drawn-out *meee*.) 'It's the Bishop!'

The Bishop of Melbury was Canon Howard's pet hate, as he had taken to ordaining women with gusto. The bishop, one Mr Brown, had been appointed by Mrs Thatcher – an appointment made in the spirit of her nonconformist upbringing. Along with her lack of humour went a lack of any comprehension of the delicacy of Anglican party politics, and she happily appointed men she believed sound – that is to say, not socialist or likely to object to national services of thanksgiving for her brave acts, as Robert Runcie, Archbishop of Canterbury, was reputed to have done after the Falklands War. She had blocked the appointment of the socialist Bishop of Stepney to the Diocese of Birmingham. finally, she was responsible for the colourless Carey following on at Canterbury, but to Canon Howard's fury she had also appointed an evangelical as the bishop who had been plonked into the traditional Diocese of Melbury.

As Luke began to contemplate the day ahead, the absurdities of many aspects of the Church of England crowded in on his thoughts. A Nonconformist woman prime minister, or even an atheist, by bad appointments could upset the precarious balances within the Church. Its head, the Queen or King, became a Presbyterian when going to Scotland, thus embracing a religion ruled by elected elders rather than bishops.

Luke was gripped by a feeling of panic, a blind attack such as had never assailed him before. At this moment all his certainties of faith and his commitment to the belief of High Anglicanism left him. He began sweating and found it difficult to breath. He wondered if he was about to have a heart attack. The final divinity lessons of the term took on a cosmic significance. Simpkins' question about God the 'prime mover' seemed unanswerable. Luke saw a universe of pure chance. Cold and unfeeling – endless empty space. How could a being that was supposed to control that immensity have any interest in Luke that morning, or any concern as to whether the priest in the cathedral was wearing vestments appropriate to the Church's year. Also, could a religion forged out of political and domestic strife, really have evolved via the Oxford Movement

32

into the purest form of the universal Catholic faith. The cosmic and the parochial questions of the last divinity classes thudded in Luke's head. Pelion piled on Ossa.

He shaved and dressed hurriedly and rushed across the cathedral close in order to attend the eight-thirty Low Mass. As always it was held in the exquisite Lady chapel beyond the high altar. This chapel was utterly plain, with thin soaring pillars framing some of the most beautiful medieval stained-glass windows in Europe. The predominant colours were blue and red, and even on dull days the effect was staggering, especially the main windows behind the altar depicting Mary with Christ in glory, attended by St Michael the Archangel welcoming them into heaven. The side windows depicted the hierarchy of angels – the seraphim, cherubim and thrones contemplating God and reflecting his glory; the angelic dominations Virtue and Power were shown in their traditional role of regulating the stars and the universe. Would that Luke could believe it that morning, or convince Simpkins.

When he reached the Lady chapel he was depressed by the sight of the bishop approaching its altar; he was wearing no vestments, just a white surplice and a black stole around his neck. Underneath the surplice, yellow corduroy trousers and brown brogue shoes protruded.

At the altar he paused to rearrange the flowers and move the four lighted candles in minute but fussy movements. Turning to the small congregation, he smiled and said, 'Welcome my brothers and sisters to this morning's Communion. We shall use the *Book of Common Prayer* service.'

Luke knew the bishop viewed it as just a memorial meal to provide a spirit of togetherness, so he kept interjecting several asides commenting on 'the fellowship of their gathering', and before the psalm for the day asked everyone to introduce themselves by name to their neighbour and shake hands. That morning the psalm asked of God, 'What is man that you are mindful of him? You have made him little lower than the angels.' Here the bishop paused and looked at the windows and lifted up an arm, pointed in the direction of St Michael the Archangel and smiled in a sentimental way, like a mother reading Enid Blyton to a spoilt child. Luke could stand it no longer and from his place at the back of the chapel quietly left to seek breakfast at his father's house.

On the lawn of the cathedral close a small boy was doing somersaults and cartwheels badly. It was William. A charming son of one of the canons who had a house in the close near his father's. He caught sight of Luke, waved vigorously before running over to him to take him by the hand. Together they walked across the lawns, William trying to skip at the same time as hanging on to Luke. This meeting lifted Luke's spirit and he felt a godsent antidote to his depression. William left him at the entrance to his father's house and skipped away onto the lawns again to try his hand at cartwheeling.

Margery Brown had arrived to clean up after the ravages of his father's early morning attack on the kitchen. She was delighted to see Luke and fussed over him, providing an excellent plate of bacon and eggs, strong coffee and a copy of *The Times* that had just been delivered. His father had gone off for the day, so Luke was grateful to get the paper first. At the end of every day, the paper's pages had been added to by comments in red biro, such as 'stupid', 'utterly despicable' and 'beneath contempt', and pictures of disliked public figures distorted with graffiti. Recently, Luke had seen his father's skilful alteration of a picture of Mrs Thatcher chatting with Archbishop Carey. The prime minister's hair had been darkened and shaped over her forehead in a Hitleresque manner, with a matching moustache, while the archbishop had developed bosoms and long black hair and pigtails. A byline added, 'Canterbury fräulein enjoys sycophantically the attention of her Führer.'

That morning, Luke was able to read a newspaper in pristine condition. On that day there was an article on a priest who had lost his faith and how he had experienced difficulties in the local employment office in getting any benefits or serious help in obtaining a job. He had been regarded as an unreal oddity by the staff. Luke began to tremble so that the paper shook in his hands. What could he do if his faith was genuinely lost?

Luke spent another hour after breakfast trying to read the rest of the paper, but his mind kept returning to the void that had appeared in his system of belief. He compared himself to a solo explorer on an ice floe that was dissolving in a sudden thaw, everywhere cracks appearing around him and an increasing fear of being dragged down into the icy waters. He was rescued by the ringing of the phone. He heard Margery answering.

'No, Canon Howard is not here, but his son Fr Luke is.' There was a pause, then, 'Fr Luke, it's one of the nuns from Melbury Abbey. She'd like to speak to you.'

Luke took the phone.

'Sister Felicity here. Fr Robert is down for the day and wondered whether you and your father could join us for lunch? Also, it would give him support, as the bishop has invited himself to come for port afterwards.'

Luke explained that his father was away for the day, but accepted gratefully on his own behalf. Afterwards Luke wondered whether it was just a coincidence that he should have been in his father's house that morning, worrying himself sick with his black despair; he could have driven away for the day.

The confraternity of Gethsemane had its main house and headquarters behind Westminster Abbey. It was in one of the many small streets between the Abbey Cloisters and Church House. It was a compact establishment with a fine chapel which could take fifty people comfortably and a refectory of the same size. Three priests lived in the house, one of whom was a man of charismatic character, one Fr Robert, known to all the community as 'Fr Bob', and who was the elected master of the fraternity and Abbot of Melbury Abbey. From this building, its organisation flowed. Meetings, pilgrimages and retreats were organised and a monthly newsletter was published, giving news of the one hundred and twenty or so members of the order. This number fluctuated from year to year, as their vows bound them only for a year, from one New Year's Day to the next. A few people left each year to marry, or else decided that they did not wish to be under the obedience required by the order.

In addition to the house in London there was a retreat house in Melbury. Like the house in London, it was owned by the confraternity and the members owed their obedience to the master only. Episcopal oversight came in the person of the retired Archbishop Humphries. Most of their members were chaplains in schools, universities, prisons and hospitals, and so were outside any official control. They regarded themselves as an elite, being praetorian guardians of Anglo-Catholicism. They were suspect in the eyes of most Anglicans and heartily disliked by its Protestant-minded members, though no one questioned their discipline or deep spirituality. Even the Protestant Truth Society failed to find any cause of scandal, save for its members' total disregard for the Anglican orders of service, as they used mostly those of the Roman Catholic Church spiced with a few Orthodox rubrics.

The confraternity had been fortunate in having a member who had died in the 1890s and left the order a family fortune made in speculating in early railway companies. He had happily accepted the nickname of Fr Puff-Puff and a portrait of him hung in the London refectory holding a smoking censer made out of a model steam engine. The order had accepted this eccentric machine for producing incense in deference to the large amount of money which had already flowed from Fr Puff-Puff. The fortune had enabled the order to publish a regular number of polemical books and fund meetings in agreeable locations to spread its message. At the moment, Fr Puff-Puff's fortune was paying for a vigorous propaganda campaign against women priests.

The fortune had been astutely invested, so that its funds were said to exceed twenty million pounds. The retreat house at Melbury was thus maintained to a high standard. It had originally been an abbey and then the manor house of Melbury. It had since reverted to its original name, Melbury Abbey. One wing of the house housed six faithful nuns of the Anglican Order of Gethsemane, founded by the fraternity in the 1890s. These nuns did the housekeeping, gave spiritual comfort to visitors and looked after the aged and eccentric permanent Chaplain, Fr Ignatius, and a small number of members of the confraternity studying there. Fr Ignatius had been a Mr Smith until he had taken on this rather more Roman name. Apart from making sure the house ran smoothly the nuns also provided excellent food. One of the sisters had run a restaurant in Walton Street in London for many years until she discovered a vocation for the religious life.

So it was here that Luke found himself after an excellent lunch of smoked salmon mousse and rack of lamb. They were sitting outside the dining room having coffee and savouring the last glasses of a 1982 Château Latour.

'Fortunately, Fr Ignatius, the chaplain, is out today – he

36

wouldn't have really appreciated this,' sighed Fr Robert. This was being economical with the truth, as the chaplain had built up a fine cellar over his twenty years in residence. 'Now, tell me your news. We hear very disturbing rumours about the college and what sounds like a disastrous appointment of the new head. I was dining in Michaelhouse, Cambridge, a month ago and heard from your old head some very alarming stories. As I was due here I thought I should see either you or your father.'

Luke told him about the college and about his forthcoming sabbatical. Fr Robert interrupted him by ringing a small handbell. Sister Felicity appeared and he removed a hot-water bottle from beneath his cassock. He suffered from a stomach complaint – though it did not affect his appetite – and whenever possible carried a hot-water bottle. It was supported from below by the cord tied round the waist of his cassock and ending in two knots, denoting his yearly religious vows chastity and obedience. The order ignored the traditional third monastic vow of poverty.

'Sister, could you refill this, please?'

Luke had heard rumours of this eccentricity but had believed them humorously scurrilous. Neither the nun nor Fr Robert showed the slightest hint that this was either unusual or embarrassing.

'Of course, Father, but in this heat you amaze me,' was all the nun said.

Fr Robert turned to Luke as if nothing had interrupted their conversation. 'Would you like some more of this Colombian coffee? By the way, there is an excellently stocked humidor here. I'm going to have a Montecristo Especial, a small one. Will you join me?'

Luke shook his head, as much in amazement as denial; no wonder poverty was not one of their vows.

When the nun returned with the hot-water bottle, Fr Robert asked for the Montecristo.

'I want to get this going before the bishop arrives – he always is such a sanctimonious fellow, shaking his head and sighing when he sees me smoking. I tell him this is my way of praising and thanking God for sending us Fr Puff-Puff.'

The nun giggled. 'I can't think that this will help your tummy, Father.'

'Don't be a fusspot! Now, Luke, what are we going to do about the college? I gather our Archbishop Humphries has temporarily stopped the Protestant enemy entering the place in the person of Mr Jones.'

Luke shook his head. 'That's only temporary. The only solution is for the headmaster to go, but he might be there for another ten years – it worries me to death.'

'Mm, no wonder you're looking peaky. Remember, you can always spend a few quiet days here.'

Luke shook his head again. 'I'm afraid I should be here under false pretences. You see I'm losing my faith, not only in the Anglican Church, but in God as well.'

'Tell me all. There is nothing unusual in your condition. A lot of our brethren come here suffering in the same way – not necessarily a dark night of the soul, but certainly one of the mind.'

After the cigar had been delivered and lighted, Fr Robert listened to Luke's problems as they walked around the garden. Luke gave him a summary of his intellectual confusion. Fr Robert made no comment as he spoke, only stopping occasionally to knock accumulating ash from the end of his cigar, holding the cigar vertically and examining it with eminent satisfaction before flicking the ash into the flower beds, where it fell with a satisfying soft plop on sundry carnations and roses. When Luke had finished outlining his problems, they had reached a small walled garden which contained a rectangular pond covered in red lilies. A wooden bench was beside it and Fr Robert went and sat down, beckoning Luke to join him.

'Well, as you appreciate, no proof of the existence of God can be so overwhelming that we are forced to accept; this would make us merely servile automata. God, we believe, wants us to come to him freely my making continuous leaps of faith. For most this faith develops slowly over the years, ebbing and flowing until in the end it is an integral and mature part of our psyche. I myself have no doubts now, and the exquisite balance of the world confirms God's existence to me.'

Luke sighed, thinking of his conflict with Simpkins in the divinity class.

'It seems to me this exquisite balance has within it some pretty nasty weights: poverty, wars, natural disasters, disease, the suffering of dying children. It's mighty difficult conveying all this to others as part of the divine plan.'

Fr Robert nodded sympathetically. 'I know it's terribly hard to take; especially when it hits one directly. I have a sister dying of a horrible cancer at the moment. Undoubtedly, corruption entered God's creation, the Fall, not just of man.'

Luke shook his head. 'Too easy – evolution, the brutal survival of the fittest I don't call that corruption, just the basis of a developing world.'

Fr Robert was silent for a while. 'We don't know that. God's plan might have been different. "There was war in heaven", and, temporarily, Satan has left his mark.' He got up and walked over to the pond and examined the end of his cigar. He took a puff, looked at the glowing ash and flicked it into the pond, where it dissolved in a small hiss of steam. He turned to Luke. 'Of course, we will pray for you, but I dare say the temporary reality of your headmaster and all his works is putting a strain on your belief. You must come here on a private retreat...'

He was cut short by the appearance of a nun leading the bishop towards them. He was dressed in a mauve tweed jacket over a purple polo-necked jersey. A large silver cross bounced on his ample paunch as he advanced towards them. He waved a hand in a way that hovered between a Benediction and a greeting.

As Fr Robert got up to meet the bishop, he said as an aside, 'There will be war in heaven now!'

Bishop Brown surged between them, shaking their hands with a limp paw.

'Goodness, am I too late for the port and coffee? How good to see you Luke, just one of the people I most wanted to see today, and you, Robert, still smoking those overwhelming cigars! Community flourishing is it, or are you all sneaking off to Rome before our beautiful women curates undermine your vows of celibacy?' He burst into a high-pitched giggle and sat down on the bench, which creaked ominously. Fr Robert and Luke regarded him in astonishment. He continued unabashed. 'Robert, I wanted to see you to ask a favour in addition to sampling your vintage port. Our prison chaplain at Thorngate is ill. Is there any chance of one of your brethren getting off their knees and standing in for two or three weeks? I know you can spare someone.' Fr Robert stood silently as the bishop's stream of consciousness continued unabated. 'Good, good, I knew I could count on you.

'Now, Master Luke, or should I say second master. I most definitely want to hear about your Melbury College quincentenary celebrations, and also about the publication of the journal of my predecessor, Bishop de Witte. Such a fascinating life I'm sure it's going to be, but first we have got to establish that it has to be a joint venture in its editing. You see, his fame is as first Anglican Bishop of Melbury – the fact he was an old boy is really an irrelevance – so I'd like to give you every help we can and offer myself as joint editor. My wife has had a brilliant idea. The book should contain a colour picture of his magnificent tomb in the cathedral as a frontispiece, with me standing in front. Don't look so amazed, Luke. You could be in it, too – by the side perhaps.'

Fr Robert interrupted the flow. 'Let's discuss this further over the port and coffee.' He could see Luke seething with anger.

As they walked towards the house, Fr Robert took Luke's arm and in a low voice said, 'Just thank him, don't get into an argument. The journal is college property and you're the sole editor – ignore him and get on with it. Take your leave when we get to the house.'

Luke did. 'So sorry to leave you but I have a lot to do as I'm going away tomorrow.'

The Bishop looked peeved and Fr Robert smiled. 'Have a good holiday and keep in touch.'

Chapter Five

The next day Luke and Alastair set off in convoy for Cornwall with Alastair's family divided between the two cars. The sun came out and blue skies greeted them as they crossed the Tamar Bridge into Cornwall. Later, the cars reverberated with the cries of 'the sea, the sea', as it was glimpsed beyond the far coastline. They arrived at Alastair's cottage in the early afternoon. There was not a cloud in the sky. The children tumbled out of the cars and rushed around, pursued by their barking retriever dog.

The cottage was a low, whitewashed building with sky-blue shutters and doors covered by a mixture of roses and honeysuckle. It faced a small lawn, beyond which cornfields followed the land rolling down to the Helford river, where small beaches and rocks lined the shore. To the left of their view could be seen the river opening out into Falmouth Bay and the ocean shimmering in the sunlight beyond. On one side of the lawn there was a small, white-boarded gazebo in which there was room for a wood-burning stove, a sofa and easy chairs. On the side facing the river was a large bow window in which stood an old ship's telescope on a tripod. Alastair's youngest son, Benjamin, aged five, told Luke it was for spotting pirates coming up the river. His mother went to the scope and, turning it to see downriver, beckoned Luke to look through it.

'See, there's Boscannon Manor.'

Luke had not expected the building to appear so near. The telescope was powerful, so that the manor looked to be only two hundred yards away instead of over twelve hundred. The Tudor building was constructed of solid Cornish stone with two massive chimney stacks at each end, and at a right angle, leading away from the river, was the more recent addition of a Georgian wing. This wing was enclosed by a high-walled garden. The wall facing the river had a door and further away a small arch at its base out of which tumbled a stream. This flowed through a field and then disappeared into a sloping wooded valley leading down to the Helford river. Luke saw the wood was full of different palm trees. It was lush and exotic. The edge of the wood overhung a small beach. On one side of the beach was a stone pier on which stood a small crane to which a boatswain's chair was attached. Underneath was moored a smart motor boat.

Luke was captivated. The powerful telescope brought the view so close it was like watching a film divorced from the distant reality. He turned back to look at the manor house and as he did so the door in the side of the walled garden opened. A young woman appeared wearing a long white dress with a red sash tied around her waist. She could have been the ghost of an Edwardian beauty. Although he could not see her features clearly, her whole appearance was enchanting, framed with the circular picture of the scope. She raised a hand to brush aside a dark fringe of hair and gazed towards the river. Then she turned to look, it seemed, directly towards Luke. He felt she must be seeing him as clearly as he was viewing her, so that instinctively he moved to look down the river at a yacht tacking in from the sea.

Benjamin pulled at his sleeve. 'Uncle Luke, can you see any pirate boats? Any skull and crossbones flags flying?'

Luke gave up the telescope reluctantly. 'I'm glad to say no. Perhaps just a pirate's wife awaiting his return.'

After unpacking they all had high tea in the kitchen, consisting of bacon, eggs, sausages and baked beans, followed by locally made Cornish ice cream. This meal created a suitably somnolent condition in the children and they were dispatched to bed early. Alastair, Charlotte and Luke then returned to the gazebo to watch the sun set over the Helford. Alastair took over a tray of glasses and ice and produced a bottle of whisky from a cupboard in the gazebo. They sat watching the white ripples on the water of the river turn pink in the afterglow of the sinking sun.

'Cheers, and God bless the Helford,' said Alastair, and continued after they had tasted their drinks by asking Luke about his progress and plans concerning the editing of the de Witte papers.

'Not as much as I would have liked,' answered Luke. 'Alastair, you kindly offered to help with translating the Latin and I would appreciate it while I'm here as I've brought photocopies of the diary. Before term ended, old Tompkins the librarian made a great to-do of it, photocopying every page for me and then, of course, locking the originals away again. He was a great help, his Latin is better than mine. Together we managed, I believe, to get the pages in chronological order and correctly dated. The first bit seemed to record de Witte being sent from the English College in Rome at the end of the 1570s. There's a fascinating description of his secret landing up the Orwell river in Suffolk. Then it becomes a record of visiting various recusant families in East Anglia, all referred to by a series of numbers in code of a sort, to hide their identities and houses. Obviously he was taking precautions in case the diary was captured. I have just translated some pages referring to his time with the Rookwood family, who lived about ten miles north of Bury St Edmunds. It appears their Catholic loyalties were discovered at the time of Queen Elizabeth's progress in East Anglia in 1578. She stayed at the Rookwood house at Euston and de Witte narrowly avoided arrest and seemed badly shaken by the incident. I've got this bit with me. Perhaps, Alastair, later on you could help me – I'm stuck with some of the translation.'

'Delighted,' said Alastair and added action to his words by refilling their glasses.

'Is there any truth about a part being missing which is now at Boscannon?' As Charlotte had asked this, she pointed towards the manor across the river.

Luke got up as he answered. 'Well, here's a real problem.' He went to the window and looked at the manor, which was now reflecting in its windows the last rays of the disappearing sun. 'Tompkins said there is a reference somewhere at the end of the diary to the papers relating to the time between August and November 1589, when de Witte was known to be at Boscannon. The reference states that they were hidden there, but I haven't found it yet. I don't know whether I told you, but in the papers I have there is a curse, a powerful one, on anyone reading the missing pages – obviously before he'd hidden them – so it is clearly important that I read them if I am to form a proper judgement of him and edit an honest "life and time" for the Queen's visit.'

'What do you think is so important about them?' Charlotte had got up and joined him, looking out of the bow window.

'I think they provide the answer to his conversion to Anglicanism – that's why the pages are vital and that's why the Boscannon family have kept them secret. Tompkins thinks they may reveal that the family was plotting with the Spaniards against Elizabeth. The Helford would have provided an excellent landing area for a series of armadas, large or small. Maybe de Witte discovered this and his English loyalties were offended. It's also possible that he saw the light about Anglicanism being a purer faith, and that's why the Boscannons won't release the pages.'

Alastair interrupted. 'I bet there's a lady involved. Wasn't he a married man when he became bishop?'

'True,' agreed Luke. 'We shall know more when I translate all we possess and we shall know it all if the Boscannons cooperate. Tompkins had no luck with the previous generation a few years back. I rang two days ago and could only speak with the cousin of Rear Admiral Boscannon. She listened and just said she would pass the message on to her cousin, referring to him as "Boss". She sounded like a hearty hunting aunt of P.G. Wodehouse's Bertie Wooster. The unspoken message seemed to be "don't ring us, we'll ring you".'

Alastair now joined them at the window. 'Splendid, the house is open to the public some weekends through the summer. We'll check tomorrow to see if it's open, then we can motor across by boat and you'll be able to charm yourself around the rear admiral and family, and, bingo, the riddle will be solved. Personally, I'm betting on a lady. *Cherchez la femme!*'

'Don't be so cynical,' said Charlotte. 'It's only because you're flirting with Rome,' she added as she saw Luke's look of pain. 'Luke, be honest, aren't all of us in our Anglican party doing the same?'

Luke hesitated for a moment. 'You don't expect me to encourage anyone in that direction while I'm still the senior chaplain of Melbury on a sabbatical, and I don't intend to let it interfere with the job in hand, reference the diary or the pleasure of being with you. Of course, we are all in torment and we just have to pray we do the right thing. Personally, I don't see much attraction in going over and I shall do my best to dissuade you both. I'm really upset to hear it.'

Charlotte hugged him. 'I think the Boscannon thing is super-exciting. No doubt we shall have time for theological dispute. Don't worry, nothing is decided.'

The fine hot weather continued. Summer had come with a vengeance in the second week of August after torrential rain had flooded the South West of England. After an early lunch they had trooped across the ripening corn fields and down to a small beach below the cottage. Peacock and Red Admiral butterflies flitted from the wild flowers, and trampolined from a bed of foxgloves overhanging the beach. A long white motor boat floated from a mooring fifty yards from the shore and on the beach a small pram and oars were padlocked to an iron ring set in a rock. In this boat Alastair ferried them in two journeys to the motor boat, each load weighing the pram so low down in the water that it seemed any serious waves from passing boats would sink them.

Alastair explained that he had hired these boats for the duration of their stay and told Luke he was free to use them on his own. It was the best way of getting to the sandier beaches across the river. The motor boat started without protest and five minutes later they were alongside the slipway on a beach below Boscannon Manor. A large sign said, PRIVATE SLIPWAY – NO MOORING, and the path leading off the beach into the woods had another large notice saying, TRESPASSERS WILL in big red letters. The following words, BE PROSECUTED, had been lightly painted out with white paint to give it a Winnie the Pooh literary reference, and this act of vandalism was completed with a biro signature saying, EEYORE RULES OK.

Alastair ignored both prohibitions and, having tied up to the slipway, led them into the wood. The undergrowth was thick, and the sunlight broke through only when the exotic ferns and palms swayed open momentarily to allow light to penetrate the mixture of closely planted greenery. Oaks and beeches above them sighed in the light breeze of the early afternoon. The path up to the manor was steep and they paused for a few minutes to admire a small lake amongst the trees into which a falling stream splashed over rocks. The whole area had an enchanted atmosphere. Luke felt as if he was in a dream. He put the sensation down to the heat and the humidity. They all stood looking at the lily-covered water. Apart from the sound of the splashing stream and the heavy breathing of the adults recovering from the climb, it was utterly quiet. Even the birds seemed poleaxed by the heat. Suddenly, the stillness was broken by the magic appearance of a kingfisher dropping down from the sky above the lake and darting under the waterfall, and then, for a brief moment, alighting on a branch before rocketing into the sky.

'Kingfisher,' they all said, except for Benjamin who shouted, 'It was a fairy, a fairy', and danced up and down in delight.

They resumed their climb up the path for another five minutes until it broke through the trees onto a wide terraced lawn in front of the manor. Already, visitors were walking to and fro, admiring the view over the woods to the river. A sign on a wooden stand in front of the house directed the public to go in a single direction, TO MANOR HOUSE AND MAZE. Alastair called them together and suggested they visit the house first to get out of the heat for a while. As he spoke, Alastair's daughter Lucinda and young Benjamin broke away and ran down the side of the house in the opposite direction, shouting alternately, 'It was a fairy!' 'Don't be silly – it was a kingfisher.' They wrestled with each other as they drew level with the long wall containing the garden on one side of the house. Benjamin ran to a door in the side of the wall. Luke could see another wooden sign there, saying STRICTLY PRIVATE, and sensed trouble. He ran after them, calling, 'Benjamin, Lucy, come back.'

As he got near, Benjamin and Lucy were wrestling against the door, which suddenly sprang inwards. The two children stumbled through and Luke saw them lurch together against a tall stepladder. As if in slow motion, the ladder began to topple to one side. On top was the young woman Luke had seen through the telescope. She was wearing a pair of baggy, faded-pink dungarees over a skimpy white T-shirt. As the ladder began to slide, she dropped the secateurs with which she had been deadheading a climbing rose and gripped the top of the wall with both hands. One foot teetered on the skewed ladder.

'Dear God,' she exclaimed as she hung there between heaven and earth.

'Help is here,' said Luke, like a character out of a Victorian melodrama. He steadied the ladder upright against the wall with one hand and proffered the other to help her down. She descended in a rush and stumbled against Luke. At that moment their lives changed.

Luke was wearing a grey cotton shirt topped by a dog collar – summer issue, Watts and Co., ecclesiastical outfitters – and his lower half was secularly clad in white cotton trousers. Through his shirt he felt the warmth and softness of the girl's bosom, and she felt the firmness of his thighs against her legs. They parted as if they had received a high-voltage shock.

Behind them, the children lay sprawled on the ground. 'I'm so sorry, please forgive us,' and similar words, sprang from Luke and the children.

'Hell,' said the girl. 'What's the point of having notices saying "Private" if you burst through like lunatics? I was pruning this "Rambling Rector" rose, not expecting young jackanapes to knock me about.' There was something old-fashioned about her choice of words. The children, who were still on the ground, kept saying, 'Sorry, sorry.'

She turned to Luke. 'I'm Francesca Boscannon,' she said, and held out her hand. 'Are you a rambling rector, too, or one of ours?' Luke looked puzzled. 'Well, you're dressed like a Catholic priest on a summer outing.'

He laughed. 'Actually, I'd say I am a Catholic priest, though my allegiance is to Canterbury not Rome. But how do you do, I'm Luke. These are the children of a friend. This is Lucinda and this is Benjamin. I'm staying with them across the river.'

The boy looked up. 'Uncle Luke, I did see a fairy, I did. Not a kingfisher.'

Francesca bent down and, taking his hands, pulled him up. 'I bet you did. There are lots in the woods here. Anyway, I'm afraid you can't stay. It's out of bounds. My husband is bound to a wheelchair. He's behind that pergola, beyond the pool, and he hates being seen.' As she said this, the air was rent by the sound of gunshot. A wounded pigeon fell nearby. The bird had one wing it could still flap, so that it staggered in a circle before falling into the pool in the middle of the garden.

47

'Who the bloody hell are you talking to? Get them off the quarterdeck! I'm drowned again, get me into dry dock.' An angry man's voice shouted from the direction of the shots.

Francesca sighed. 'I'm afraid I must ask you to leave now. Here comes Joseph pushing my husband's chair.'

At the same time a woman appeared out of the house through open French windows.

'Francesca! Damn you, I thought you were looking after Boss this afternoon while I keep the yobs from pinching the knick-knacks. Instead I see you're enjoying some gentle pruning and gossiping. As always it's Nancy who does the dirty work. It seems Boss is soaking again.' She set off to join the gardener, pushing the rear admiral towards them.

Francesca looked despairingly at Luke. 'Incontinence is the least of my troubles.' She held out her hand. 'Please go.'

Luke saw that it was bleeding and had a thorn in the flesh under her thumb. He took out a handkerchief, fortunately unused, and gave it to her. 'Can I help with that thorn?'

'Golly, I hadn't noticed – shock, I suppose.' She laughed lightly and added, 'Thank you.'

Luke took her hand. It trembled slightly. He knew she was looking at him all the while, examining him closely. Above the hand held out towards him, he could not avoid seeing the outline of her breasts through the light material of her top.

He felt his own hand tremble. 'This is absurd,' he thought. 'Please excuse my cheek,' he said, trying to speak in a calm manner, though he knew his voice was betraying him. 'Before we leave, I must ask you a favour. I'm here to begin a search for an important historical document believed to be in the manor here. I have not yet got any positive answer from your husband – perhaps...'

He was interrupted. Cousin Nancy came into view, followed by a gardener pushing a wheelchair in which sat Rear Admiral Boscannon. The woman was wearing jodhpurs and a red-checked shirt. She had unkempt brown hair, with wisps blowing in front of her nose.

The gardener was a short red-cheeked man with a kind face, dark thick hair and a tight brown suit, obviously dressed up for the public viewing of the manor. The rear admiral was sitting hunched in the wheelchair. His face was white with barely controlled fury, but when he spoke his voice was icy.

'Francesca! Why the hell are you not in the house watching the visiting peasantry? And who the hell are these?' He glared at Luke and the children. 'This part of the manor is not open – out of bounds – so bugger off before this revolver fires by accident and removes your manhood!' This threatening and insulting speech was delivered in the same icy tone, which made it even more disturbing.

Luke formed the impression of a powerful man. He was wearing a white naval shirt, with faded rear admiral's epaulettes. He had short-cut grey hair above a square face, and his mouth was cruel. His eyes were steel blue, set astride a pointed nose with pinched nostrils. His arms were muscular and his shoulders broad and strong. Luke surmised that he exercised rigorously the top half of his body. He could not see the body below the waist, as its weakness was covered by a dark blue rug.

As he formed these impressions, he said, 'I beg your pardon for our accidental intrusion, but I find your words unpardonable in front of these children.'

The rear admiral breached the barrel of the revolver and began to load it. The children got behind Francesca in a rush. She murmured, 'I'll do what I can. Please forgive the unpleasantness.'

'Get out,' shouted Nancy, and the rear admiral shut the breached gun and held it across his chest, ready to fire. His voice was as cold as the gun's steel barrels. 'I advise you to take that as an order. Don't push me to use this.'

Luke bowed towards the wheelchair and touched his forelock like an Irish peasant. 'God bless you, your honour. Sure to goodness it's too lovely a day for such harsh words.'

When they got outside the walled garden onto the long terraced lawn, they found the others waiting for them. The children had run out and even Luke, after a mock bow, had walked quickly after them. He had no doubt the rear admiral had a psychotic nature – whether due to his injury or not, he had no desire to find out. His threat had sounded genuine.

'That sounded welcoming,' commented Charlotte.

'Yes, well I'm afraid any cooperation from the rear admiral and his beastly female petty officer is now unlikely. I could gladly kill you, Lucy and Benjamin.' Luke shook his fist at them in mock fury imitating the rear admiral.

'Maybe,' replied Lucy, 'but I think that nasty man will do it for you.'

'Horrid, horrid people,' added Benjamin.

'Well, one can still see the house and then do the maze,' said Alastair.

The house was disappointing. A series of rooms led off a long dark corridor. Although the windows were open to the view of the river, the house seemed damp and stale and obviously only the wing of the building facing the walled garden was occupied. The first two rooms were reception rooms, filled with overlarge Victorian furniture covered mostly in brown velvet or leather and overlooked by stern ancestors. Several of these were dressed in naval uniform or were priests or nuns.

The third room was more interesting. It was about thirty feet long, and at one end a bookshelf covered a door which opened to reveal a small Catholic chapel beyond. It was furnished in a baroque style with several overdramatic Spanish statues of saints set in niches in the walls. The gardener, Joseph, stood uneasily on guard in front of a large open fireplace. He had been co-opted to help keep the public at bay. He turned out to be surprisingly informative once his Cornish burr was deciphered. He told them that in recusancy times the chapel had no windows and its entrance was hidden by the bookcase, but added that provision had been made for the hiding of the vestments, crosses and Mass vessels, as well as the resident priest. He paused dramatically, stepped to one side of the fireplace and, picking up a brush, swept away ash covering the large hearth. He then removed a stone on the side of the fireplace revealing a small wheel from which ran an iron chain. He began to turn the wheel, waving the onlookers to stand back. One of the large hearthstones began to sink. It dropped about three feet before coming to rest as the top step of some stone stairs leading into a tiny room below, six foot by six foot square. The only light came from two flue pipes in the wall and from a sanctuary lamp burning in front of a crucifix.

'You can go down one at a time. There's not much room, as you will see. It's said that two priests hid there for a week without food or water when that dreaded scourge of Catholics,

Queen Elizabeth's friend Topcliffe, repeatedly searched the house and had his men occupy it for a week. He had information that the priests were here, but the family had a fire going above these steps. That happened only a few years after they had hung, drawn and quartered St Cuthbert Mayne in November 1577 up at Launceston.' The little man sighed. 'Terrible times for the faithful. You will see the crucifix down there is sixteenth century Spanish.'

Alastair's son, Anthony, put up his hand. 'What happened when people were hung, drawn and quartered?'

'Nothing nice,' answered the Cornishman. 'first they were bound to a hurdle and dragged by horses through the streets from their prison to their place of hanging, often from the Tower of London to Tyburn. They did not die when hung – there was no breaking of the neck, just strangulation – but before passing out they were cut down and disembowelled. They were then beheaded and their bodies quartered and displayed or flung into a nearby pit.'

'I feel sick,' said Lucy, taking Luke's hand.

Luke was the last to enter the tiny space. He stood still and fixed his gaze on the exquisitely carved figure of Christ attached to a dark green painted cross. The sanctuary lamp gave a seeming movement to the face as it flickered in the draught. Luke began to say the words of the Anima Christi prayer. For a moment he thought he heard someone else coming down the steps behind him. He felt a close warmth. He turned, inexplicably hoping that it might be the young wife of Boscannon, Francesca; but he turned to find no one. Some time later he thought perhaps it had been de Witte. Certainly he stood longer, wondering whether the priest had had to hide there with only the crucifix for company. When he got up the steps into the library, Alastair was there.

'The others have gone to the maze. I'll join them now. Perhaps you want to examine the chapel?'

Luke did, but he did not find any atmosphere there except for an over-sweet, sentimental Catholic piety that was common in the nineteenth century. The Cornishman stood at the back watching him, making sure nothing was pocketed by Luke. He was fairly certain that Luke was an honest visitor, but, two years before, a petty thief had come disguised as a clergyman,

51

though his act had been abysmal. The new young wife of the rear admiral had found him out by asking him to say the Lord's Prayer with her in the chapel. The rascal had not even known the words. However, he thought Luke appeared a gentleman and the genuine article, so he was glad to talk to him.

Luke asked him if the library contained any old bound papers, or parchments, or vellum sheets. He had noticed that some of the shelving was fronted by glass doors with brass grids behind and faded green material hiding whatever was there.

'I can't tell you, sir. I've only seen this cupboard opened once, and that was when the auctioneer came just before the rear admiral married.'

'Auctioneer?' Luke's voice rose with anxiety.

'Yes, that's right sir. The rear admiral wanted a new boat to impress his Francesca maiden, his bride-to-be.' Luke was charmed by this Cornish description. The man continued, 'Tragic waste of money. Its boom cracked his spine a month after they were married. Anyway he sold some paintings and fine pieces of furniture and I believe some old papers and books. They say the auction raised a tidy sum.'

Luke's anxiety increased. 'You don't know if a diary kept by one of the recusancy priests living here was sold or is still here?'

'Can't say I do – only the rear admiral can tell you or the auctioneers if it was sold.

'You've been most helpful,' said Luke and slipped him a pound coin. 'You can't remember the name of the auctioneers?'

The Cornishman scratched his head. 'Came from London ... religious sort of name...'

'Ah, Christie's, perhaps,' said Luke.

'Could be,' replied the man. 'I'll try and ask the rear admiral's cousin, Miss Nancy, later. Not now – she's in a right state. Usually is, come to that.'

Luke tried to find the others in the maze. He felt that finding the diary was going to be even more of a search than he had anticipated and told Alastair what he had learnt.

Next day Alastair rang the local estate agent to confirm who had auctioned the Boscannon contents. 'Christie's', came the answer. Luke rang Christie's to find most of the experts were on holiday or were away pursuing potential treasures to sell. A secretary in the book department was eventually found and promised to see if they had an old catalogue of the sale and send it to Luke. For the present he could do no more than edit the diary he had from the school or, if possible, learn from Francesca Boscannon where the rest of it was to be found.

Chapter Six

The next day was overcast. Alastair and Charlotte packed all the children into their Volvo estate and set off for Falmouth, leaving Luke to work on the diary. Already he had established that de Witte had embarked on his diary at the suggestion of one of his fellow priests at the English College in Rome, so that future students there could have some picture of the missionary life awaiting them in England. If possible he was to send it in parts back to Rome, but on no account were places and people associated with the hidden life of the Catholic Church in Elizabethan England to be revealed unless already public knowledge.

The diary began with a dedication to Cardinal Allan, the brilliant Elizabethan Catholic who had brought the English College in Rome to the forefront of the mission to Britain. To gain some deeper knowledge of the life of the missionary priests in those days, Luke had already absorbed several books. The more he read, the more apparent it became that it was a world parallel to that of modern times, where millions had been hunted and persecuted and tortured by Nazi and Communist regimes; a world where one's beliefs had to be hidden; a world of the informer offered bribes by the government; a world of rigged trials, of financial pressure and the threat of bankruptcy. Worse still, imprisonment, torture and a brutal death.

De Witte's diary was made up of quarto sheets of different materials; parchment and paper and vellum. That is to say that each sheet was folded twice, then cut to make four pages, and these were then sewn together. In some quartos the thread had gone, but fortunately the order was clear from the dating.

The first quarto he was editing that day described how, in the autumn of 1579, de Witte and two fellow priests had sailed across the North Sea, in a Dutch boat taken at Antwerp, bound

54

for Ipswich in Suffolk. It was slow work, but Luke was pleased after an hour to have produced a description to his landing.

By God's grace a mist came to hide our anchoring on the Orwell river at two in the morning. The captain had us rowed in the ship's small boat to land on the southern shore. A long, mud-covered pier greeted us. In great haste the sailors bid us farewell and God speed, and so we stood offering great thanks to God and Our Lady in protecting us on our journey. Then the mist cleared to reveal in the moonlight an inn, a place called Pin Mill and the Inn called the Butt and Oyster. Many boats lay around on their sides in the mud. Dogs began to bark and we made haste inland up a long lane surrounded by small dwellings, with more dogs abarking. We were to find lodgings at a nearby hall, Ewarton, where a faithful family were expecting our arrival. It was nearly an hour before we reached it, but we found to our dismay many men in the road and the house ablaze with lights. The pursuivants were before us, searching every cranny. An informer in Antwerp must have sent word of our coming. May God be praised, we had not arrived on the day appointed, but a contrary wind delayed our passage. So warned, we hid in a barn nearby. Master Thomas from the house found us there safe the following night and took us in and hid us in a safe and secret place.

At first Luke had to use his Latin dictionary, but gradually he became more fluent in his translation as the phrases and words became familiar. What was obvious was the sense of menace overhanging this life.

De Witte was constantly on the move. He was described as a country gentleman and directed to minister to Catholic families in East Anglia. Luke found the succeeding descriptions lacked interest, as, for reasons of security, de Witte was not prepared to describe people or places, so that the entries were merely bland accounts of dates, Masses and numbers attending. He was mentally more stimulated later that morning, when he came to a passage in which de Witte described an incident that was public knowledge. In the summer of 1579, Queen Elizabeth made a royal progress through East Anglia, staying at a succession of houses en route to Norwich. Luke, in his background reading, had already learnt how she had stopped in August 1579 at the house of the Rookwood family at Euston, near Bury St Edmunds. Although the family were known Catholics the royal party chose this house. Hindsight suggests the government intended to make the incident that occurred an example to warn others in the area. Towards the end of her stay, the head of the family was presented to the Queen and de Witte described the scene.

My master, Rookwood, was called before the Queen in his own hall. A cruel courtier cried out, 'Thou art an idolatrous papist – it is a disgrace to Our Majesty thou comest here.' To the horror of all, he was taken away to prison. Later, this selfsame persecutor claimed a piece of court plate missing and instigated a great search throughout the house. God's mercy on us. In the nearby barn they found our Mass vessels and a statue of Our Lady. This last treasure was taken to the Queen awatching dances in the courtyard, taken with much obscenity and jest and thrown onto the fire burning there. How low our country has fallen into impiety. May I be saved from a similar fate to Our Lady's image.

Luke could sense the fear. This last sentence appeared to have been scrawled in haste. The whole description was written in a jagged style which he found difficult to translate and edit into meaningful language. He moved on to an easier task. He decided to turn to the latter part of the diary. In 1581 de Witte arrived in Cornwall and, after his conversion in 1583 to Anglicanism, the diary was written in English. Luke had already dipped into it and found it had a more colloquial style. It charted de Witte's meeting with Anglican divines after his conversion at Boscannon, his subsequent appointment as a Canon of Melbury Cathedral and his rapid promotion to bishop in 1587. He found it a relief to be able to scan the pages of the English and get the gist immediately, so he was annoyed to find a quarto dated 1588 that had reverted to Latin. He was about to put it aside and search for any references to Boscannon. So far he had drawn a blank in that quest and it confirmed that this period was covered by the part of the diary that was either at Boscannon or had been sold at auction.

However, he began to translate the 1588 quarto. Some of the words had been underlined and they caught his interest. They referred to a hundred and thirty ships off Calais and Philip of Spain. De Witte was writing about the threat of the Armada. Luke quickened his translating with mounting excitement as it told of the approaching Armada.

Some one hundred and thirty ships are abreast of Calais and there is a great fear they may land but thirty leagues from Melbury. My Lord Burghley today sent a messenger to take to safety the treasure of the Cathedral and make most secure the Wessex crown and jewels and Cathedral plate.

'Good God,' Luke exclaimed aloud. He went to the sunlight streaming through the gazebo window as he struggled to read the next entry dated three weeks later. The photocopied page of the diary shook in his trembling hands as he continued to translate.

It was a thing well done, thanks to my plan and Master Robert. Only I know the riddle of the attack on the great chest as it went on its way to safety at Berkeley Castle. Thanks be to God, much blood only and no death. The answer lies with the other secrets at 71-18-51-110-42-53-53-18-53.
God sent me Master Philip at this time.

With his Latin dictionary Luke slowly checked each word before writing out the paragraphs in full. He had stumbled across one of the great puzzles of the lost hordes of treasure, exceeded only by the loss of King John's treasure in the Wash. The task of editing the diary had changed in a flash from a mere scholarly exercise to an historical coup. In its pages could lie the answer to the whereabouts of the lost crown of Wessex, used in the medieval coronation of kings in Winchester Cathedral, and once at Melbury; also, the gold Mass vessels and jewelled copes that had been locked away in the treasury of Melbury Cathedral after the Reformation. Luke remembered that the cathedral archives had recorded the capture of the small troop taking the cathedral treasure chest on the cart to Berkeley. They had been surprised in thick fog in the Vale of Pewsey, just outside Bishops Cannings. During a bitter fight, one of the attackers had made the horse dragging the cart gallop away into the fog. It was found later abandoned outside Devizes – the chest empty of treasure but filled with many copies of a book by Robert Southwell arguing the merits of the Catholic faith.

Luke could hardly breathe he was so excited, his mind racing over the possibilities. Obviously, de Witte knew who was responsible for the outrageous attack, but was he a beneficiary, or was the treasure to be ransomed for a cause or hidden, to be shared later? He remembered from the cathedral history that someone came at the end of the century demanding a ransom, but he turned out to be a rogue who under torture confessed to pretending to know where the treasure had gone. Rumours abounded. Even Topcliffe, the dreaded torturer of Elizabeth, had been suspected, so that in the vale there was a rhyme which ran,

> In Pewsey Vale, at Bishops Canning
> Topclife gave God's jewels a tanning.

Not only might the diary give the answers, but it appeared to point to a place where the whereabouts of the treasure could be found if only the curious numerical reference could be deciphered.

Luke decided he must calm himself by making a cup of coffee in the house. As he got up he passed the bow window and looked across to Boscannon Manor. As he did so, the door in the walled garden opened and a large dog ran through it, followed by Francesca. He forgot his desire for coffee and moved swiftly to the telescope. He saw first that the dog was a borzoi, probably young, as it was charging round the terrace; second that Francesca was wearing khaki shorts and a matching shirt. He took in a stunned breath which he exhaled in a low whistle.

Unfortunately, his sight of them was short-lived as they dropped out of view into the wood leading down to the river. Luke did not move. He again rationalised his next decision. He decided he must meet her again to find out if she had any information about the diary. He wanted to see if she was going to appear by the river, so that he would know which way she was going to walk. He would then take the boat across, land ahead of her and walk back to meet her. He waited impatiently by the telescope to see whether she appeared at the top of the beach. After five minutes the dog emerged with a stick in its mouth, quickly followed by Francesca Boscannon. For a moment she paused, looking straight ahead at the pier. He was afraid she might turn around and disappear back into the wood. However, he saw her tapping the side of her leg with a stick and quite obviously calling the dog, which was casting around on the beach. It returned to her, and both of them set off along the southern side of the river and headed downstream towards the sea.

As soon as her direction was assured, Luke found himself running out of the cottage and down to where the pram was pulled up on the beach below. In spite of his haste, he had remembered to pick up the key of the motor boat moored out on the river. Ten minutes later the motor boat and pram were heading towards Falmouth Bay and the mouth of the Helford river. It was then that he caught another glimpse of Francesca and the dog.

Luke was concerned to find the shore of the river was devoid of beach at this point. Small cliffs topped with gorse, bracken and thick hedging was all he could see and his alarm increased when Francesca disappeared from view as the path was lost in the thick undergrowth.

He had to motor for another five minutes before he saw a small rough beach on which he could land, having anchored the motor boat offshore. The tide seemed to be running fast out of the river and he had some difficulty in rowing the pram to the shore. He calculated he must have been travelling at about twelve miles per hour, as the fast-running tide was carrying the boat with it, and so Francesca was probably a mile away from him as he finally squelched ashore on the seaweed-covered beach.

With difficulty he pushed inland to find the footpath through the thick scrub that lay at the back of the beach. He was sweating and, scratching himself, he began walking upstream to where he hoped Francesca would be, and was rewarded by the sight of the borzoi running towards him, still with a stick in its mouth. When it saw Luke it stopped, dropped the stick and began to bark excitedly, dancing to and fro, blocking Luke from progressing. Francesca's distant voice added to the commotion.

'Rasputin, Rasputin...' In a minute she appeared running round the corner of the path, and the dog put its tail between its legs and sank down on its haunches facing Luke.

'So sorry!' Both Luke and Francesca said the same words together.

She laughed. 'Golly, it's the rambling rector again! What are you up to today?'

'Just exploring this side of the river, hoping to find a deserted beach. Given up and came ashore for a walk.'

She looked at him quizzically. 'It's well met because I wanted to learn more of your scholar's quest. My enquiries at the manor were not well received. Let's walk on to where your boat is moored – it's too sweaty on this path here. We're surrounded by flies and tall undergrowth.'

Luke led the way back to his landing place. Although he had only been gone half an hour he was alarmed to see the motor boat out of the water, wedged between two seaweed-covered rocks. The fast current of the tide had dragged the boat and its anchor.

The girl laughed. 'We'll have plenty of time for a chat – about four hours until the tide floats you off those rocks! You seem a bit of a "landlubber rector".'

On one side of the beach was a patch of deep grass. The girl led the way there and sat down facing the river, pulled up her knees and rested her chin on her hands. Luke noticed she was wearing sensible walking shoes and long khaki socks to match her shirt and shorts. She had laid a small riding crop beside her once the dog had settled in the shade. Luke decided at that moment that she was the most beautiful woman he had ever met. He imagined her dressed as part of a smart African safari, but the neat cut of her clothes seemed quite natural on her, even though she was on a rough walk by a Cornish river. For a while they just looked at the river, watching a steady procession of yachts and motor boats. The borzoi rose from its haunches and poked its long nose into Luke's crutch.

Francesca laughed. 'He obviously thinks you're okay. As you

probably realise, he's called Rasputin and he's very young.' Luke pushed the dog gently away and stroked its neck. A silly ditty came to him, but he felt at ease immediately on this second meeting, so quietly he said,

'There's no disputing
He's called Rasputin,
For all can see
The Tsar's pedigree.'

Francesca laughed again. 'That's funny,' she said, and Rasputin began wagging his tail and jumped up and rushed around barking until she managed to seize his collar and drag him to her side. Luke was seized with envy for the dog.

'Now, spill the beans,' she smiled encouragingly.

Luke told her all he knew, and the reasons why he was editing the diary, but held back that morning's discovery about the treasure. When he had finished he turned to her.

'Tell me, why did your enquiries on my behalf cause a problem?' He tried to sound casual.

The girl laid back in the grass and stretched herself before putting her hands behind her head and looking up into the sky. In answering, she told Luke about her recent life.

'I married Philip Boscannon three years ago, just before he retired from the navy. My father served under him as a lieutenant commander at the Admiralty. I met him at a naval party in London. He asked me if I would cook and crew on his boat for his summer leave. I was at a loose end between jobs and love affairs, also absolutely skint – always have been, I'm afraid. Lieutenant commander fathers don't have spare cash, and my men friends were a feckless lot without a bean. The idea of getting away from it all and working for a tough naval father figure seemed a good idea at the time, and with no expenses I could save a little money. We started here and then sailed the boat for two weeks up channel to Plymouth where Boscannon was to end his naval career. He moored his boat and me up the Tamar and told me he wanted me to remain as crew for a further three months until winter set in. To cut a long story short, we had a last sail one long weekend in October and survived the devil of a storm. The rest of the party, another naval couple, remained below decks being sick. The mainsail split and we limped into Plymouth on the jib and the motor. As we headed up the Tamar he proposed to me and said he would buy a new yacht as a wedding gift to us both. I didn't know him at all really, but the storm showed his strengths and Boscannon Manor had charmed and impressed me. So, perhaps because of the emotion of returning safely to land, I accepted. Also we were both Catholics – not very serious ones – but it means you have the same mental foundations.

'The following year we were married at Boscannon, and a new forty-foot yacht was anchored off The Inn at Helford Passage – a surprise for me – and we were waved off on it by our guests and sailed away to the Isles of Scilly for our honeymoon. At the end of that summer, three naval friends came down for a weekend. Philip took them off to sail across to St Mawes for lunch at a posh restaurant there and I think they all drank too much. It was a rough day with a gusting wind and on the way back Philip had gone to untangle a painter attached to the jib. One of the party at the tiller was larking about, trying to grab a bottle of whisky. A gust of wind caught the boat, the mainsail jibbed and the boom caught Philip in the middle of his back. Now he's a paraplegic, as bitter as a rotten almond and so am I sometimes. I'm telling you all this because I want you to know I'm fascinated by your quest and would like to help, but because of this disaster to my husband I'm not close to him and never got to be so. I have to share looking after him with a difficult cousin – one Nancy Boscannon. You had a taste of her up at the house. So you see, I don't have the persuasive powers of a beloved wife to conjure up your diary for you, though I'm not sure if it still exists, at least in the house...'

Luke interrupted her and she was startled by the intensity of his voice.

'We've got to find it. The whole task has changed radically. I've discovered something unbelievably important in the diary. Not about what happened to the priest at Boscannon but of national historical importance. I can't tell you now, but it's dynamite.' The words tumbled from him.

Francesca's eyes widened. 'Well, I'll see what I can do. Philip goes to Truro for physiotherapy on Fridays. Will you still be here in two days' time?' Luke nodded. 'Nancy and I take it in turns to take him and it's hers this week, but she was talking about swapping it. If we don't, you can come over when they've gone – they'll be away for three to four hours. We'll have a good search and I'll give you a snack lunch. I'll know by tomorrow night, so give me your phone number. I'll probably have to pretend that I'm ringing my dress shop, so if the visit is on I'll just say you can deliver the dress as soon as possible. If this Friday is out but next is okay, I'll say please deliver the dress next week.' As she began to walk back up to the path along the cliff top she turned and waved. He returned it by raising an arm, but she had already turned away.

As he waited for the tide to float the boat off the rocks Luke's thoughts raced over a series of fantasies in which fame and fortune for the discovery of the royal crown and jewels would lead to some relationship with Francesca, forged by the fire of trying to unravel the mystery of the hidden treasure. He knew it could be dangerous. She gave off a remarkably composed air of resignation, but her life with a brute of a crippled husband made her vulnerable. His own relationships with women had been reserved since he had been ordained. He had been searching for a suitable fiancée to be a schoolmistress and cleric's wife. Before leaving Cambridge he had a six-month affair with a friend's sister, but it had burnt itself out. Currently he was developing a relationship with the young matron in the school sanatorium, but she did not impinge on his senses in the same way as Mrs Boscannon.

Eventually, the trapped boat floated away from the grip of the rocks in the current of the rising tide, and Luke rowed out in the pram to retrieve it before it dragged its anchor again. He returned to the beach below Alastair's cottage at full throttle, anxious to share the diary's revelations about the missing royal treasure of Melbury.

Alastair's innate Scottish suspicion of miracles put a dampener on Luke's excitement.

'Are you sure this is really part of the original diary, not a fake addition put in by some jesting scholar in later decades? These pages, post conversion to the Anglican faith, seem curiously out of keeping with the first quarto's measured Latin. They're in a jocular style of contemporary seventeenth-century English.'

Charlotte was sitting in the bow window of the gazebo and interrupted them; she had been studying Luke's translation of the morning relating to the missing treasure.

'Maybe he became jocular having switched from being a hunted Catholic priest to a comfortable Anglican bishop; like leaping from being Graham Greene's priest in *The Power and the Glory* to Bishop Proudie in Trollope's *Barchester Towers*.'

Alastair dryly commented on this interruption. 'You can see she read English at Oxford.'

Charlotte continued unabashed. 'Well, at least you could get a handwriting expert to verify that it's all written by the same author. I think it's a staggering development.'

Luke nodded. 'Spot on. An excellent idea.'

Alastair's dour Celtic mood was not mollified. 'Don't get carried away, man. Certainly it lifts the finding of the diary into a different dimension, but if it is discovered it still may not give a minute map reference to the hiding place of the treasure. Even if it did, it's likely de Witte's fellow conspirators would have moved the treasure on his death, or alternatively the shifting structures of the building over the century could have obliterated the treasure in dampness and rubble.'

Luke was not to be deflated. 'Maybe, but a gold crown, chalices and jewels and rotted vestments would still survive.'

'Aye, I can see your drift now.' Alastair was shaking his head. 'But just remember, the owners are still around. The Queen and the Church will reclaim their property, though I have no doubt you will get a reward and a one-minute slot on the TV news. Still, let's look at the coded reference to its place of hiding.' He had taken a piece of paper and having written down the numbers was shaking his head. 'Substituting one number for a letter just produces gibberish, and it seems that even if a number represented a word known only to de Witte it would not make sense. Still, if we look at the numbers and make them pairs we find something of interest ... 71-18-51-110-42-53-53-18-53. We have 53 occurring three times and 18 twice, and in the name Boscannon we have *N* occurring three times and *O* twice. Eureka, maybe it does refer to Boscannon. So you could be right to concentrate your research there.

They all beamed with excitement.

Charlotte clapped. 'Ali, you are clever after all!'

Luke laughed. 'Well, it's a hell of a boost to my task of editing the diary. I must find the missing parts and at present I'm relying on the lady of the manor to get me an invitation to root around when her antagonistic husband and his relation are out. Fortunately I met her by chance this afternoon and she's agreed to help.' He told them of his walk and meeting Francesca.

Alastair smiled and raised his eyebrows meaningfully. 'A chance meeting, how lucky. Fancy getting the boat across on an ebb tide just to walk on the other side.' He swung the telescope and pretended to study Boscannon Manor.

The telephone rang in the house. Charlotte got up but the ringing stopped. A moment later Alastair's son, Anthony, appeared.

'Sorry to disturb you, Pa, but a cranky woman just rang and asked if I was a Mr Luke in the Max Mara dress department? I said she must have the wrong number but that I do have a Mr Luke here, the Rev Luke. She apologised and asked me to give him this message. Tell him the dress can be delivered on Friday on approval as discussed.'

Luke blushed. 'Thank you, Anthony.'

Anthony looked astonished. 'Golly, you're not working part time in a mail-order dress business, are you?'

'Of course not – just a private joke.'

Alastair put his hand on the boy's shoulder. 'Don't worry, there are a lot of them about – private jokes.'

The boy shook his head in amazement and went back to the house to watch *Top of the Pops*.

Alastair hooted with laughter. 'I'm going to fix three strong drinks. You can have the day off on Friday and take the boat again. Charlotte, you had better find some pins for Luke so that he can fit the dress properly around the lady's delectable figure!'

'Don't be a beast, Ali. Get us the drinks.'

As he walked out the door he whooped again with laughter. 'No one will believe this.

'Don't mind him, Luke.' Charlotte got up and went over to Luke and gently touched his flaming cheek. 'I know you'll find the diary, and the treasure, too. It's fantastically thrilling, but be careful not to find more than you can handle. I'd hate you to be hurt.'

Luke shook his head. 'It's become an obsession, I know. What is imperative is that we tell no one about the treasure, not even family, otherwise Boscannon will be besieged by the media. It could be hell.'

Charlotte smiled. 'Jolly trying for Mrs Boscannon as well. Luke, you know Al and I are very fond of you. I'd hate to see you get hurt. I'm a woman and I can see what is beginning – you are very impressed by Mrs Boscannon.'

Luke blushed. 'Well really! I'm very impressed by the thrilling idea of finding treasure.'

Charlotte laughed. 'Come on, that could cover finding the treasure of Mrs Boscannon's affection. She sounds in a hell of a marriage and you are attractive. Don't forget I learnt something of life from my English degree: I don't want to see a friend turn into a Mellors besotted by a Lady Boscannon Chatterley!'

Luke blushed a deeper red. 'That's ridiculous.'

Charlotte tweaked his nose. 'Of course it's ridiculous and I don't want to see you so. Come, let's go and get those drinks...'

Chapter Seven

Next morning was another glorious summer's day. A phone call came for Luke from Francesca.

'Did you get my message? Good.' She laughed. 'Sorry, Luke, I'm just happy. The others left five minutes ago so come over as soon as poss. Come through the garden door.'

Luke felt a surge to delight at this easy intimacy. He didn't question where the rapidly accelerating familiarity was leading.

Half an hour later he was opening the door in the wall and entered the enclosed garden where Francesca had been dead-heading roses. He saw her on the far side to the large pond through which ran a stream. She was wearing a wide-brimmed black straw hat. Her dress was white. She looked towards him, removing her sunglasses and putting them in a flat basket she was holding in one hand. On seeing him she put the basket on the ground and came to meet him. She took both his hands and kissed him on both cheeks.

'You look nice in mufti.'

Luke was wearing a light-blue shirt and matching jeans. He felt absurdly happy.

She took his hand. 'Come and look at my roses first. After Rasputin they are my joy. See these Damask roses – aren't they lovely?'

Luke nodded. 'My father grows them in his house in the close at Melbury. He tells me the crusaders brought them to England from the Middle East.'

She smiled up at him. 'How exciting and how lovely, your father living in the cathedral close at Melbury – I know it.'

She led him to another group of roses. 'I'm told these are the oldest – Gallica roses grown by the Greeks and Romans.'

They walked slowly from one flower bed to another. At the

67

edge of a bed of soft pink roses was a line of burgundy red flowers with small drooping fronds of colour.

'What are those?' asked Luke.

She blushed, reflecting the colour of the flowers. 'Love-lies-bleeding.' A thousand images crowded their thoughts as they both were lost for words. 'Do you know this rose?' She broke the silence and picked one of the pink roses.

Luke shook his head and she looked pleased at his ignorance.

'It's "Omar Khayyám", raised from the seed of a rose found on his grave – isn't that exotic?' She picked one. 'Wonderful perfume but not a particularly good rose.' She had stopped and with one hand held the flower under her nose and turned to face Luke and stood looking at him intently. Her other hand still held Luke's and slowly she moved the rose for him to smell. 'Isn't it beautiful?' They were standing very close to each other and they said nothing. She squeezed his hand hard and they both pretended to look at the rose, but in reality were looking into each other's eyes, searching to find approval for their unspoken attraction for each other. The spell was broken by the distant sound of a stable clock striking the half-hour. Francesca let go of his hand. 'I suppose we'd better pursue your scholar's quest for the diary. Let's have a drink first, I've got some champers.'

She led the way into the house through the open French windows. A bottle of champagne and two cut glasses stood on a silver tray in the drawing room. This was a panelled room with soft-grey-painted wood, and contained chintzy covered chairs and a four-seater sofa. It had a cool air of comfort in contrast to the dank public rooms Luke had seen on his first visit. Francesca asked him to open the champagne. It was a Bollinger.

'Here's to finding what you want,' said Francesca as she raised her glass to her lips.

'Amen to that,' Luke replied, 'though for most of us it's difficult to say what that is.'

Francesca looked at him quizzically. 'Come and sit down.' She patted one of the cushions on the sofa indicating where he should go. He sat down and she leant against one of the arms. 'Tell me, do you feel the need to act all the time like a parson or priest or whatever you like to call yourself? I mean, saying "Amen to that" and making an opaque spiritual remark.'

Luke found it difficult to follow her change of mood. He judged she wasn't angry, just in a direct way asking a question that genuinely puzzled her.

'Well, I don't act the part, but I suppose one falls into a religious mode of speech when one is immersed in it all one's working life. Like Guards officers who develop habits of speech. I'm sorry if mine grated.'

'Not at all, I'm really interested. Some of our priests talk as if there was no spiritual dimension, especially if they are Irish and racing mad. It must be a terrible strain having to be nice to people and always acting in a spiritual way.'

Luke laughed. 'It's bloody sometimes, I can tell you. I've got a sarcastic master problem and it doesn't sit easily under my dog collar.' He realised he had never spoken to anyone like this before. It seemed absolutely natural.

'I can understand. It's like that for us being Catholics. People expect us to be better than the rest of the population and get a satisfaction from the situation if we're not. Pagans have a much easier life, though a lot of them are dead underneath the surface. Come on, let's finish this bottle and then attack the library. I tried to find out more for you from Philip at dinner last night, but he shut up like a clam. His beastly cousin, Nancy, ticked me off in the kitchen afterwards. She said that if I had read the history of the house properly, I would know that the Elizabethan recusant priest here called de Witte had left the church to become a Prot and abandoned the then lord of the manor to the mercy of the authorities, who chased him to death. The man had the cheek to marry his widow. So it was a no-go area to try and help some outside prying eyes uncover a Catholic scandal by looking for his diary. She added a funny thing, saying, "anyway, there's a legend that the diary was bad karma," you know, a curse on anyone reading it. And, even more peculiar, she said Philip had done so before his accident, though she believed he had subsequently sold part of it with some pictures and furniture that were auctioned. Because of this I never got to mention it again. Hardly encouraging news for you.'

Luke felt again the chill that had struck him when the school librarian had pointed out the malediction the first time he had handled the diary.

The girl stood up straight. 'Come on, drink up, I've got something better to drink with our lunch, but first the library. I have at least found a copy of the auction catalogue, so you may be able to see what might have been sold relating to the de Witte papers. Also, Philip's father had someone catalogue the library just after the war and I've found that as well.'

Luke was not certain later whether it was the effect of the champagne or just a surge of delight that Francesca was assisting him in the chase and had found the auction details and catalogue without being asked. Anyway, he found he could no longer keep from her the possibility of the diary leading to the lost Melbury treasure.

'Francesca, thank you for your valuable help. If you're going to continue assisting me I think I have to tell you about something pretty shattering – a discovery I found in the diary. You'd better sit down, but you must promise to tell no one else.'

Her eyes widened at the seriousness in Luke's voice and she sat down beside him.

'My lips are sealed, so you can tell me.'

When Luke had finished telling her about the treasure, she gasped, '*Dio mio!*'

Luke burst out laughing and she joined in. Their laughter swept away the restraint that had been making their conversation tense after being so close when looking at the 'Omar Khayyám' rose.

Francesca sat up straight and smoothed her hair. 'Okay, Sherlock Holmes. I'll fetch the catalogue and auction particulars and you can study those while I get us a bite to eat. A moment later she returned with the library catalogue written on lined paper, yellowed with age, and the auction particulars from Christie's. The latter contained the following description: *A calf folder containing four quartos of parchment. The calf folder branded at the top with de Witte's family motto, 'If God be with us, who can be against us.' One quarto in Latin, one in English and two consisting of numerals presumed code.* There was a tick written against the lot number and the sum of £160.

'Oh, my God,' sighed Luke. 'Sold – we must find the buyer.'

He turned to the library catalogue. The contents of the library were listed in a fine italic script. He came to the description of the de Witte diaries. It differed from the auction particulars, listing three quartos in English instead of one, each quarto being given a date. The one in Latin and two in code were also catalogued.

So, there were still two in English that Philip Boscannon could have retained. These at least would still be in the house, and perhaps those sold could be traced and the buyer found. Even if they could not be bought, at least he should have a chance to edit them. His train of thought stopped as Francesca came back into the room with a tray. He got up to help her.

'Put this cutlery and the glasses on the table. I hope you like steak tartare. I'll get the rest. I've lifted a bottle of '82 Laffite from the cellar. Could you open it?' She handed him a corkscrew as she turned to go back to the kitchen.

Half an hour later they were sitting back on the sofa having consumed not only the steak, but her husband's exquisite bottle of wine. They were both pleasantly mellow and were trying to sober up on strong black coffee, though an accompanying glass of Grand Marnier was not assisting. Rasputin was stretched out in the sun by the open French windows, snoring gently.

Luke turned to her. 'When you exclaimed "*Dio mio*", why did you do so in Italian?'

'Well, I'm half-Italian. It's my passionate side coming out. My mother was Italian.' As she finished the sentence she turned and kissed him fully on the lips. It was a totally natural happening, and he returned her kiss with even greater ardour. It seemed he was now on automatic human pilot, his dog-collar persona left on the ground. Then it seemed for them that time had ceased to exist. Their tongues made contact, tasted each other and explored. At last she broke away and lay back on the length of the sofa. She took his hand and pulled him down to her. Their hunger for each other amazed them both and although their only contact was their lips and the pressure of the upper part of their bodies, they were rapidly approaching an inevitable climax. Francesca was making little mewing noises and Luke was groaning, lost in the tide of passion. This state of uncontrolled bliss was broken by the noise of the dog growling. Rasputin had been disturbed by their behaviour and had padded round to the back of the sofa, put his front paws on it and pushed his nose firmly between Luke's writhing shoulders.

Luke sat up in astonishment, followed by Francesca, who pushed the dog away, saying, 'Jealous beast!' She got off the sofa and took the dog by the collar. 'You come with me, you must repent in the kitchen. Luke, I'll be back in a jiffy – you're beautiful.' She blew him a kiss as she disappeared through the door, taking the reluctant Rasputin. As good as her word, she was only gone for two minutes.

Luke took her hand and pulled her down so that he could start kissing her again, moving from her lips to nuzzle her neck and gently biting the lobes of her ears. She began mewing again until she ended with a cry that died to a whimper of pleasure. She broke away.

'I'm going for a swim.' She pointed to the large pond in the rose garden. 'When I'm alone in the summer it's the bestest thing I'm able to enjoy. It's always a little cool because of the stream running though it but it'll clear our heads and then we can get back to relaxing on the sofa.' As she was speaking she was taking off her clothes slowly, throwing each item on to one of the chairs. 'Come on, lazy.' She stood before him completely naked. Her skin was spotless, like silk, and her body magnificent. She had a tiny waist over well-formed hips. A flat tummy led to firm breasts. 'If you don't join me I won't help you with the diary ever again, let alone kiss you.'

Luke stood up and tried to grab her wrists but missed, and the alcohol in his system unbalanced him as she pushed him away and he slumped back onto the sofa.

'Come on, groggy legs,' she said, and walked out through the French windows, adding, 'no clothes, please. Prudes not allowed in my sacred pool.'

Luke rapidly got to his feet and tore off his clothes as far as his underpants. Her slow undressing – in fact a calculated striptease – plus his unrealised passion made it impossible to remove this last article of clothing. He was in a state of rampant excitement. He ran out of the room into the garden and, seeing her ahead swimming gently, did a racing dive and swamped her, giving her no time to protest at his bulging underwear. In a moment she had swum to him and flung her arms around him.

72

'You brute, what are these?' In one swift move she had pushed him over and at the same time slipped his pants down to his ankles. In order to swim he had to kick them off, and as they floated to the top she seized them and flung them out of the pool. They landed on top of a nearby rose tree. She swam over to him, put her arms round his neck and then rubbing her whole being against him whispered, 'Who's a lovely boy, then?' before putting her hands on his shoulders.

Luke placed his hands round her waist and was about to lift her up before thrusting against her, when they both froze. Behind the far wall of the garden was a drive leading to the front door of the house and they heard the sound of a car crunching over the gravel. A door slammed. The voice of Nancy boomed over the wall.

'It's no use complaining to the hospital, Philip. We'll write to Matthew about their incompetence – isn't he the chairman of the hospital board? I'm sure he'll have the matter investigated.'

Francesca put her finger to her lips and whispered, 'Oh God. Something obviously wrong at the hospital. What bloody luck!'

Her whispers were interrupted by barking and then Rasputin appeared, bounding out of the French windows with Luke's trousers in his mouth.

'Hell,' Luke hissed under his breath, 'who let the dog out?'

Francesca took his hand and pointed to the gazebo in the corner of the garden. 'Get behind that, now. I'll try and get your clothes together.'

Luke clambered out and sped behind the building, dripping and shivering with cold, and, he admitted later, also with shock. He heard Francesca shouting, 'Rasputin, come, good boy, give to Mummy. Oh, *do* come here.'

A moment later she appeared behind the gazebo clutching her own clothes and his shirt, shoes and socks. She was also trembling and began to dry herself with the shirt.

'Hey!' Luke exclaimed.

As she pulled her clothes over her half-wet body she whispered, 'The bloody dog ran out of the garden with your trousers.'

'Thanks a million,' muttered Luke. 'What about my pants?'

She shook her head. 'I couldn't reach them.'

'Thanks another million. I'll be arrested for indecent exposure.'

'Shut up, you rambling rector ... or erector...' She looked at him and started laughing.

Luke looked at her in astonishment and laughed. 'This is no time for crudity. Do something, girl.'

'Right. I'll get Nancy and Boss in the kitchen for some tea and light conversation about hospital cock-ups. When they're at the trough, I'll come outside and call Rasputin three times. That's a signal for you to foot it up the main stairs. My room is first on the right at the top. Go in there – there's a bathroom en suite on one side, but there's also a door leading out of it into Boss's room, so don't use that, for God's sake. You'll hear us coming, as the lift doors make a hell of a clang when it stops on the landing and we get Boss's chair out.'

'I'm shitting myself already,' said Luke, 'at the thought of my French-farce dash up your stairs.'

'I love you.' She kissed him on the lips as she left him.

A few minutes later he heard Nancy's voice. 'There you are – you've obviously had fun. We've had hell. The hospital failed to tell us the appointment was cancelled because the stupid physio is sick. People in hospitals cannot be sick. Boss is in a foul mood. Where's your luncheon friend? You didn't tell me you were expecting a visitor.'

'Oh, quite unexpected. An old school chum, Ursula Standfast. I'm afraid you've just missed her. Great to see her and super surprise. Being on holiday at St Ives, she thought she'd come over. I'll make you some tea. Sorry about the hospital.'

Both Francesca and Luke prayed his underpants would not be noticed, gently gyrating at the top of the rose tree next to the pool, but fortunately, at the mention of tea Nancy turned and went back into the house.

Luke waited a few minutes and sprinted to retrieve his underpants. Francesca had thrown them onto the top of a thick rose bush. Luke noted with an ironic snort a label identifying it as 'Maiden's Blush'. He tried to disentangle the pants without tearing them on the copious thorns. He succeeded, though a large thorn pierced the finger on which he wore his signet ring and a piece lodged itself deep behind it. He began to bleed copiously, staining his underpants. He sprinted back behind the gazebo to put them on. They were still damp from the pool, and now his blood and consequently the

74

words 'deflowered virgin' kept interrupting his thoughts as he planned his campaign. His first task was to stem the bleeding on his little finger. He didn't want to leave a trail of blood in the house. He tried to ease off his signet ring, revealing as he did so a deep gash from the embedded thorn. The finger was beginning to swell and the ring was reluctant to move. His efforts were given greater impetus by the sound of Francesca calling Rasputin three times. He tugged frantically at the ring. It shot off the end of his finger and rolled onto the stone floor of the gazebo. He froze in horror as it disappeared between a gap in the large stones covering the floor. He went to look but could see no sign of it. There was a garden spade leaning against the wall of the gazebo. Luke picked it up and gingerly lowered it into the gap and it dropped without check. He tried to ease up the stone with it until it threatened to break. The size of the stones required at least two men with crowbars to lift it. Luke sighed. 'What a day.' He marked the crack in the stone with the spade.

The priority was to get to Francesca's room. He looked round the corner of the gazebo and ran for the house. When he got to the French windows he stopped, took off his shoes and tiptoed to the hall. He caught sight of himself in a long looking glass. He held his still-bleeding finger cradled to his shirt. Having lost his trousers he had no handkerchief from which to make a tourniquet. He was a dishevelled and shocking figure with tousled hair and blood smeared on his face that was now staining his shirt as well.

'My God,' he breathed. 'I could be the first choice for the ghost in Hamlet.' He shot across the wooden floor of the hall. As he passed the kitchen he heard Rasputin barking and scratching at the door and, over the noise of the dog, he heard Boscannon shouting, 'Hell, woman, that empty bottle is one of my last Laffite '82s. Do you know what that's worth? Two hundred and fifty to three hundred pounds!'

Cousin Nancy butted in even louder. 'Was worth,' she said, then, 'I'll get your slippers.'

Luke knew that he could not get up the stairs if Nancy was coming out of the kitchen, as its door was the nearest one to the bottom of the long staircase. However, he remembered the downstairs layout sufficiently to make a quick dash to the cloakroom which, conveniently, was under the stairs.

Unfortunately, Luke had not heard Boscannon say that he had left his slippers in that room as Nancy went to get them. Luke had just sat down to relieve himself on the lavatory when he heard the door handle turn, but, as he'd had time to lock it, he was temporarily undiscovered, though he had difficulty in suppressing any noise of tinkling into the lavatory bowl. He broke out into a sweat as Nancy tried to open the door with increasing vigour. He heard muttering and then the sound of her footsteps returning to the kitchen.

Luke realised he only had a few seconds before she returned with Boscannon; no doubt armed with his gun. He threw open the window and then he opened the door a crack and, seeing the hall was empty, shot across it into the drawing room, throwing himself behind the sofa where earlier that afternoon he had embraced Francesca. He wondered what she was doing at that moment.

Nancy was addressing the others in the kitchen. 'Sorry, Boss, the loo door is jammed or someone is in there, so I can't get your slippers. Francesca, your visitor hasn't passed out in the loo, has she, after all the wine you've consumed?'

Francesca shook her head vehemently.

Boscannon said, 'Get my gun in case we have a burglar in there.'

Nancy went off to his gun cupboard in a room off the kitchen which also housed her riding kit and his fishing rods. She returned after a couple of minutes and Boscannon led the way. He nodded to Nancy to try the door again. She did and it opened.

'Bloody hell! Something odd here. I could swear it was locked.'

Boscannon told her to stand aside and motored over to the lavatory and opened the cover. He bent forward. 'Someone has just peed in here. Do you have an explanation, Francesca?' His eyes had narrowed as he spoke.

Francesca averted her face from his gaze. 'Sorry, yes, I just popped in here before joining you in the kitchen. I'm afraid I was in a hurry to help you.'

Boscannon exchanged disbelieving looks with Nancy. He

lowered his voice and said, 'You're a bad liar. If I discover whatever has really been going on, I'll flay you! Let's just do a recce of the rest of the house, in case we have a burglar. I haven't shot one of those yet! German U-boat crew, yes; burglars, no.'

He swung his chair round and motored towards the drawing room. At that moment Rasputin had managed to paw open the kitchen door and bounced past them into the room ahead. Boscannon reached the doorway first to see Rasputin disappear behind the sofa. Luke patted him gently, then firmly pushed him away. Rasputin broke into excited barking and leapt over the back of the sofa and descended, knocking over a coffee table on which stood a vase of flowers.

Boscannon began an icy blast. 'How many times have I told you, girl, to keep that dog out of the main part of the house. Come here, you bloody animal, and you, you stupid girl, clear up that mess.' He had caught the dog by its collar and it was nearly strangling itself as it fought to get free.

Francesca cracked. Picking up an ebony ruler she rapped Boscannon's knuckles so that he let go of Rasputin, who bounded out of the still-open French windows. Francesca ran out after him, with Boscannon screaming obscenities as he motored after her.

A moment later, Nancy ran through the room and out into the garden. Luke seized his opportunity and sprinted up the stairs. When he reached the top of the stairs, he opened the door on the right. Its contents confirmed that it was Francesca's bedroom. In contrast to the rest of the house it was decorated in a Laura Ashley chintzy style. The bedspread matched the curtains and the top of the bed had suffered a population explosion of teddy bears. Her dressing table was crowded with family photographs, family weddings and christenings and a lot of school groups holding tennis racquets. Luke went to the chest of drawers and opened the top to find a pile of handkerchieves. He took one and made a tourniquet around his bleeding finger. As he was doing this, Francesca came into the room. She cast her eyes over him, smothering a giggle and said, 'If you don't mind me saying so, I preferred your first appearance as Chaplain of Melbury.'

Luke's sense of humour had not deserted him. He laughed.

'Look, I've got to get out of here or face a public uproar. Where are my bloody trousers?'

'Darling, I don't know.'

'Well, for Christ's sake, find them – or a substitute.'

At that moment the lift gates on the landing opened with a metallic clang.

'Oh God, Nancy and Boss. Don't go next door whatever you do.'

Luke snorted. 'This farce gets more ridiculous – why don't you just introduce me to the family?'

They heard the door of the bathroom open and Nancy's voice boomed, 'I've done enough. Francesca, take over to change Boss.'

'Get under the bed, Luke.'

He slid under the valance without further protest. He heard Nancy shouting, 'Francesca', and a weary reply, 'I'm coming.'

For several minutes all that Luke could hear were the sounds of running water, flushing lavatories and low murmuring voices from the adjoining room. At one point, the door between the two rooms had opened and Francesca had looked in to make sure Luke was out of sight. She returned to the bathroom but failed to shut the door behind her. It clicked open after she left, so that Luke could hear every word.

'You might show Boss a bit of sympathy. God, what a life, can't get out of this chair, stuck in this hell. I've had an absolute shitty day – stupid place – and then coming back to find you'd poured away my Laffite '82 – what the hell were you playing at, girl?'

'My life's not a riot here, so if a pal comes unexpectedly I want to entertain. I didn't know it was so valuable.'

'Balls,' snorted her husband. 'Anyway, that makes it a day for a bit of a treat for Boss. Get on with it. You know what I want, don't just stand there like a stuffed dummy. Take your shirt off, I need to see them, see them hard.'

'Boss, I won't. Not today, please.'

'Do as you're told, girl.'

Luke heard the sound of the chair motor hum into action.

'Let go of my wrist ... Oh God, Boss, that's one of my best silk shirts.'

'Don't bloody care, show them to me. Go on.'

'No! No! No!'

Luke wanted to leave his hiding place under the bed, but he had to suffer this appalling exchange as he knew his appearance would make the situation even worse.

Boscannon started screaming, 'Nancy, Nancy', above the sound of Francesca's sobbing. Another door opened. 'What the hell's happening now. Boss?'

'Get the bitch out. She won't help me get to bed and rest.'

Then the door slammed between the bathroom and the bedroom, and he heard the sound of a key turning. Beyond the door the sounds of shouting increased in volume.

Francesca entered the room and collapsed by the side of the bed, sobbing convulsively. Luke put out a hand and took her wrist, whispering, 'Don't worry, I'll help. Don't worry. Please Francesca, trust me.'

After a few moments she regained control. She disengaged her wrist. 'Just stay here. I'll get a pair of Boss's jeans from the laundry, though they won't be ironed.'

Luke continued to hide under the bed. He felt contaminated by the revelations of Francesca's marital life. He had promised help, but how could he with his limited resources? It all seemed beyond him. Anyway, he couldn't cope with the scandal that would result were he to take Francesca away to his own life.

The bedroom door opened.

'You can get out now.'

Luke got up from under the bed.

'Nancy's putting Boss to sleep and in a moment she'll go down to the kitchen to get him a large whisky. I'll give the word when she returns to his room and then you'll have to leg it.' Then she started laughing as Luke clambered into the unironed jeans. The legs reached just below his knees and the waist flapped around him – it was at least four inches too large.

'I'll find you a belt.'

She went to her wardrobe and brought him a black leather belt. She stood close in front of him as she threaded it through the loops on the jeans and then pulled it tight to fasten it so that Luke was brought forwards to touch her. She was nearly his height in her heeled shoes, and they stood breathing heavily. Luke stirred involuntarily and once again they were kissing, their passion overwhelming them. Her breasts were revealed through her torn shirt. Outside the room they heard a door shut.

'Nancy's going down now.' Reluctantly, Francesca broke away. 'When she goes back to Boss's room I'll meet her on the landing, and as she goes in I'll say, "Thank you, Nancy." That's your signal to skedaddle. I'll ring you as soon as I can. You've got to stay in my life. Promise?'

Luke kissed her forehead. 'Of course, I told you, don't worry.'

'God, you look a sight.' She went into the bathroom and returned with a flannel and towel and removed the dried blood on his arms and dabbed at his stained shirt. 'You'd better have something else.' She produced a navy polo-necked jersey from the back of a chair. 'There, that suits you.' From the landing came the sound of the lift moving. 'That's Nancy. We'll exchange clothes as soon as possible. I'll try to find your trousers. Don't forget the important part of today – we've found each other.' She touched his cheek and went out of the room, leaving the door ajar. A moment later he heard her say, 'Thank you, Nancy.'

Luke looked out onto the landing. Francesca was standing outside Boss's bedroom door, her hand on the door handle. She motioned Luke to move with a jerk of her head. When he got to the bottom of the stairs he turned round – she had not moved – and she blew him a kiss. Luke ran back into the garden and onto the path through the woods to the jetty and the beach. Fortunately, the boat was afloat.

When he got back to the cottage it was after six. Charlotte came out of the kitchen.

'We were beginning to worry...' she said, and then she saw his clothes. 'What on earth?'

Luke blushed. 'Slipped in the water, so the lady of the manor helped me out with these togs. Unfortunately cut my finger too.'

Alastair also appeared. 'Not got into too deep water, I hope,' he said, and laughed ironically.

After dinner Luke found it difficult to adjust to the homely family atmosphere. His mind was in turmoil. Before going to bed he walked to the bottom of the garden. It was a warm, moonlit night, and a soft breeze was blowing down river. In the distance he heard a car leaving from the direction of Helford Passage and voices from The Inn at the waterside. A single light could be seen from Boscannon Manor. Luke rested a foot on the low wall before him and murmured a remembered line from The Merchant of Venice. ' "When the sweet wind did gently kiss the trees and they did make no noise, in such a night Troilus methinks mounted the Troyan walls, and sighed his soul towards the Grecian tents, where Cressid lay that night." '

Then, kicking the wall, he said, 'God, I'm hopelessly in love. Not possible, it must be a delusion. Can't be the male menopause, I'm only thirty-nine. It's time I got back to Melbury and my duties.'

Next morning, his sober reflection was aided by a call from his father's home. It was Margery.

'I'm afraid your father's had a bad fall and broken his right arm. He's in hospital now and they say they will keep him overnight. Could you come back tomorrow, as I've got my mother coming to stay and she's a bit frail? Sorry to spoil your holiday with this news.' Luke went to break the news and found Alastair and Charlotte in an embrace in the kitchen. Alastair was waving a letter in his right hand.

'I've just heard from the provost that I'm to succeed you as master in charge of cricket during your sabbatical.'

Luke's face lit up. 'I can think of no one better, but I'm afraid I've got only bad news – my father's broken his arm and I have to leave your idyllic existence here.'

This news was greeted with genuine sadness.

Luke packed hurriedly. He knew if he delayed departure he might get a call from Francesca and he had no idea what he would say to her. By ten o'clock he was on his way back to Melbury.

Chapter Eight

Luke's journey to Melbury took longer then he expected. The traffic was heavy all the way and the road from Taunton to the A303 was blocked by an accident involving a caravan and a bus. He arrived at his small house in Melbury, tired and dispirited. The house seemed stale and lifeless after the liveliness of the holiday cottage in Cornwall. He felt lonely and was tempted to ring Boscannon and try to speak to Francesca. This he resisted after a considerable struggle. He knew continuation of their relationship would lead not only to serious complications in his life but serious sin.

His depression was deepened when, having changed clothes and had some tea, he had visited his father in Melbury hospital. While changing, he had deliberated as to whether he should wear his cassock and decided that this time it was the right garb. Because his father was over seventy he had been put in a ward full of geriatrics. When Luke arrived in the ward he saw his father lying forlorn and shrunken. He sat gently on the side of the bed and quietly took his good hand.

'Father, what have you been doing to yourself?'

'My dear boy,' his voice quavered. 'How good of you to leave Cornwall and come. I understand from Margery you will collect me tomorrow morning. It can't come too soon. This place is full of gibbering old maniacs. They should be in loony bins.' At this he lowered his voice and, pointing to a bed opposite, whispered, 'That creature used to work behind the bar in the Black Swan. Phoney poofter, thinks he's the Earl of Wessex and gabbles gibberish all the time – listen to him.' His father tapped the side of his head with his good hand, then took Luke's arm and whispered again. 'It's a bloody disgrace people like him being in a public ward. Last night when I was coming round from my arm being set, I saw him removing the vase of roses

82

that Margery brought me. I was too fazed to say anything, but I gather he wrapped the roses in a newspaper and gave them to the ward sister.' His father glared across at the ex-barman, who was now beckoning to Luke. 'I should go now before he gets you in his clutches.'

Luke kissed his father's forehead and waved goodbye to the barman. This prompted a cry of 'Padre, please, I need your help.'

'Oh God,' thought Luke. 'Now I'm trapped. If I had not been in a dog collar I would have pretended not to have heard. Now the whole ward will damn the Church if I leave without speaking to him.'

'Let me introduce myself.' The man seized Luke's wrist as he moved to speak to him. 'I'm the Earl of Wessex, the Earl of Wessex, the Earl of Wessex.'

'Very pleased to meet you. How can I help?'

The man leaned forward, still gripping Luke's wrist. 'Come back when it's dark. I want you to marry me to one of the sisters. She's agreed to be the Countess of Wessex.'

'Ah, I see. Well, unfortunately I have another wedding tonight. Let me see the time...' At this Luke prised away his wrist from the man's hand. 'Perhaps tomorrow evening. I hope you sleep well tonight, get your strength up.' He backed away and made a rapid exit, hearing shouts of 'I'll pay you, I'll pay you a thousand pounds. Must be tonight, though.'

Luke knew he had failed in his duty of compassion, but his worries had drained him.

When Luke got back home he opened his mail. There were gas, electrical and phone bills, all bigger than expected. 'Perhaps I should go back and do the wedding,' he mused. Next morning he returned to collect his father. It was a beautiful August day, and with a sigh of satisfaction his father greeted the cathedral close as they drove under the arch that led to the broad sweep of the lawns at the west end. His father's house overlooked this swathe of green which, apart from young William doing handstands, was free of people. Luke helped his father gently out of the car so that the injured arm was not knocked. He led him through the small front garden where the heady scent of flowers greeted them. His father exclaimed with delight when the front door was opened by Margery. She had managed to get a friend to be with her mother so that she could be there when they arrived. Luke went back to the car to collect the small canvas bag containing his father's belongings. He noticed how little it contained; a Bible, a book of prayers, slippers and some frayed pyjamas, an old toothbrush and shaving things, that was all. He felt that even had his father been going for a longer stay at some plush hotel, that was all he would have taken.

After lunch, he went back to his house to collect what he needed to stay with his father. It was agreed he would stay for a week until Margery's mother returned to her own home. While he was packing he had two phone calls in quick succession. The first was from Christie's. He had made contact with an old Melbury boy who he knew worked there. He was head of the manuscripts and books department and now, back from holiday, had rung to tell him who had bought the de Witte quartos. It was the English College in Rome. The bids had been made by one of the staff there, a Fr Hammond.

Luke thanked him profusely. Inwardly he was delighted. Not only was it in good hands, but maybe the English College in Rome had information about de Witte that would help him in his quest.

He cheered up a little as he contemplated the information about the English College in Rome. His task of editing the diary came not only with payment, but expenses. He would contact their Fr Hammond and make a visit to Rome as soon as his family commitments allowed. He had just finished packing when the phone rang again. He cursed silently before answering.

'Father Luke? You're a beast, Father Luke. You took me to the edge of paradise and then evaporated.'

'Francesca, I'm so sorry.'

'Yes, I know about your father's arm. Your friend Charlotte told me. I didn't have her number but I drove round this morning. She's nice. Since you left I've been in hell, frantic. I hate you so much for not ringing, because I love you. Now I've said it again and I know to you I was a dangerous holiday thing, but I can't help it. I'm obsessed with you, can't get you out of my mind.'

'Darling, I can only say how sorry I am for not getting in touch, but I didn't know what persona I should adopt if someone else answered the phone...'

She interrupted him. 'God! Use the same shop-assistant guise until we think of something else, like the police or the Prince of Wales, anything, so at least I would know you cared.'

'I was going to write.'

'Don't you dare! They examine my post like the Inquisition. I know Nancy sometimes steams open my letters. Though duty keeps me they suspect I want to break out. I won't, so don't worry. I'm not going to bolt and park myself outside your door and cause a scandal, honest, but please Luke we must keep in touch – I can't live without that.'

Luke knew he must play for time. He was pretty certain her undertaking not to bolt hid a desperate desire to do so and at this juncture he didn't know what to say until his own emotions were under control and he could make a rational decision.

'Look, I must stay with my father until the end of the week. Then I've got to arrange a trip to Rome.' He explained the news from Christie's. 'After that, I'll come down to Cornwall and stay nearby. Perhaps we'll have better luck next time with the library if you can get the house to yourself again...

'Is that all you can think of, using me for your research? first I'd rather have better luck in my bedroom – that's having immediate treasure. Hell, my phonecard's running out. I'm in a box in Helston. It smells.'

Luke was worried. It seemed his romantic future with Francesca was to proceed without delay. She was not going to allow time for clerical doubts to intrude.

'Darling, when can I safely ring you?' The phone went dead at this question. Luke was filled with anxiety, fearful as to what he would say when and if she rang. He only had to wait two minutes.

'I've moved to another box with coins. It's even smellier. Darling, thank you for calling me "darling". Give me your father's number so I know at least I can have a word, just to hear your voice. You don't have to gush love if your Dad's at hand.' Luke was overcome by her need and obvious love. He gave her the number. 'Money running out. I adore you. Can't wait to see you again.'

It was two weeks before Luke could leave for Rome. His father had taken a long time to recover from the shock of the broken arm and his treatment in hospital, and it had been necessary for Luke to help with the return home of a testy invalid.

He stayed in his father's house to help Margery. Because of its small size it was impossible to have a completely private conversation, so that when he rang Francesca he was unable to express his feelings for her. Numerous times Francesca called while Luke's father was in the same room and he was obliged to confine himself to pleasantries. One morning Francesca had exploded with anger.

'For God's sake, this morning I'm alone in this morgue. Can't you get to a phone box and tell me you love me?'

'Of course I do. I promise after my visit to Rome I'll come down and tell you in person.'

'I want to hear it now, for heaven's sake. If you love me, find a reason to leave your father and phone: if I don't hear from you in the next half an hour I'll come to you whatever the problems here or with you.' She had ended by slamming the phone down.

Luke looked at the buzzing phone with surprise.

'Father,' called Luke, 'I have to go into town to the bank. We'll lunch when I get back.'

In fact he went straight to the town's best hotel, The Golden Hind, where he remembered there was a phone box in the reception area. As a housemaster he had been regularly entertained by parents, and the Golden Hind's good dining room had provided a base for parental ambitions to be launched at Luke in the hope of gaining some favour for their children. When he arrived there, the manageress of the hotel was standing behind the reception desk.

'Good morning, Fr Luke. We've missed you while you've been away. It's nice to see you again.'

'Thank you. My father's phone is out of order so I wondered if I could use your box naturally I'd like a drink and a chat afterwards.'

'What a nuisance and what a coincidence. Your father has just telephoned to book a dinner table for four. Obviously phoning from a friend's. How is his arm?'

Luke flushed. His lie about the phone sounded thin and he had also discovered that his father was planning a dinner party of which he had not been informed.

The phone box was small and Luke felt constrained again as he phoned Francesca's number. He got her immediately. He noticed the manageress taking a long time to arrange some flowers on a table just outside the box. He was convinced she knew there was something of interest to be heard having disbelieved his excuse about the telephone. He put up a hand to shield his voice as he spoke to Francesca. Out of the corner of his eye he could see the manageress still hovering, removing and rearranging flowers, for no good reason as far as he could make out. He tried to explain the situation to Francesca and whispered that she was constantly in his thoughts. She had replied that she hoped he would do better in the future and that an uninvited visit from her had been avoided by a whisker. Luke was perspiring when the conversation ended, due only in part to the confines of the box.

The manageress saw his condition and later told her husband that she thought Fr Luke must be in a spot of trouble with a woman.

Chapter Nine

A week later Luke was at Heathrow boarding a plane to Rome. Once on the plane he had to admit to a sense of release from the responsibilities of everyday life. Family were no longer able to reach him; bank managers junior chaplains and other irritants were cut off. He planned to stay in Rome for a week, though he had no idea how much of that time would be taken up by the diary.

Alastair had recommended a small hotel called the Shelley, which welcomed English visitors and had a reputation for good Italian food. This was located behind the Borghese Gardens. Its rooms turned out to be simply furnished. He had a single bed, a carafe of water on one side and a vase of roses on the other. He thought of Francesca and her rose garden. On the ground floor was a small restaurant on one side of the reception area and on the other side a bar, from which a tiny courtyard garden could be reached. The garden contained pots of hibiscus geraniums and hydrangeas in between which were half a dozen wooden tables and chairs. Somewhere a canary sang sweetly.

After a good dinner Luke sat in this garden feeling relaxed and tried to picture what the English College would be like and the priest there, Fr Charles Hammond who had possession of part of the diary. He had spoken to him on the telephone. It had been a brief and, Luke thought, rather a curt conversation. Fr Hammond had acknowledged the fact of the diary and his part in acquiring it and then agreed the date and the time of their meeting.

As with most preconceptions of people and places the reality was to prove quite different from Luke's mental pictures. The English College itself was in a narrow street in an architecturally undistinguished area of Rome. Luke had imagined it amongst a series of national colleges, grouped close to St Peter's like a

Roman version of Oxbridge. The reality was a nearly blank facade broken only by a large entrance door. He later learnt that the college had grown out of an earlier English pilgrims' hostel. After the Counter-Reformation, national colleges had been established to train priests to reconvert countries that had lost the faith. Irish, Scottish and English colleges had been established in other centres as well as Rome. English colleges were established in Valladolid in Spain and Lisbon in Portugal, as well as nearer home in Douai in Northern France.

Luke rang the bell at the gate of the English College and was ushered in by a monosyllabic Italian. Luke stated his appointment with Fr Hammond. He was led into a hall and left standing. The Italian shuffled off to a room by the front door and a telephone conversation ensued. Luke assumed he was announcing his arrival. five long minutes passed. He studied various plaques on the walls of the hall, commemorating visits from English cardinals and one from the present Pope. The plaques were topped by carved cardinals' hats or papal tiaras.

A door opened in the distance and a priest appeared.

'Fr Luke. I'm so sorry for the delay. I'm Fr Sanders, assistant to the rector here. Unfortunately, Charles had to go to the Gregorian, our university in Rome. He just rang to say he was on his way back. If you're interested I'll show you around until he returns.'

The priest, Fr Sanders, was an engaging middle-aged Englishman, full of enthusiasm for his college. The inside of the building proved a delight, built around an internal courtyard garden. It was hard to imagine the rigorous regime of Elizabethan times and the bitter internal political battles that Luke's studies had revealed to him.

However, in the main chapel those times came alive as Fr Sanders described the leaving ceremony of the missionary priests which had taken place beneath the large painting hung behind the altar: those brave souls had accepted with ardour the dangerous life ahead in spite of the certainty of imprisonment or martyrdom for the majority.

After their tour, they sat in a painted dining hall awaiting the return of Fr Hammond. Fr Sanders collected two coffees from the kitchen. Luke told him briefly about the purpose of his visit and then declared himself as an Anglo-Catholic, which he admitted was an uncomfortable thing to be since the Church of England had allowed the ordination of women. He added that it made the Roman Catholic Church especially attractive to people of his persuasion.

Fr Sanders ignored the Roman prefix. 'The future development of the priesthood in the Catholic Church is not certain, though our Pope rules out changes for the moment. Personally, I would not welcome an Anglican coming here to be trained if that was the only reason for his conversion, and the advice I give any Anglican priest wanting to convert to our faith is to live the life of the Church as a layman for a while. Our ethos is totally different, you know – not so cosy, I think.' At this he offered a friendly smile and continued. 'We had an ex-Anglican here recently. He just couldn't acclimatise himself and soon returned to his old ministry – one, I'm sure, that would bring great blessings – though certainly his time here was not wasted, either for him or us.'

They were interrupted by the Italian from the front-door office, and Fr Sanders told Luke that Fr Charles Hammond awaited him in the library. 'You should get on well together, both of you being priests and schoolmasters.'

'Fr Hammond is a schoolmaster?' Luke looked surprised.

'Didn't you know, he was headmaster of Brockhampton Abbey School for five years and recently the prior of that abbey, but his love of Benedictine history made him a natural to be in charge of the English congregation's archives, and being over seventy he was due for less arduous responsibility. He stays for a month a year. He trained here before joining the Benedictines and so he feels at home, and our library has a lot of material useful to him. He's a charmer and has a fund of wonderful stories.'

Fr Sanders got up and led Luke to the library. When they entered, the tall slender figure of the Benedictine Fr Charles had his back to them. He was standing at the top of some library steps while gently removing a document box. He turned and gave them a warm smile and jumped down with surprising agility. He came towards Luke holding out both hands to him. It was difficult later to analyse his instant appeal, but Luke decided that it was the combination of his clear blue eyes under a shock of white hair and an expression that was lively and yet ascetic, though the liveliness dominated with a constant suggestion that he would surely recount something extremely funny, were it not for the seriousness of the matter in hand.

He also had the engaging quality of appearing to be extremely interested in the person he was with and in what they had to say. From the first, Luke and Fr Charles forged a genuine friendship. Luke later reflected that it was a sort of intellectual love at first sight that included each other's characters, too. They sat facing each other across a table in the library with the document box unopened between them: to an outsider it would have contained some old, stitched parchment; to the two men, it was part of an essential history of a man of interest to them both, but particularly to Luke, who was hoping for a clue to the treasure.

Fr Charles explained his interest. De Witte had been trained at the English College but he had lived for a while with Fr Robert Stackpole, a Benedictine recusant priest, after he had left Euston Hall in Suffolk. Any document relating to early membership of the English College was of course one the College would like to possess, but as far as de Witte was concerned, there was a matter of greater interest to Fr Charles. His apostasy was well known, but there had been rumours at the time of his death that he had not died an Anglican, and Fr Charles had become fascinated to find in his studies of contemporary documents how often this rumour occurred; some sources hinted at a voluntary martyrdom, though no written evidence yet supported this, hence his interest in acquiring any de Witte papers. In fact he had been on the verge of approaching Melbury College so as to study their parts of the diary of de Witte. The two men began with a strong mutual interest, though trying to find different answers.

Luke then shared his knowledge, save for the reference to the treasure. He held the mental reservation that the quarto relating to the treasure would not be offered to Fr Charles to study. However, he did raise the question of the code.

Fr Charles sat up straight at its mention. 'We had another quarto prior to those acquired in the sale, given by the father of the present owner of Boscannon and some of that is in code. Aggravating, as it refers to the exact time of de Witte's conversion to Anglicanism at Boscannon Manor. I've got a friend at the Vatican Library, an expert in old codes, and he's looking at it. His conclusion so far is that the numbers refer to letters or words starting or ending pages in a book possessed by de Witte. find the book and the code is broken. Could be anything, a breviary or herbal, or the life of a saint, and probably written in Latin.'

Their discussion was interrupted by Fr Charles announcing the general need for a good helping of lasagne. Carrying the box, he led the way to a nearby square and, like an arrow, went to a small cafe in its corner where they were greeted like royalty by the owner, who waved them to a table in a prime position. When they were seated, Fr Charles turned to Luke.

'So why do you think de Witte apostatised and became an Anglican?'

Luke did not answer immediately. 'Well, I suppose from the scant evidence so far, people might say *Cherchez la femme* – he marries the squire's widow. But it wasn't necessary to leave the priesthood of the Church of Rome to have a woman, then or now, I understand...' Fr Charles wrinkled his nose with an expression of disapproval. Luke continued. 'I actually think it was genuine. Rejection of the overwhelming claims of the papacy or the Catholic Church's plotting with the Spanish, and perhaps seeing the middle theological way as right, as against the corruption of the Church – indulgences, etc – and its political interfering.'

Fr Charles shook his head. 'What about blue funk at the idea of being hung, drawn and quartered. The persecutions intensified when Elizabeth's chief persecutor, Topcliffe, got going. De Witte's diary reveals a fastidious man much given to hygiene and concern with his appearance. See here.' Fr Charles opened his book and pulled out a sheet of paper. 'This is in English in the journal.' He passed across the excerpt, which was written in a neat italic script. It described de Witte preparing to dress for dinner at Boscannon and his care in washing first and in trimming his hair.

Luke looked surprised. 'I've not come across that fastidiousness in the parts of the diary I have translated.'

Their conversation was quelled by the arrival of two men carrying electrically amplified accordions. They started to sing, '*O solé mio*', and Father Charles joined in louder than anyone.

'I think this meal should end with a coffee and brandy to celebrate our meeting.'

The music moved on to play *'Volare'*. Before the musicians could open their mouths Fr Charles began the song. Luke joined in. He had not been so happy in an uncomplicated way for weeks.

At the end of the music Fr Charles got up and put the document box into Luke's hands. 'I have to go back and meet someone at the Gregorian. Study this and let's meet tomorrow. Come to my Mass, nine-thirty at the college, and we'll breakfast here afterwards and compare notes. I don't think this quarto helps your view of de Witte.' He made a small sign of the cross towards Luke and turned to stride off through the crowds milling in the square.

Luke ordered another coffee and opened the box. The extract of the diary was still in Latin. The quality of the script was variable, some of it barely legible, as if scrawled in a great hurry. He would need the help of a Latin dictionary and a magnifying glass, both of which were back in his hotel. He decided he would visit St Peter's first and then go to his hotel and translate the diary.

It had been some twenty years since he had visited Rome. He had come on a combined Catholic and Anglican ecumenical pilgrimage soon after being ordained. His mind back then was set in its belief that High Anglicanism was the purest form of Catholic Christianity, and he had viewed St Peter's with a jaundiced eye, seeing its vast size and baroque architecture as vulgar, and, in addition, tainted by its source of building funds being the outrageous sale of indulgences over a long period.

That afternoon his appreciation was less superficial. He was moved by the obvious evidence of the Church's worldwide appeal in the mixture of races represented in the basilica crowds, praying and contemplating. There was also a vitality in the groups of pilgrims moving in and out, particularly among groups of young priests and nuns – an animation not seen in the gentle visitation of clergy to diocesan events in Melbury Cathedral.

Luke found a group of young filipino pilgrims saying the rosary in a side chapel. He stood at the back, moved by the intensity of their responses as the Ave Marias were recited staccato at a machine-gun speed – obviously they had many religious sites to visit before the afternoon was finished. Luke envied their simple acceptance of the faith. No theological scruples about papal authority, the Marian doctrines, the primacy of conscience. The faith they had inherited was enough to help them into heaven. Luke left them to visit the crypt and St Peter's tomb below the high altar. He prayed for his family, for Francesca and for success in editing the diary and finding the Melbury treasure, and then prayed that he might regain his faith in God and prayer. On his way out he passed the statue of the dead Christ in his mother's arms. Michelangelo's Pietá. He stopped and in his contemplation he saw Francesca holding the flower love-lies-bleeding.

He arrived back at the Shelley, taken by a taxi whose driver acted as if pursued by the Furies. Luke had to suffer an attempt by the driver to extort a surcharge of five thousand lire because the hotel was on the far side of the Borghese Gardens. He entered the hotel to cries of anti-clerical violence from the frustrated driver.

The rough-and-tumble life of Roman taxi drivers was soon forgotten. Luke changed into casual clothing and settled down on his bed to translate the diary.

The first page described the arrival of Topcliffe and a posse of pursuivants at Boscannon. The manor household had been warned in advance by a Catholic fisherman rowing across the Helford, while the pursuivant party had the long ride round the Helford to the Lizard peninsula via the village of Constantine. This visitation had led to de Witte's week of incarceration in the secret room below the hearth, while the visitors lodged themselves in the stables, entering the house without warning at all hours. They would search thoroughly, tapping walls and floors, moving pictures and bookcases, and driving long metal needles into areas they thought might be hollow and concealing Mass vessels or a priest. De Witte recorded his relief and thanks at their eventual departure to Launceston, where they were to arrest St Cuthbert Mayne, who was martyred there: hung, drawn and quartered.

De Witte's next entry was a description of this fearful death. The code appeared after this entry. Luke wondered if it recorded some dread he was unhappy to put into English words. Then came a gap in the dates. The third page was dated two months later. Luke translated it with quickening curiosity, though with some dismay. The first paragraph produced:

This evening My Lady bade me walk with her in the long gallery. She told me of her high respect for my person and my appearance and bid me sit with her and read some poetry. She told me my voice was fine and also my thighs well formed.

This last sentence was scrawled. The next paragraph continued, *Later that evening, My Lord Boscannon being absent, she desired me in her chamber to help her in her devotions...*, then six lines of code followed, wavering in all directions. A final line in Latin read, *May the precious blood wash away the stains of my sins.*

Cherchez la femme seemed no longer necessary if one put an adulterous interpretation on this event. Luke tried to look for alternatives. De Witte could be recording spiritual weakness under the recent visitation of the pursuivants. The last page gave some comfort. It recorded the visitation of an Anglican cleric, a Dr Austin. He had come to instruct the household in the reformed faith. He also brought news of the failed Babington Plot, the foolish Catholic attempt to displace Elizabeth. De Witte also recorded Dr Austin giving them a solemn warning that any family sheltering a Catholic priest would suffer certain imprisonment and probable death. Again the diary repeated De Witte's unexplained agony and desire for forgiveness. He had been presented to Dr Austin as tutor to the Boscannon boys and had confessed failure to dispute with the cleric as he denounced the Catholic faith, though his Lord Boscannon openly railed against these heresies.

The next day's record read, *My Lady fears for Her Lord's outspokenness and advises that both she and I confess to Dr Austin our desire to follow the Queen's faith in spite of her husband.* Two lines of code followed, then a long scrawled paragraph.

The pursuivants came this day to take My Lord. He jumped from the casement and took one of the horses. All followed as in a hunt, My Lady and I behind. The pursuivants lost him in the woods above the river. My Lady knew whither he would go. We caught up with him, he crying to us, 'You are false traitors of the faith,' as he jumped a wall into the woods so as to reach the river, but the horse slipped as he cantered down the causeway to the boats. It stumbled and My Lord fell into the water after hitting the stone side of the pier. 'My back,' he cried as he tried to swim, but he began to sink, and I was about to run into the water when My Lady held me, saying, ' 'tis for the best.'

Two lines of code followed.

Luke got off his bed, stunned. He went into the bathroom. He felt drained. It was as if he had been present. To him, de Witte had become like a well-known acquaintance who suddenly had been dragged into some sordid and murderous scandal. He looked at his watch: it was seven o'clock. He decided he needed a bath, then, in fresh clothes and with a strong drink he would try and sort out the revelations of the day.

In his bath Luke looked at the thorn's scar on his finger and relived that day with Francesca. He longed to speak with her and decided he would make up a persona that could legitimately ring her from Rome – perhaps an acquaintance wishing to have the phone number of one of her Italian relatives.

Chapter Ten

Luke first went to the bar and ordered a vodka and orange juice. He felt restored after his bath and change of clothes. He was wearing a camel-coloured linen jacket, cream cotton shirt and nicely pressed chinos, which created the picture of a successful young tourist.

A waitress taking a drink to the dining room gave him a lingering smile of admiration.

'*Santo cielo! Bene!*' she murmured as she passed him.

He did not understand the compliment but blushed, his vanity flattered. He picked up his drink and walked into the small garden. He sat by the statue of a plump Venus, behind which sat the canary in an elaborate cage. A couple were in one corner talking volubly above the noise of a Vivaldi concerto being relayed by hidden speakers. In the other corner it was darker, but Luke saw the back of a young woman. She was looking into a handbag mirror as she adjusted her hair, which was dark and tied behind her head with a black velvet bow.

Luke felt there was something familiar about her. As he was wondering where to sit, he realised she was looking at him in her mirror. She turned to him.

'Luke.' She spoke softly so that his name was barely audible above the music. Then she gave him a delicious smile as she got up.

'Francesca! What on earth...?'

Before he could say another word, she put his drink on the table and flung her arms around him and kissed him passionately, her mouth opening to receive the kisses he found himself returning. Eventually they broke apart, noticing that the other, Italian couple were watching them, their conversation suspended.

Francesca led him to her table. They sat facing each other, holding both hands, Luke noticing her large brown eyes sparkling with pleasure, her full lips slightly open, moist from their kissing. They did not speak: there were no words to express their happiness. Luke leant forward and touched the corner of her mouth that turned up slightly when she smiled and then traced with his finger a line to a nearby dimple.

Luke offered her a sip of his drink. 'I think we need to catch up with developments over dinner – they have good food here.'

'I know, I came here with one of my cousins the day before you arrived, just to check you would be all right here.'

'Great Scott! How the Dickens did you know I was coming here? I hope you didn't ring every hotel in Rome.'

Francesca burst out laughing. 'You are a quaint thing – "Great Scott" and "Dickens" – you remind me of my grandfather. Of course not, I just rang your father's house and a nice lady there told me where you were staying.'

Luke got up. 'I'll go and fix a corner table for us, then you can confess all.'

Francesca replied, 'I don't need absolution yet.'

As he moved into the light, Francesca admired the way his jacket hung on his broad shoulders. She took another sip of his vodka and orange and noticed her hand trembling a little in her excitement.

Luke returned with menus. 'That's fixed. By the way, what does "*Santo cielo, bene*" mean?'

'"Goodness gracious, that's good." Why do you ask?'

'Someone in the dining room said it.'

'About what dish?'

Luke laughed at her question. 'I'm afraid I can't tell you. I'm not sure whether it's available. Anyway, I've got you a vodka and orange for yourself to save mine evaporating any more.'

They ordered prosciutto and melon, followed by a lobster risotto. A bottle of Soave completed a delightful Italian dinner. Their conversation was superficial. Luke described his visit to the English College and Francesca answered questions about her Roman relatives but there was a brittle quality to their words. Underneath ran a strong emotional current. Both knew this new meeting, unexpected by Luke, was one that would set the course that would lead either to the end of their relationship or into another, more demanding existence: a world of passion, a world of consuming psychic force. They both found difficulty in swallowing their food and the bottle of Soave was finished before the risottos. Francesca took his hand as they awaited coffee to finish their meal.

He wanted to stand up and take Francesca to the lift and to his room, but knowing it only had a single bed, and his official occupation of the room was as a cleric on single terms, held him back, so strong was his priestly conditioning. He tried to return to a more mundane world.

'Where do your cousins live in Rome? Is it far by taxi? Naturally I'll see you home to them.'

Francesca lowered her eyes and a smile hovered about her lips. 'They live out towards Tivoli, a bit far, I'm afraid. I didn't want to spoil the evening, so I'm staying here.' Then her mood seemed to change and she became serious. 'Luke, I'm frightened. Where is this love going to take us? I can't keep you out of my thoughts. I want you in my life. Is this wicked?'

A waiter brought their espresso coffees and the bill for Luke to sign. The cups were very small and the contents quickly drunk. Luke signed the bill before answering.

'I don't know. Of course I want you too – the rules seem irrelevant. Perhaps things will become clearer. Meanwhile, I think it's time we went to bed – I feel the excellent wine might cloud our judgement.'

She smiled. 'Maybe, maybe not, but I agree, to bed – I'm tired.'

Luke went to his room on the second floor after seeing Francesca to her room on the floor above. They had kissed until she pushed him gently away.

He felt the stubble on his face and shaved. He cleaned his teeth and, leaving his pyjamas under his pillow, put on a hotel bathrobe. For a moment he paused as he began to turn the handle on his door. He knew going to her would mean that they would become lovers. He stopped and went back to the window, his mind in turmoil. He was conscious of his heart beating. He tried to pray, but as he did so he caught sight of a couple kissing passionately beneath a tree in the street below him. 'It's meant to be,' he thought, and went to Francesca.

When he reached Francesca's door he tapped lightly three

times. It immediately opened. She was looking beautiful in a white silk dressing gown, but he could see she had been crying and moved to take her in his arms. She shook her head and held him away. She closed the door slowly, saying, 'We'll talk tomorrow, please forgive me.'

Luke was dumbfounded. He had taken the most difficult moral decision of his life and had been handed a wet blanket. He knew his religious nature should have welcomed this turn of events, but he felt only fury. He returned to his room and in frustration flung himself on his bed, muttering, 'Women, bloody women!' After a while he got dressed and returned to the bar. He ordered a large whisky and, having knocked it back, walked out of the hotel to wander aimlessly around the neighbourhood until weariness overcame him and he returned to a fitful sleep. He was woken at seven-thirty by the ringing of the phone in his room. It was Francesca.

'Darling, I'm sorry. I'm in a mess. Help me.'

Her plea for help dissolved all his anger. 'Darling, I understand. Let's meet at lunchtime.' He explained that he was expected at the English College and that after Mass he had an important meeting with his Benedictine fellow sleuth in pursuit of the diary and its hidden clues to de Witte and the treasure.

'Well, if you prefer the company of the dead, I don't know if I shall he able to keep resurrecting you, but I'll forgive you just this once,' she laughed. 'I'll expect you back here at lunchtime.'

Luke's state of romantic euphoria was more difficult to sustain in the quiet atmosphere of spiritual energy present in the chapel of the English College. His new friend, the Benedictine Fr Charles, had been chosen to say the main Mass of the day, as it commemorated an Elizabethan Benedictine martyred in England. Though none of the students present that morning expected to be martyred, they responded to the various parts of the service with meaningful ardour.

Fr Charles preached a short sermon. He thanked the college for the privilege of being with them that morning to celebrate one of his order's martyred sons. That saintly life demonstrated heroic courage and virtue and he had no intention to belittle it, but he said that the Elizabethan martyr's life was lived out on a clear battlefield where the enemy was known. For his

100

brothers there that morning, their lives were to be lived fighting on a battlefield that was far from clear; a field obscured by the shifting mists and fogs of fast-changing social mores and theological strife. These inclement conditions would be the background to their priestly lives and would sap their strength. The damp would enter their bones and martyr them too, but with loneliness as they fought the spirit of the age – the Zeitgeist of rampant materialism and the pursuit of pleasure at any cost to health and happiness, which was especially ruinous to families in their future parishes. They too would suffer much, but like the martyr they were celebrating that day, they would be redeemed and given strength by the Holy Spirit of God and the prayers of their heavenly brethren. Their devotion to their calling would produce that peace of spirit which passeth all understanding and with which no earthly joy could compare.

His sermon was thus only two minutes long, but he asked that they should sit for a few minutes in silence together before proceeding with the Mass. They were to be uncomfortable minutes for Luke as he wrestled with the thoughts of his earthly joys with Francesca. In the end he reasoned that his calling at that moment was to crack the diary of de Witte and Francesca was part of the team now; moreover, she needed him in her martyrdom of a marriage. Even as he concluded his meditation with a sigh of resignation, it was not, he felt, a scenario filled with peace passing all understanding.

Fr Charles collected him at the end of Mass and they returned to the restaurant in the square for a late breakfast of coffee, orange juice and toast. After their initial intake of coffee, Fr Charles asked Luke how he had succeeded with the diary and what were his conclusions. He hoped it hadn't kept him up too late.

'Well, it was more than I expected,' said Luke and shook his head. 'I'll reserve my judgement for the moment, but the description of the death of his Lord Boscannon and the ambiguities concerning his relationship with the wife were rather a shock.'

Fr Charles nodded sympathetically. 'It does look as if you had rather a rough night worrying about it – here, have some more coffee. Now, tell me more fully what you and Melbury College hope to produce from your labours and I'll lay my cards down. I think we know the directions each of us are facing in, but I do believe we should work together as far as possible. I think you have the greater part of the diary.'

For a moment, an uncharitable thought flashed through Luke's mind. Did Fr Charles also have knowledge of the missing Melbury treasure? Was it a popish plot to find it first and was he trying to get as much information from him as possible? The remark about Luke's possession of the greater part of the diary seemed a little sinister if he interpreted Fr Charles' interest in that way. However, as their discussion developed Luke decided this suspicion was pure paranoia: Fr Charles' interest was obviously spiritual, though in a way that Luke regarded as on the edge of eccentricity as far as devotion to the English Martyrs was concerned.

Fr Charles was interested to know how Luke would deal with the incorporation of the quarto he had provided, with its obvious indication that de Witte's conversion was due to funk and seduction by his mistress, Lady Boscannon.

Luke explained the details of his commission from Melbury College. He would edit the diary fully; it was then up to the college to decide whether to produce it in full or in a sanitised version. Whatever conclusions one might draw from the latest revelation in the quarto Fr Charles had provided, Luke knew that the last parts of the diary showed de Witte as a conscientious Bishop of Melbury and as a good husband to the widow of Boscannon. Taking the totality of his life, Luke judged it worthy of some celebration, though he doubted whether it would be used as propaganda in exulting the Anglican over the Roman Church. He would be in a better position to judge when he had completed the work. What he wanted to know was the real reason for the interest of Fr Charles and the English College in Rome in this apparent failure of a missionary sent to England. It must be more than just the rumour of de Witte returning to Catholicism.

Fr Charles picked up his empty coffee cup and seemed to study intently the residue of grains inside it. 'I don't know how Catholic your Anglo-Catholicism is with regard to belief in the close involvement of saints in our earthly existence? Some of us believe that God grants spiritual favours via our intercession with the saints – asking those who have gone

102

before us into heaven to help us. I assume you must know that in the Church's process of canonisation – it is usual for a proven miracle to be recorded before beatification is declared officially, followed by another miracle and the assent of the Pope before the person can be raised to sainthood.

'When the English Martyrs were canonised, the need for proven miracles associated with them was lifted due to the passage of time and was anyway unnecessary, as martyrdom is seen as automatic evidence of saintliness.' Fr Charles paused. 'Last year I visited Quebec. On the memorial to Wolfe and Montcalm there is an apposite inscription 'Courage was fatal to them. History made them heroes.' He called for more coffee and continued: I'm therefore passionately interested in de Witte, to me the repentant sinner at the last days of his life, returning to the Church of his youth, though we have no proof of it. But this is the explosive part: the English College library has some letters from contemporary Catholics, one from a man and his family living in Melbury after de Witte's death. They infer, though there are no details and again there is no proof, that for some reason they invoked the help of de Witte's prayers to save the life of an injured son who was dying after falling from a horse. He apparently survived, and they regarded it as a miracle. There are other letters confirming answered prayers, and some came from Cornwall. Why, why should they invoke de Witte if he died a heretic Anglican bishop? I long to know, and the English College equally would like to know, for here they would have a martyr who answered prayers and was responsible for miracles. My conclusion is that there was a last-minute return to the faith and that he died for it.' Fr Charles leant forward and took Luke's hand. 'I beseech you, if you find this to be so in any part of the diary, or if you find proof from contemporary sources, please, I beg you in the name of our joint Saviour that you tell me. It is important to me personally in a way that you may find curious.' Fr Charles withdrew his hand and looked into his coffee cup again. He was obviously embarrassed at revealing his emotions in such a way in front of a fellow Englishman. He seemed agitated. 'I'll tell you one day.'

'Don't worry,' said Luke. 'Now I know the reasons for your interest, I'll give you whatever I discover, even if it does reveal that de Witte returned to Roman allegiance and subsequent martyrdom, though I doubt its possibility. He has a fine Anglican tomb in the cathedral – hardly likely if he had Poped.'

Fr Charles laughed at this expression and got up. He shook Luke's hand. 'Keep in touch. I'll let you have some photocopies of anything of interest and I'll let you know if our code expert at the Vatican Library comes up with any clues to crack the code.'

Luke found a taxi and directed it to return him to the Hotel Shelley. The driver threw up his hands and began muttering about the traffic and the problems of getting to the other side of the Borghese Gardens. It was obvious that taxi drivers did not expect to get custom on the way back to the centre of Rome. Luke repeated the name of the hotel and added, '*pronto*'. The driver sighed as if being ordered to ascend Everest without the aid of oxygen.

Luke sat back in his seat and tried to file in his mind the contrasting events that had happened since his arrival in Rome. The quarto provided by Fr Charles had undermined his hopes of presenting de Witte's diary as the simple story of an Elizabethan Catholic priest turning to Anglicanism and becoming a bishop through his own outstanding qualities. However, it was the ethos of the English College and the enthusiasm and spirituality of Fr Charles that unsettled him most as he journeyed back to meet Francesca. It jarred against the smooth journey he expected going back to her. He kept saying to himself, 'We need each other so much.' He counted on being with her in a few minutes; all other problems would be put to one side and resolved eventually. He decided that they would delay lunch and go immediately to her room.

When he arrived at the hotel he was handed a message from Francesca. *Darling boy, have had to go out. Several boutiques have demanded my presence – my legacy under threat – whoopee! Join me for lunch at one-thirty – Trattoria di Luigi, just down from the Spanish Steps. Can't wait to reunite our ecumenical relationship.*

Luke read this with a mixture of amusement (mild) disappointment (strong) and annoyance (very strong). His total reaction was similar to his feelings whenever a favoured pupil at Melbury disappointed him by being wayward and unreliable. He went to his room and changed out of his priestly garb and into the clothes of the previous evening to enter again his new world as the lover of a beautiful young woman who unfortunately needed to learn a few school rules.

He had to wait ten minutes for a taxi to come to the hotel, so he was late in arriving at the restaurant. The Trattoria di Luigi was in a street opposite the Spanish Steps which was mostly occupied by fashionable boutiques, and the taxi took several minutes edging through the crowds walking in the middle of the road. Luke became increasingly frustrated and angry that they were not meeting in the calm of the hotel courtyard. He entered the restaurant in an unhappy frame of mind.

Although it was nearly two o'clock the restaurant was packed. Several people were standing inside the door awaiting tables. The hubbub of excited customers and waiters was deafening: it was obviously extremely popular and in fashion. Most of the girls looked like models and the men like svelte pimps. There was no sign of Francesca.

A man dressed in a very sharply cut pinstriped suit and carrying a large pad approached Luke. 'You have a reservation, *signor?*'

Luke nodded. '*Sì, Signora* Boscannon.'

The man studied the reservations. He noticeably curled his lip. 'Very sorry, no such name here.'

Luke began to perspire. The noise and the heat was taking its toll. He tried his own name.

The man smirked, 'Ah, ah, *Padre?*' Luke nodded weakly. 'This way, your lady not arrived yet.' In the man's smirk lurked a thousand scandalous articles in sleazy newspapers, entitled, 'Priestly Casanova in lay dress lunches unsuspecting model!'

The table was at the back of the restaurant, next to one occupied by a corpulent Italian man in his sixties and an anorexic platinum blonde, circa eighteen. He was stroking her arm with one hand and eating asparagus with the other. Luke longed for the normally half-empty dining room of The Golden Hind in Melbury, where he would occasionally have a chump chop with his father out of term time.

His reverie was interrupted by the arrival of Francesca. She was holding several large carrier bags sporting the names of the leading Roman fashion houses. She placed them by the side of the table and flung her arms round Luke.

'Forgive me, sweetest one,' she whispered several times, and then kissed him fully on his lips. The corpulent man was distracted by her beauty and effervescent arrival, and choked on a particularly large piece of asparagus. Francesca pulled round her chair next to Luke's and, putting her arm round him, rested her head on his shoulder. 'I've had a heavenly morning. Hit the bullseye everywhere I went. What bliss it must be to be able to do this every year – but don't worry, what I've got will last and last. It's all simple and in excellent taste, except for the lingerie.' She sat up and tweaked his ear. 'Don't look so disapproving, my love. When I can get away to you from my Boscannon mental home I want to live, and I don't suppose many more legacies will come my way. Don't be angry. I know I'm late, but isn't this place fantastic?'

Luke tried to smile. She prattled on and then a waiter came.

'*Due sogliole alla griglia*, and salad,' she said, 'and house Verdicchio, *per favore*.' She turned to Luke. 'This is on me. I promise you, the sole here are the best,' and then, noticing Luke's glum demeanour, she added, 'Now, tell me, what ails thee, owner of my very self?'

'Not these last few hours, I think,' grunted Luke.

'Darling, you were out playing with your obsession, so I thought what about me? Don't spoil it all.' Francesca looked suddenly so crumpled that Luke's anger and frustrations melted. He drew her to him and kissed her ear.

Francesca turned and kissed him on the lips again. 'You are lovely, but naughty. You must learn to wait for treats. Didn't your nanny tell you...'

Luke laughed. The corpulent man overheard and looked peeved, like a small boy with a less attractive ice cream than his neighbour's.

Francesca added, 'Don't rush your food when it comes. Now, tell me about your morning and I'll tell you about mine.'

When they returned to the hotel, Francesca said, 'You can come to the room and give me marks for each of the clothes I have bought. I'll give you a fashion show.'

Luke shyly asked, 'Please may I be your photographer?'

Back in her room Francesca was like a child. Luke was

106

reminded of his sister pirouetting in a new party dress in front of a wardrobe looking glass, aged five, totally enchanted by her own image.

Francesca was less innocently narcissistic, but took equal delight in her changing reflection as she paraded her new suits, coats and dresses, joyful that everything looked perfect and relishing Luke's endorsement of her purchases. She made him sit on a small chair in the bedroom and made her entrances from the bathroom where she had taken all her carrier bags. Luke asked if he could photograph her as she came and went. She made a passable imitation of a model displaying a fashion house collection. Luke awarded her ten out of ten without reserve.

She came over and kissed him. 'It's sweet of you to approve. We will find occasions to wear all these, won't we?'

Luke nodded, but was unable to think where or when.

'Now for the grand finale – it may take a minute.' She disappeared into the bathroom and five minutes later appeared transformed in a black negligee. Her hair was piled high on her head and she had sensuously exaggerated her make-up. He asked her to hold her pose as he loaded a fresh film into his camera.

He moved closer to her and could not hide his desire. Immediately, Francesca turned away and went across to the window. She slumped in a chair, leant forward and buried her face in her hands. She began to sob convulsively.

'Sorry, sorry. It's no good...'

Luke stood for a moment, stunned. He went to comfort her but she put up her hand to keep him away.

'Oh God, it's no good.' She got up and ran into the bathroom and locked the door.

Luke stood at the door, his head against it, and spoke softly. 'Francesca, darling, give it time, it'll be all right – I promise.' He was torn apart listening to her distress.

Eventually she moved towards the bathroom door and he heard her say, 'Luke, I'm afraid I can't come out. Please be patient. I need time.'

Luke sighed. 'I will try to be, but it's getting too confusing. I'll leave you now if that's really what you want.'

He returned to his room. There was a message slipped under his door and a light was flashing on his telephone. The message

107

read, *Your father has rung several times. Please contact him urgently.* Luke picked up the phone and pressed the red flashing button. The operator repeated the written message. Hell, thought Luke, some further disaster has happened to my father.

He rang as instructed. His father answered the phone. His voice was angry.

'Where have you been hiding? The hotel had no idea.'

Luke immediately felt like a boy again, caught by his father committing a serious misdemeanour.

'Sorry, father, had to go out to follow a lead, it meant getting back late last night.'

'Hmph,' was the immediate reply. 'I asked the hotel to check your room at nearly midnight. I hope you're not involved in any hanky-panky. Never trust Latin hot-blooded girls.'

God, thought Luke, I hope he can't sense my blushing. Visions of Francesca appeared in his mind. He addressed himself to the phone.

His father's voice was querulous. 'So, no high jinks, I hope?'

Luke made a bad attempt at a light laugh.

'Whatever do you mean? I'm here in Rome engaged in a piece of historical research, aided by a splendid Benedictine...'

His father interrupted, 'Can't hear you. What's that about Benedictine? Dangerous stuff – I read in a magazine at the dentist last week that it's drunk with ice by the fast set in Italy.'

Luke looked at the ceiling in despair. 'No, father, a monk not a drink!'

His father ignored this reply. 'Watch out for the faded aristocracy in Rome – totally degenerate. Are you mixing with them?'

'Of course not, father, don't be ridiculous.' He began a long explanation involving unexpected clues leading to a sudden visit to a library south of Rome near Tivoli with a member of the English College. Luke's attempt at a fictitious explanation caused a snort of derision from his father, who interrupted him.

'Tivoli is east of Rome. Whatever are you up to? Anyway, cut it, you're needed back here. Margery is ill and I need some heavy shopping done. More importantly, you've got an emergency with your junior chaplain, Fr Peter. We think he's having a breakdown – nervous and moral. A nun was spotted the night before last entering his house just before midnight. The man's a moron, though I didn't think women were a problem for him. As for the identity of the nun, the place is in an uproar because yesterday a similarly dressed nun – she was wearing a black habit, not a brown one like the Gethsemane nuns – caused a riot and a punch-up in Mr Jones' church.'

Luke interrupted. 'Crikey, what happened, and who saw her entering Fr Peter's home?'

His father replied. 'The provost and his wife saw her entering Fr Peter's house. They were walking back from a dinner with the dean. But what happened? You may well ask. The cleaner in Emmanuel Church sees this nun praying, goes into the vestry to get some polish and returns to see the nun placing a crucifix and six wooden candles on the plain Protestant altar table. The cleaner, puzzled enough by the presence of a praying nun in that happy-clappy tabernacle, is alarmed and goes off to get Mr Jones. When he, plus wife, arrives, he evidently screams like a banshee and tries to catch the nun, who by then is running for the door...'

Luke interrupted again. 'Who told you all this?'

'Let me finish, boy – but if you must know, it's Margery. She's friendly with the cleaner. Anyway, Mr Jones catches up with the nun and tries to restrain her. Then to his surprise he gets a left and a right, knocking him to the ground and leaving him with a black eye and a cauliflower ear. The nun leaps on the cleaner's bicycle parked by the church steps and is never seen again. The bike is found by the public lavatories. Result is a case of grievous bodily harm, and the police are being harried by an hysterical Mr Jones to make a quick arrest.'

'Father, are there any clues, and what does Fr Peter say about his nun?'

Luke's father sighed again. 'Don't keep interrupting, I haven't finished. The nun was wearing dark glasses, and the only clue was a large carrier bag she was carrying to transport the candles. It had Watts Ecclesiastical Outfitters printed on it. The provost rang Fr Peter the next day to ask about the nun. Fr Peter told him the seal of the confessional forbade him from saying anything, and, when the provost exploded at that answer, he evidently burst into tears and put the phone down.

Since then he's gone to ground. No answer to the telephone and apparently left. The police are getting a warrant to question him and, if necessary, search his house. Fr Ignatius from Gethsemane said Mass in the school this morning but you must come back to help, otherwise the wounded Mr Jones will get a foot in the school chapel. Also Fr Peter obviously needs help and therefore we need you back today not tomorrow.'

Luke sighed. 'I'll get the first plane I can.'

He wearily scribbled a note to Francesca. In it he briefly explained the reason for his departure and promised he would see her again in Cornwall as soon as he could find the time to rent Alastair's cottage. He packed his case and went to her room, half praying she would not answer the door. His prayer was answered and he left the note under the door.

When he arrived home he rang the hotel to speak to her but they told him she had left. Without knowing her Italian relatives' telephone numbers, he had lost contact. It was in a deep depression that he faced the prospect of getting in touch with Fr Peter.

Chapter Eleven

When Luke arrived back in Melbury, he first went to see his father to find out if there was any further news. There was none so he set off for Fr Peter's house in spite of there being no reply to his constant phoning.

By the time he reached the house it was dark and there was no sign of life. He knocked and rang the bell and, getting no answer, he prised open the letter box in the front door and called out.

'Fr Peter, it's Luke. I'm here to help – I know about the nun.'

When he said the word 'nun' he thought he heard a gasp in the hall beyond. He repeated the message but got no response, so he walked round the house, and apart from imagining he saw a net curtain move – it could easily have been a draught – there was no sign of the junior chaplain. When he returned to the front of the house he found a police car parked with its lights flashing. A police sergeant was looking through the house window and when he saw Luke he straightened up.

'Aha, the Reverend Peter Stobbs, we've been looking for you.' He turned to the police car, beckoned urgently, and a young constable got out and joined them. The sergeant nodded to the constable to stand behind Luke to cut off his retreat.

'Sorry, Officer, I'm not Fr Peter Stobbs. I'm second master at Melbury College, and senior chaplain.'

The sergeant looked at him suspiciously. Fortunately, Luke still had his passport in his jacket and was able to prove his identity and assure them he also was searching for Fr Peter.

The police sergeant left him saying, 'A real mess when you have an outbreak of GBH among members of a body preaching peace and love.'

* * *

At dawn the next morning Luke returned to Fr Peter's house and positioned himself behind a shed at the back, where he could see the kitchen. A bottle of milk stood by the back door. At six-forty-five the door opened slightly and a hand came out to retrieve the milk. Before the door could be closed Luke pushed it open, knocking Fr Peter over in the process. Luke then closed the door behind him and went to help his junior chaplain to his feet, but he lay there in a foetal position and began to sob uncontrollably.

Luke locked the door and patted Fr Peter's back. 'Don't worry, I'm here to help. I think it would do no harm to get Dr Morris to come and give you something.'

Fr Peter lay sobbing, so Luke telephoned the college doctor and explained the situation. Half an hour later the doctor and Luke were taking him to a private psychiatric hospital near Salisbury. As they were leaving, a police car came down the street with its siren wailing. The doctor gently asked Peter about the nun and the only reply was, 'Such a courageous woman, braver than I could ever be.' This was endlessly repeated like a mantra.

Later that day Luke returned to the chaplain's house, as he had kept the key to the back door. He needed to satisfy a suspicion that had struck him on the drive to Salisbury when he had noticed that Fr Peter's hands were bruised. He searched the house and found under the mattress of a bed in the spare room a large carrier bag imprinted with WATTS & CO ECCLESIASTICAL OUTfiTTERS. Inside was a complete nun's black habit and white wimple.

For a while Luke sat on the bed convulsed with laughter before realising that he must get home and destroy the evidence of the identity of the fighting nun. At dusk he made a bonfire of leaves in his garden before going to his father's house for dinner.

He shared his secret only with Alastair and his father, and later with Francesca. The mystery of the battling nun passed into local legend and a local cartoonist produced a postcard showing a nun knocking out a lifelike representation of Mr Jones, depicted with cauliflowers instead of ears. It sold like hot cakes and was entitled 'The Church Militant'. Mr Jones tried to sue on grounds of libel, and failing in this attempt made him more determined to win the battle to take over the organisation of the school chapel services.

Having destroyed the evidence of Fr Peter's alter ego, Luke contacted all members of the college chapel committee. It was agreed that Luke should take all the services until a satisfactory replacement was found and that the committee should meet the next day in London at the grace-and-favour flat that the retired archbishop, Dr Humphries, enjoyed in his retirement in the cloisters of Westminster Abbey.

Luke then went to the school to find Alastair just as the morning lessons ended. His heart lifted as he walked through the cloisters and corridors thronged with boys leaving their classrooms en route for lunch in their houses. He did not realise how much he had missed the life of the school. The sounds and scents of a school community were unchanging and to Luke it was a heady mixture, heightened when several of the boys smiled with spontaneous pleasure when they saw him. His progress to meet Alastair in the common room was continuously interrupted as he stopped to exchange greetings.

He reached the common room just as Alastair was leaving to go to his house. Luke was greeted with a yelp of delight.

'Scots wahey! What draws you back from the fleshpots of Rome? Don't tell me you've seen the light and are coming back as a cardinal! Join me for lunch and tell me all your news.'

Luke kept back any discussion to Fr Peter or questions about the state of the school while he sat with Alastair amongst the boys of his house, and confined himself to telling his friend about Fr Charles and the progress with the diary. It was not until he went with Alastair to his study to have coffee that he told him about Fr Peter. When they had finished laughing about the extraordinary sequence of events, they agreed the breakdown of Fr Peter created a dangerous opportunity for the head and Mr Jones to destabilise the religious ethos of the school.

Luke asked about further developments in the school. Alastair told him that the integration of Lady Edwina's girls' school, was going well, much to his surprise, but the sixth-form college was a disaster due mostly to a disproportionate number of Russians. The head had certainly succeeded in bringing a large

113

influx of Europeans via his contacts and agencies. The latter had brought in a mixture of forty French and German pupils who had been spread throughout the houses, but the head's contacts in Russia had produced another forty mature boys who had gone straight to the new sixth-form house in the town. Of these, thirty were from new rich families, and Alastair reckoned that all were spoilt and unpleasant and possibly the most undesirable had Russian mafia connections. The remaining quarter of the intake were a complete contrast: charming, but from pathetically poor families, these had come supported by scholarships from a Russian Orthodox religious foundation; their poverty originated from professional families ruined by the economic crisis in Russia or having fathers who were poor Orthodox priests. The rich majority bullied the poor mercilessly and caused disciplinary mayhem with drunken sorties around the town. Alastair said they should be sent back to Russia as soon as possible, but the head could only bask in the economic success of increasing the numbers in the school and the college council was eating out of his hand. The only area independently protected by the college statutes was the chapel committee, and Alastair warned Luke that the head was rumoured to have circulated a proposal to the council to have it abolished. He wished Luke and the council well and had no doubt he would hear more at the meeting scheduled for the next day in London. As Luke got up to leave, Alastair said, 'By the way, you know our cottage in Cornwall is free at the moment and we'd be delighted if you kept it aired if you want somewhere quiet to work on the diary, plus the attraction of some gentle boating on the Helford.'

Luke grasped Alastair's hand warmly and said, 'That would be wonderful. I hope to start work on the diary again next week.'

'Good man,' said Alastair. 'The keys are here whenever you want them – and the keys for the boat are in the cottage.' He was too reserved to spell out the obvious.

Luke felt deeply depressed as he walked back to his own small house: the troops of Midian seemed to be gathering strength. His depression was not helped by a humid cloudy day, unusual for autumn. He decided he needed a siesta and then he would see if he could find Parker that evening in the Black Swan. He would be able to give him all the town and school gossip which might be useful in any future outbreak of hostilities with the head.

Luke found sleep eluded him. He was profoundly disturbed about events in the school and could see no resolution to his future relationship with Francesca. He only knew he desired to be with her more than anything else in the world, his very being craved her urgently. He knew his years of voluntary celibacy had entailed repressing his nature and that he was naive and inexperienced with women. Francesca attracted him not just physically but, with her character, emotionally entranced him – he felt intuitively completed by her. In the meanwhile the Fr Peter crisis had separated them, but his mind was filled with images of her and to his clerical dismay he found his dream life had become riotously erotic. Most mornings he awoke to find evidence of nightly excitement.

As Luke lay on his bed seeking sleep that afternoon, he recalled a vivid dream in which he and Francesca were in a storm on a yacht on the Helford. A wave had burst over them, soaking their clothes so that they had had to descend into the cabin to change. They could only find oilskins to cover their nakedness. As they finished redressing, the boat ran aground and the scene of the dream changed instantly to their lying together on the cliff edge, making love while watching the yacht break up on the rocks below.

This dream continued to haunt his waking hours and made his lack of contact with Francesca unbearable. He got up and phoned Boscannon. To his relief it was answered by the gardener, Joseph, who had shown them the secret priest-hole beneath the hearth when they had visited Boscannon. He offered the information that Francesca was abroad and it was not known when she was due home. Luke gave him the message that she was to contact her dressmaker as soon as possible.

Luke was so frustrated that he knew he would be unable to sleep that afternoon. Instead he went for a walk to watch the school boats practising on the river. When he reached the straight stretch where the eights could race each other, he was engulfed by a sudden thunderstorm, which had been preceded by a small hurricane of humid air. He was drenched to the skin and, as he walked in sodden clothes and squelching shoes, he could think only of his dream.

Luke felt depressed in spite of a bath and a change of clothes, but hoped a meeting with Parker in the Black Swan would take his mind away from worrying about Francesca. He knew he would learn the latest gossip about the town and school.

He entered the Black Swan wearing his black cassock; this caused no comment – it was understood that the cathedral and college clergy wore their cassocks whenever possible as witness to their priestly role, a custom which infuriated Mr Jones, who rarely wore even his clerical collar. Luke noticed a group of Slavic-looking boys taking up most of the counter of the main bar and apparently sharing a bottle of vodka, concluding that this was his first sighting of the Russians. Seeing no sign of Parker, he went to the back of the inn to the 'snug bar' as it was appropriately named. It was heavily beamed and had a large inglenook fireplace in which logs were simmering and hissing, infusing the room with the smell of burnt pine. There he found Parker on an old oak settle, holding court to the delight of a small gathering. Luke recognised two of the college groundsmen and the head porter and the keeper of the college stores. He was greeted warmly and a whisky was ordered for him. A place was made for Luke on the oak settle next to Parker.

At first they just exchanged pleasantries about the weather and about his progress in editing the diary, until Luke pressed the right gossip button by asking about the number of clocks Parker still looked after in the school. Before answering, Parker knocked the ash angrily out of his pipe into the fireplace; the lower portion of tobacco in his pipe was damp and sizzled as it dropped into the fire.

'Father, it grieves me to say only three clocks. The Tompion in the headmaster's study, your old Perigal clock and one outside the college council chamber. Just think of it, I used to look after forty timepieces! It's barbarous replacing them with clicking electronic monsters. On top of that I have to endure being in the headmaster's room sometimes when he's there, and you know, Father, he's developed an increasing BO problem

116

– no doubt all his nastiness oozing out. And some of his phone calls are embarrassing in the extreme – he seems to think I don't exist. Why only today he was drooling down the phone to his wife, "Darling Bubbles this and Darling Bubbles that…" and next minute talking to a "Sandra" in a most lascivious manner.' The room had fallen silent save for the gentle sizzling and crackling of the fire.

'Tell Father what you heard about the statue,' interjected the head porter.

'Well, that was a stunner.' Parker took centre stage but delayed speaking by refuelling his pipe and thus building up the expectations of his audience.

Luke felt a prickling sensation at the back of his neck, a reaction he experienced when fearful or angry. He was possessed of both emotions at that moment as he rapidly reviewed in his mind the significance of the statue of Our Lady.

The statue in question was that of Our Lady of Walsingham. It represented her sitting on a throne, wearing a crown. She held the Infant Christ on one side and the sceptre on the other. Walsingham had, in medieval times, been the premier Marian shrine in England and was located in the north of Norfolk. Its significance in the Church of England was as a place of pilgrimage for Anglo-Catholics. In the 1920s a High Church priest had revived Marian devotion there with manifestations of extreme Catholic practices more associated with florid Latin devotions. An Italianate church in miniature had been built around what was said to be an original holy well. Outside were other objects of Catholic devotion, and the comings and goings of Anglican nuns and monks and occasionally resplendently garbed bishops in purple robes and much lace. The Roman Catholics were represented in Walsingham by a simple chapel on the outskirts, and were usually bemused and astounded, if not actually scandalised, by the Anglo-Catholic establishments. However, the statue was to be found in more sober High Church circles, and devotion to Our Lady was seen as marking one as an Anglican and sympathetic to the view that the Church of England was the rightful Catholic presence in the kingdom. To have the statue removed would destroy the outward sign that this was where the college stood doctrinally. He was jolted out of his thoughts as Parker unfolded the drama.

Parker raised his eyes to the tobacco-stained ceiling.

'Well, last week I was alone in the head's study when the telephone rang. It has an answering machine and I heard the Revd Jones' voice. He said he had investigated the legal status of the statue of Our Lady of Walsingham in the college chapel, that it had been a gift in 1925 to the headmaster of Melbury and his successors, meaning he could remove it and burn it at any time, just give him the date and he would help. Horrible, Father, and he ended by laughing in a really obscene manner.'

Luke had to get up and put his glass of whisky on the mantelpiece. His hand began to shake involuntarily. He turned to the room, the others looking at him expectantly.

'Gentlemen, over my dead body. Thank you, Parker, I think I'll go to the front of the house to calm myself before I leave. Please have another round on me – I'll tell the barman to take your orders.'

This produced an enthusiastic barrage of 'Good luck, Father' and 'Let us know if we can help.'

When Luke returned to the main bar he found it full, and the majority of the customers appeared to be the Russians, all of them wearing Melbury scarves and cravats. He tried to get to the bar to tell the girl serving to replenish his friends in the snug, but his way was blocked by a tall thickset young Russian who was leaning over the bar trying to kiss the girl.

Luke tapped him on the shoulder. 'Excuse me...'

The Russian turned around. He had a bottle of vodka in one hand, which he waved about wildly before lurching forward and putting a large hand, the size of a side plate, at Luke's throat. His grip was like a vice. For a moment he rocked Luke back and forth, trying to focus his vision, then with a roar of laughter released his grip and embraced Luke in a Russian bear hug. 'Little Father, little Father,' he guffawed, and started slapping Luke's back.

Two smaller Russian boys intervened and one took Luke by the arm and led him to a small table. 'Sorry about him. I'm Alexei. I'm at college. You priest?'

Luke could not speak for a moment – the throttling had left him gasping for breath. Eventually he answered in the affirmative. The young Russian proceeded to give his life history and his opinion of England and the school.

'Stupid peoples here and stupid school. I here for year. I go to London most weekends and stay at Claridge Hotel. I go showrooms for trying cars. Tell them I need trial of cars for my father in Russia. Last weekend I had Bentley Turbo. Little problem, I crash it but no one hurt. Police came but I had taken driving licence and passport of big Ivan there.' He pointed to the throttling Russian. 'He will get surprise soon. Never missed his passport, drunk in bed all weekend, so when police arrive it will be big laugh.' At this he began to slap his thigh and then asked, 'Which is best hotel in London, Claridge or Connaught? I like both.'

Luke was secretly amused. 'I think you ought to know that I am senior chaplain of the college on a sabbatical. What's your name?'

The young Russian looked temporarily put out until he said solemnly, 'Joseph Stalin', and collapsed in paroxysms of laughter. Luke joined in. He thought how absurd it was that the school was profiting from this influx of wild Russian boys, enjoying their life with a gusto that he could not help but admire.

Chapter Twelve

Luke slept fitfully that night, dreaming of drunken Russian boys trying to steal the statue of Our Lady of Walsingham. In the dream he was unable to stop them as he was held by the throat by Mr Jones. When he awoke he had the beginnings of a sore throat and felt feverish; he wished he did not have to go to London for the meeting of the chapel committee.

The journey to London distracted him from his worries. On the way to the station he was entertained by the taxi driver, whom he knew well, telling him of the gossip in the town about Mr Jones and the nun. 'They say a jilted former girlfriend arrived in Melbury to try and gain his love by threatening suicide in front of the altar unless he returned her passion. He did, but she hit him, saying, "That's for leaving me in the first place!"'

Luke murmured at the end of this tale, 'I don't think it was anything like that.'

By the time he reached the station further outrageous versions of the episode had been recounted.

As he stood on the station platform waiting for the eight-forty-eight train, he heard the musical sound of the cathedral bells chime the three-quarters and remembered his father reciting to him A.E. Housman's lines at least once a week in the school holidays as the town clocks chimed the quarter hours. *He stood and heard the steeple sprinkle the quarters on the morning town.* Then he would add, 'Sprinkle the quarters, isn't that just lovely!'

It was and it is, reflected Luke.

The train came in on time. Its destination was Waterloo and when it arrived in London he had half an hour before the meeting of the chapel council, so he was able to walk from Waterloo over Westminster Bridge to the Abbey. En route he wanted to visit a photographic shop which he had noted on arriving at Waterloo on a previous occasion. It advertised ONE-HOUR DEVELOPING. He had been unable to have the films processed which he had used in Rome, and it was obviously tempting fate to have them developed anywhere in the Melbury area. Yet he wanted to get them to Francesca; though the taking of them ended embarrassingly, it had been her idea, and there were others of their time in Rome.

Luke put on a pair of dark glasses and entered the shop. A middle-aged woman was at the counter and a young girl was behind her at the end of a machine, peering into it, watching continuous reels of film passing before her before they appeared as developed prints. Luke broke into a sweat as he handed over the two films and heard himself saying, 'Could you develop these, please, by this afternoon – two copies of each. My twin brother has broken a leg and asked me to get them done.'

The woman put the films in an envelope. 'Name? They'll be done by three o'clock.'

'Mr J. Brown,' answered Luke and blushed.

The woman gave him a receipt and he bolted out of the shop.

His destination was Archbishop Humphries' grace-and-favour apartment in a hidden courtyard off the Abbey Cloisters. Luke remembered there was a little known door into the Abbey Cloisters via St Edward's Chapel. He decided he would go to the chapel first to pray and prepare himself for the meeting.

The chapel is small, dark and mysterious, its atmosphere spiritual compared with the main part of the Abbey with the tourist hordes shuffling through its nave. There was no one else in the chapel and the only sign of life was its sanctuary lamp flickering by the altar. Luke tried to pray. Was he in a state of separation from Christ because of his love for a married woman? He made an act of contrition but felt it was hollow: his mind was distracted by his memories of Rome and the expectation of seeing Francesca's image in the photographs, and distracted by his theological doubts.

The sound of Big Ben striking twelve brought his prayer to an abrupt end – it was time for the meeting. Luke jumped up and opened the door that led into the cloister. He walked rapidly towards Deans Yard and just before reaching it turned left into a small cloister containing the archbishop's apartment. When he entered he was ushered into a small panelled dining room with purple velvet curtains. The rest of the council were already seated at the table drinking dry sherry and nibbling cheese straws. All eight members of the chapel council were present, including the late headmaster of Melbury, Canon Frobisher, who was complaining about the train service from Cambridge. Fr Robert, head of the Gethsemane Order, was also there and nodded benignly at Luke.

The archbishop declared the meeting open and took the chair. The first item was the threat to the college chapel services. He confirmed that no changes could take place in the pattern of worship in the college chapel; alterations could only be proposed by the chapel council, but first had to be submitted to a vote of past and present members of the school. If no proposals came, there could be no change. In the present circumstances there was, therefore, nothing the headmaster could do. The chapel council elected its own eight members and the council itself was established in the college Statutes, which could only be altered by an act of parliament.

When the archbishop finished, he beamed happily and said, 'So the Protestant headmaster Henshaw is powerless to change college worship.' There was a small murmur of satisfaction and Fr Robert said, 'Deo gratias', which Luke inwardly echoed. 'So let us now discuss arrangements for the unhappy absence of Fr Peter.'

Fr Robert said the Gethsemane Order would provide temporary chaplains and added that an Orthodox priest would come from Oxford once a month for the Russians. They would appoint a new assistant chaplain if Fr Peter's state of health was not restored, and they hoped Luke would return as chaplain when his sabbatical ended.

The archbishop topped up the sherry glasses, asked if there was any other business and looked at his watch. He added that Fr Robert was giving one of the excellent lunches at Gethsemane HQ in Tufton Street and confirmed that they all knew the way out through Deans Yard.

Luke put up his hand. 'I'm afraid we may have a tricky technical situation with the statue of Our Lady of Walsingham.'

Reluctantly, the archbishop motioned the members to listen

to Luke. Luke told them what he had gleaned the night before from Parker. The council members expressed various sentiments of shock and surprise and questioned whether the head could really lay claim to where the statue should be. Luke suggested that though he might not have the nerve to destroy it, he could remove it to his house and put it in his cellar if he wanted. He went on to say that the chapel council should write him a warning letter, and that surely this evidence of plotting with Mr Jones should make them question his suitability as head and they should convey as much to the provost.

The archbishop put up his hand. 'I think you are going too fast, Fr Luke. We know your feelings about Henshaw, and this so far is hearsay. I suggest we get Bridges, our ecclesiastical lawyer, to give us a counsel's opinion – he's just taken silk. Fr Robert can liaise with him, as they are both in London. We can discuss this further over lunch.'

Luke felt put down and wished he could find some excuse to slip away before they walked over to lunch, where the conversation would be dominated by the archbishop telling them tales of derring-do in the African mission field. Fortunately they were joined for lunch in the Gethsemane refectory by a tall aesthetic-looking priest in a black cassock.

'Ah, just the man.' Fr Robert jumped up as he entered and introduced him to them all as Fr John Price from Canada. 'He's come to give a series of lectures to the Forward in Faith movement, to warn them of the terrible changes to Anglicanism in Canada since women priests appeared there. Give us a summary, John. It will make your flesh creep.' Fr Robert sat down and nodded encouragingly. Tales followed of strange services and almost pagan priestesses. 'It seems only by founding new Anglo-Catholic communities, new churches in fact, that our Catholic faith can be saved. As you know that's one way the Forward in Faith movement sees as a possible solution: a new Anglo-Catholic Church of England.'

Fr John was obviously one of a number of heroic priests trying to save their vision of Anglicanism, and he told them how small communities of dispossessed Anglo-Catholics were founding new centres of worship.

All this and the following discussion depressed Luke. It would obviously lead to a breakaway church, and the history of such

123

bodies was not happy. Old Catholics breaking from the Catholic Church of their original faith in the nineteenth century, and Old Believers in Russia, were just shadows. If only the Catholic Church had made positive moves to bring in Anglo-Catholic communities and their priests. If only it had the courage to create a Uniate Anglo-Catholic Church, it would have brought thousands into the family of the universal Church. It had happened in the Ukraine, why not England? Luke suspected the row at the 1998 Lambeth conference over the ordination of gay priests and bishops would have put an end to any consideration of a Uniate solution. If it was not to happen, did Luke's destiny lie in going over to Rome.

The council moved from the refectory to enjoy coffee, port and cigars in the Gethsemane hospitality room. A log fire and comfortable sofas provided a pleasant background for the archbishop to resume his missionary tales. The spiritual welfare of the college was forgotten in the haze of port and cigars. The whole meeting seemed to be an excuse for a comfortable lunch party. Luke seethed inwardly: they should be planning the removal of the head, not, surprisingly, relying on the status quo of the college chapel statutes. The head and Mr Jones were not going to be defeated by these. Luke had a horrible premonition that alternative college services would be promoted in Mr Jones' Emmanuel Church. How would they cope with that. He interrupted the archbishop to raise this possibility. The archbishop looked exasperated.

'You are being overdramatic! You have heard how the college statutes protect our position. We shall fight when need be, not before, and fight through the proper channels, not by getting personally excited. Robert, raise this when you meet with Bridges. However it does seem unlikely to me. Don't look for demons Fr Luke.'

'Oh, my Lord!' Luke's voice was scathing. 'I don't have to look in Melbury College or indeed in the diocese. Our "adversary the devil goeth about like a roaring lion seeking whom he may devour"!'

It was not until three o'clock that the meeting broke up, and Luke received little warmth from the members as he took his leave. He retraced his steps to Waterloo, all the time worried about the films being developed. When he went in to the

124

photographers', the same woman and girl were there. He handed over his receipt. The middle-aged woman looked through a sheaf of envelopes before handing Luke one envelope.

'There should be two,' said Luke. He tried to sound calm but inwardly he was panicking. Were the photos of Francesca so revealing that they were going to be declared obscene, and had the police already been summoned. Luke had a vision of himself appearing in the Melbury Magistrates' Court, where the provost to the college sat as a JP. Another ecclesiastical scandal in Melbury, and, heavens, what a joy for Mr Jones and Henshaw!

The woman replied, 'Sorry, we're very busy today and Sharon here was sick at lunch.' She turned to the ailing Sharon. 'What's happened to this one?' she said, and put the receipt for the missing film under the girl's hand. Sharon looked as if she was going to be sick again, crouching over her machine. Luke noticed she had a boil starting on the back to her neck. Sharon looked at the receipt.

'Doing it now, for heaven's sake.' She bent back to her eyepiece as the film clicked through the machine. She lifted her pale face and stared at Luke for a moment, who was standing blushing on the other side of the counter. She put her hand to her mouth to stifle a giggle.

'Sorry about the delay. Reverend,' said the middle-aged lady. 'This girl will be the death of me.' She went to the end of the machine and started to put the developed photos into a yellow plastic envelope. She appeared not to see them and passed the envelope to him. 'Just check they're yours. That'll be twenty pounds...'

'Oh, thank you, I'm sure they're okay.' If they had been two hundred pounds Luke would have paid with a cheque just to get away, though he thought twenty pounds was outrageous. He did not look at the photos, they were destined for his fire.

Luke opened his door to find a pile of letters awaiting him on his return home. The post had arrived after his departure that morning. He was tired and depressed. He went to his sitting room first and lit a fire, then poured himself a large whisky and picked up the letters. He went back to the sitting room and sat down to read them, the glass of whisky by his side and his briefcase on the floor, containing the photos to be burned when the fire got going.

There were three depressing bills amongst the five letters, but the other two made him stare at them with anticipation: one was from Rome and one from Cornwall. He could not decide which to open first. Rome won. It was from Fr Charles, and it was brief. His code-breaking expert had begun to crack the problem, and already the part of the diary in his possession was yielding up its mysteries. The expert unfortunately had had to go to Israel on another matter, but could Luke come to Rome in two weeks' time?

The second letter was from Francesca and was not so brief.

My Darling, your message about ringing my dressmaker gave me life when I returned here to Boscannon. I prayed it was you. It obviously was after I first checked my genuine one, who was surprised to hear from me. I tried ringing twice, but you seem to be out all the time and now I have lost my nerve. You see, I have feared you might regret our love since you left me in Rome, that your sense of duty has taken you away for good or that you are going to become a Catholic priest – so many good reasons against us. I am writing this from a friend's holiday cottage near Frenchman's Creek. I look after it. When the letting season is over I come here and it gives me some place of refuge. So write to me here, Dove Cottage, Frenchman's Creek, Helford, or, if you are still going to keep me in your life, ring me tomorrow or the day after, I'll be here at three o'clock for an hour or two – the number is 013260 231235. All the love the world has ever known, to you, from me, your Francesca.

Luke sighed and looked at the flames of the fire as it took hold. He took the photographs from his briefcase and began to look at them one by one. When he had been praying that morning, he had found it difficult to remember all her features clearly. It seemed that his emotions had played havoc with his memory of her. The photographs rapidly restored her to his mind. They had captured her in many moods – laughing at him as they were sightseeing in Rome, ecstatic with her mass of shopping bags posing for him in the courtyard of the hotel, looking meditatively at him with her face resting in her hands like a Pre-Raphaelite beauty – but, finally, capturing her essence were the pictures of her modelling for him in her room, looking beautiful and sensual. Luke switched off the light and took a long drink. In the flickering light of the fire he tried to plan his future. He began to pray. It had to be without Francesca. Slowly he began to feed the photographs into the fire. He had burnt half when he came to the picture of her in the courtyard of the hotel. He stopped the burning and prayed again.

An hour later he knew he would go to her in Cornwall and eventually he was sure he would make his life with her in some way. Perhaps she would get an annulment; the Church of Rome was being more liberal in granting them to cope with the rising numbers of its members seeking divorce. In those circumstances it could be possible for him to marry her. Exceptional cases of Anglican clergy being able to marry after divorces were being allowed. The Church in Wales was even suggesting second marriages in church.

Luke sighed and went into the kitchen to scramble two eggs and refill his glass of whisky. Afterwards he went to bed, taking the remaining photographs of Francesca with him. Before sleeping, he lay daydreaming of marrying Francesca in a small Welsh mountain church.

Luke started the next day by going to his old second master's room in college. He remembered he had left his tennis and squash rackets in its adjoining cloakroom. Everything had to be moved to the house that had been assigned to him after he had given up his housemaster's role.

The house the school had provided for Luke was one of the small modern houses for assistant masters that had been built in an estate to one side of the playing fields in the 1980s. It was without character, but had a small garden, and he had already planted some 'Omar Khayyám' roses after his visit to Boscannon. He had moved all his books and belongings from the second master's room in the school into a small study in this new house.

Already he had filled five packing cases with books and now only had to empty his filing cabinet and collect his sports gear from the cloakroom adjoining the second master's room. He aimed to complete the task by the end of that morning, but just as he got to the door of this room he was delayed by the regular Friday visit of Parker, who went straight to his Georgian bracket clock.

'I can't crack this one – five minutes slow this time.' Addressing Luke's back, he went on, 'It's a diabolical liberty. Our head, *the brigadier*' – he said the name with a sneer – 'has had all our old clocks sold and replaced with one of these new-fangled, centrally controlled, electric time systems. Clocks clicking, not ticking, except of course for the Tompion clock in *his* room. Forgive me, but it's typical of him looking after his own comforts. And then bringing his wife in as his secretary and getting rid of dear old Margery Brown! She served you and the old head so well. But how does he justify bringing in some sergeant major as his chauffeur and shadow, prancing around in army uniform and getting rid of all our clocks? Our much beloved head, Canon Frobisher, is very shocked, I understand. A tragedy for the school when he got suddenly made master of Michaelhouse last year.' Parker was moving from first gear to top as the words tumbled from him. 'I understand from the college porter that this new head's secretary, his wife, is an absolute pain...'

Luke finally turned round. 'Please, Tom, I don't think this sort of talk helps us at all.'

The reprimand was ignored and Parker continued unabashed. 'Sorry, Father, but really – to announce that the clocks are going in order to save costs, when he indulges himself in that way, is scandalous. I can't think what the college council were thinking of, bringing in this retired military windbag!'

Luke groaned inwardly. He agreed with every comment his visitor was making. 'Tom Parker, you cannot expect me to listen to tittle-tattle. You know the reason for the appointment. Numbers have been falling and the college was accumulating a dangerously large debt. The council decided they needed a management expert, and the brigadier had, I believe, a distinguished army career. More to the point, over a period of five years after leaving the army, he put that management school at Sedgebury University on a sound footing.'

Parker snorted. 'Distinguished army career! Army educational corps, then brigadier in the catering corps – does that justify a man throwing out a wonderful collection of clocks, just to save me coming in one day a week? Anyway, we know the timetable of the school is always controlled by the chimes of the cathedral clock – it doesn't matter if some of the classroom clocks are a bit poorly occasionally. This man would have been no more than a bombardier in a decent regiment.' He laughed. 'I gather that's what he's known as by the boys, "HM the Bombardier".' He continued relentlessly. 'He's out to destroy the whole ethos of the school. I gather his speech at Founders' Day outlined a blitzkrieg. He gloried in saying he's going to turn the school upside down and send it whizzing into the twenty-first century: girls coming to the school, aiming at two out of the ten houses first, then up to fifty per cent of your numbers, I understand. What about his aim of watering down our Anglo-Catholic heritage to make the school attractive to everybody? I know we've got to watch the numbers in these funny times, but heavens, didn't he even talk of a house for Nonconformists? Hymn-shrieking Methodists and the like, you'll be having soon. This is an Anglican school with a tradition of producing bishops going back to Queen Elizabeth the first. Though I know we are meant to encourage the numerical spirit.'

Luke pursed his lips. 'Just having Anglicans doesn't ensure perfection amongst either boys or staff.'

'We are all sinners, of course, but I prefer mine Anglican,' Parker blithely continued. He knew he would eventually get a reaction and would extract some indiscretion to add to his rich collection of school gossip. 'Also, Father, the bombardier – sorry brigadier – wants to remove the blessed sacrament reserved in the Lady chapel and that the statue of Our Lady of Walsingham has to go as well?'

Luke's face went white with anger. 'When in God's name did you learn this?'

Parker picked up a magnifying glass, which he applied to a clock. 'Well, I can't actually tell you, but I heard it from a reliable source.'

Luke breathed in deeply as if to cleanse himself. The clockmaker decided to lob one last verbal grenade.

'I also heard he wants to appoint a woman chaplain at the same time as girls arriving in the school.'

'Now, come on, who told you that? I demand to know – that's beyond a joke.'

Parker inwardly hugged himself at the success of this suggestion. 'A very reliable source – our much-loved old headmaster.'

'When did he say this, and to whom?'

'Well, to me, Father, just after the speeches in the school hall. We walked down to the college grub together for the staff coffee party. Such a warm man. He told me I looked tired, but I told him that with the school clocks being thrown out I should soon have time to regurgitate myself.'

Luke raised his eyebrows. 'You mean resuscitate yourself, and I think a while back you meant ecumenical, not numerical.'

Parker looked away sulkily and picked up the magnifying glass again. 'If you insist, Father. Anyway, the master of Michaelhouse said it was bound to happen. God bless him, I'm sure you wish he was still head. Anyway, words to that effect. He told me the brigadier was already making enquiries for suitable women candidates for the assistant chaplaincy, girls or no girls.'

Luke went to his desk and sat down wearily. He picked up a tool from Parker's work box and studied it for a moment. 'You're making it up just because you know my strong views about women priests – or women pretending to be, more accurately.

Parker was triumphant. 'It's true, Father, but I forgot. I'm very sorry, he told me not to tell you. He said you'd had so much to put up with lately, what with the new head arriving. Anyway, I'm off now. I hope I've finally fixed that clock.'

Luke was left to consider Parker's understatement about the impact of the new head. Exchanges between the head and himself had been negligible since the Foundation Day speeches. During these speeches, the provost had paid tribute to Luke's work as an outstanding housemaster, chaplain and cricket coach and went on to say how much the school would miss him, wishing him a fruitful sabbatical and ending by looking forward to his return as second master in a year's time. These remarks had led to a sustained round of applause from all present, save the headmaster and his wife.

Luke had put the contents of his filing cabinet into the packing cases and then went into his cloakroom to collect his cricket bat, pads and tennis rackets. He closed the door behind him to give him more room to put the items into a final packing case. He had just finished when he heard the voices of the head and his wife in the room.

'Right, lass, that sanctimonious bugger Howard seems to have done his packing.'

'Good riddance to him,' chimed in the wife.

Luke froze in the cloakroom. He knew he should cough or make some noise to alert them to his presence, but he was so angered by their conversation that he decided he would surprise them if they continued in a similar vein. For a moment he could only hear them moving furniture and packing cases, their voices muffled by the sound.

'There,' said the head, 'your desk will be best here, then when you're sitting behind it you can see my room through the open door. Then over here we can have a big couch like the one we had at Sedgebury Business School, and you know, Bubbles, what that's intended for...' Luke then heard coy giggles from Angela Henshaw. 'What's it for, Bubbles?'

'Oh, Puggy, it's for when you're feeling powerful, like after your committee meetings at the business school.'

'That's right, lass, and what was my rule for the secretary of a powerful man?'

'Oh, Puggy...'

'Come on, Bubbles.'

'Oh, Puggy – no panties!'

Luke crossed himself in mock horror. 'What a couple,' he breathed silently to himself. He seemed fated to overhear appalling marital exchanges, though unlike Francesca's this was not tragic, just farcical.

'Right, Bubbles. That will be the rule on Friday mornings. No committee meetings here but that's the time I'll deal with the naughty boys, with Sergeant Major Carter assisting me. I have to have someone present in case one of the little pricks accuses me of taking advantage of them – but, by gum, it makes me feel powerful!'

Brenda Henshaw replied, 'Oh, Puggy, you're a real man.'

'I know, my lass. So, Bubbles, no pants on Friday mornings.'

More oohs and giggles followed. Luke heard the sound of his desk being slowly moved as Brigadier Henshaw pressed his wife over it.

'Are you wearing pants now?' The sound of the head's voice increased by several decibels, and again louder. 'Tell me, are you wearing pants?'

Luke opened the door and entered the room. 'Of course, Headmaster, well brought up people usually do...' he said, and sauntered nonchalantly out of the other door.

Later that day a note was delivered by Sergeant Major Carter to Luke's home.

After your disgraceful and insulting behaviour in eavesdropping on my wife and I, it would be best if we do not meet again. I shall endeavour to prevent your return to this college. You are forthwith sacked as second master. Have no doubt, I shall prevail in my reforms. Your formal dismissal as senior chaplain will follow after the next meeting of the college council, which will take place at the end of the summer vacation.

Next morning, Luke tried to edit more of the diary but he was distracted about what the decoding of it in Rome might reveal and even more distracted at the prospect of speaking again to Francesca. His long-term plans to share his life with her looked bleak now that he was to lose his job as second master. He reflected that finding the treasure was becoming even more imperative.

At two-forty-five he found he could not locate her letter with the telephone number, but having searched frantically in his bedroom, remembered he had put it into his briefcase the night before. He tried to say a prayer that whatever was meant to be should be granted to them and accepted, adding, please, God, may things work out that we may be together for the rest of our lives.

He rang the number at three o'clock.

Chapter Thirteen

When the telephone rang in the cottage, Francesca was sitting on a sofa. Rasputin was lying next to her, pressing her into a corner. Normally she would not tolerate that, but she was desperate for any emotional support. The telephone had rung, and for a moment she had hung back, overcome with the fear that Luke might be ringing with the intention of telling her that he could not see her again. She sat mesmerised, looking at the phone like a rabbit transfixed by a snake. Rasputin whined beside her, breaking the spell. She tried to get up to take the call but the weight of the dog stopped her. The phone stopped ringing. The silence seemed deafening. From outside came the faint sound of the wind in the trees and distant seagulls. She sat by the phone waiting for the call to be repeated. She disentangled herself from the dog and moved to the phone.

'Let him ring again, please ring again,' she kept saying to herself.

Rasputin began to whine and lay on the sofa regarding her with his head between his paws. The phone rang again. Francesca had her hand on it but sprang back as if electrocuted, then slowly moved forward to pick it up. It was cousin Nancy.

'Francesca? I thought I'd eventually find you skulking there. Some walk I'm sure you've had with Rasputin from the car to the front door. Anyway, for God's sake, get back here, Boss is in a foul mood and I've had him for two weeks while you've been carousing with your relations.'

The disappointment, plus the unexpected summons from Nancy, was too much. She could not speak.

'Hello? Francesca, I know you are there. Speak!'

Francesca slammed the phone down. It rang again. It was Luke. He had decided he would ring every five minutes during

133

the next half-hour until he got an answer, and if there was no reply he would leave a message at Boscannon to say that the dressmaker would be coming to her area once he had been told a suitable time and date.

Fortunately, Nancy's call had shocked Francesca out of the world of romance. She had decided that if Nancy rang again she would let her Italian blood rip. She'd had enough. There had been a full-time nurse at Boscannon while she was away, and Nancy's constant carping had gone too far.

Francesca snatched up the phone and snapped, 'Yes!'

Luke was temporarily stunned, but after a pause said, 'Is that Francesca?'

The answer was a long sigh, followed by them simultaneously saying, 'My darling.'

Their phone call lasted nearly half an hour. Their conversation was a mixture of endearments and news. Luke told her about the possible cracking of the code in the diary and that he had to return to Rome, but that he would then return to Alastair's cottage. Francesca burst into tears of joy at this news.

Luke took a deep breath. His will did not seem to exist: he was driven by his need for Francesca. 'If you can join me again, just for a day or two, I'm sure things will be right this time – I'll write the script!'

Francesca was silent for a moment; then, resistance gone, her words poured out. 'Oh, Luke, of course, though I demand a lead part in the play. I'll see what I can do to get away.' She went on to tell him about Dove Cottage and how lovely it would be for them when he came back to Cornwall. When Francesca put the phone down, she took Rasputin in her arms and hugged him.

The phone rang again. Francesca picked it up hoping it might be Luke again. It was Nancy.

'What the hell are you up to? You've been on that phone for hours. Don't you understand plain English? Get back here.'

Francesca was so happy she burst out laughing. 'I'm coming, you shrivelled old prune,' she said, and then put the phone down.

At the other end, Nancy stared, outraged. 'The girl is mad. One day she's going to get her impertinence thrashed out of her.' She stormed off to tell Boss.

Francesca went over to an old record player in the corner of the room. She found some dance music and danced a jig, with Rasputin an uncontrollable partner.

Luke had a window seat on his flight to Rome. It gave him the doubtful advantage of viewing their approach to a stormy sky over the Alps. Dark clouds were boiling over the mountains, depositing the first heavy snows of winter. The plane began to shudder in the unstable air. The captain's voice came over the intercom in tones reminiscent of a wartime gung-ho bomber-command hero.

'Please fasten your seat belts – teeny bit of turbulence over the hillocks below.'

The plane began to buck up and down, like a massive rodeo horse. Luke thought what an idiot the pilot was to fly into this situation. A young stewardess tried to hang on to a food trolley that had tipped over into the row in which Luke was sitting. The contents of some food trays deposited themselves on the seat next to him. The aircraft's engines began to roar as the captain tried to climb above the storm.

As Luke pulled his safety belt tighter, he wondered what metaphysical safety belt could secure his ground existence. Henshaw had destroyed his future as second master, and the college council, mesmerised by the headmaster's success in increasing numbers, would force the chapel committee to sack Luke as senior chaplain. Luke could only foresee a future as an impecunious priest or schoolmaster. The former option was threatened by his recurring bouts of disbelief, not only in the Anglican Church, but in God as well. Anyway, what future would there be for him if he was cited as co-respondent in a Boscannon divorce? It was obvious that if Francesca joined him again in Rome, they would become lovers, even if his beliefs were restored, where would he be left spiritually?

His faith had been shaken by reading that day in the *Spectator* about the growth of a Neo-Darwinism based on a theory of the genetic programming of human existence. An Oxford professor of biology had said that because the world was genetically predetermined, it was therefore a form of child abuse to allow Christianity to be taught to the young. Heavens! No doubt if this professor was programmed to become Führer

135

of a Fascist England, he would put in jail the Queen, parliament and teachers for having allowed Christian instruction in schools. Luke shook his head and drank back the double whisky he had been hanging on to as the plane swerved and bolted through the black clouds enveloping them. Blackness was becoming increasingly illuminated by flashes of lightning. Luke thought of the treasure: finding it would secure his survival. His reverie was interrupted. The captain's voice boomed over the intercom again.

'Sorry, folks, we are on our way to climbing out of this bumpy turbulence. Just keep in your seats, nothing to worry about, and make sure your safety...' He meant to end with 'belts are fastened', but he was interrupted by a couple of muffled explosions near the plane, and simultaneously the sky was lit up with blinding flashes of lightning. Luke saw ribbons of electricity chasing along the wings. The plane was plunged into darkness and seemed to be dropping like a stone. Luke was mesmerised by the wings flapping spasmodically in the continuing flashes of lightning. Behind him, women began screaming in panic and an ashen stewardess ran towards them sideways down the plane, clutching the seats as she went. They were in the middle of a tremendous electrical storm.

Luke began to pray, rapidly putting aside his intellectual doubts. 'Lord, forgive me for the sins of my life. Christ who calmed the storm on the Sea of Galilee, save us now, and I firmly resolve to serve thee better if we survive.'

Soon they cleared the clouds. Looking back, Luke saw that the sun was colouring their surface, which from above was a vivid mixture of purple, red and a sinister olive green where explosions of lightning below could be seen, popping up like depth charges in some cosmic battle.

It was a relieved body of travellers who moved rapidly to the exit when the plane had landed in Rome.

Luke arrived at the English College in time for a merry lunch with Fr Charles and some of the members of the college. The memory of his flight faded. Afterwards they took their coffee to the library to await the arrival of the cryptography expert from the Gregorian University. The room was lined with shelves packed with finely bound books spanning several centuries of learning.

Fr Charles led him to a long table and took from a large briefcase their portion of the diary, now carefully wrapped. He laid out some of the parchment pieces on the table, explaining that those were the ones in code. He then went to a glass case containing several valuable books; he unlocked it and lifted out a large red-bound missal. He placed it on the table and then took out from his briefcase the auction catalogue for the Boscannon sale. He opened it and passed it to Luke.

'When we bought our part of the diary at that sale, I also bid for this Mass book and got it surprisingly cheaply, thus does the modern age appreciate religious artefacts. I've underlined the lot number.'

Luke read the sale description: CANON MISSAL ET PRAEFATIONES etc. ROME (VATICAN) 1555, RED MOROCCO GILT WITH A CARDINAL'S COAT OF ARMS, DEDICATION TO A FATHER DE WITTE.

Fr Charles told him how the dedication had caught his eye and that he thought it would have an interest. He found from the archives that Fr de Witte had served as a chaplain for a brief period in a cardinal's palace, and he had been given this just before leaving for England. As they were talking, a tall priest entered the library. Fr Charles leapt to his feet and introduced Fr Jeronimo. Luke liked the look of him immediately. He was young and pleasantly rotund, and his eyes twinkled behind gold-framed glasses. His handshake was firm.

'This is our code breaker extraordinaire, and we must make allowances for his being a Jesuit.'

Fr Jeronimo laughed. He sat down, beaming around him, his eyes now attentive in a face crowned with a shock of thick grey hair. Fr Charles told the other priest that they had only just started, so would he like to explain how he had broken the code.

Fr Jeronimo inclined his head and said, '*Grazie*. Well, this missal is the answer. When Fr Charles contacted me, I asked if there were any books with the diary belonging to Fr de Witte and he said only the missal. This puzzled me because he died an Anglican, but then of course he had been Catholic at Boscannon and no doubt this was hidden there before he left. Now look at each page.

'Page number one. The main text is printed in black but

these red letters introduce each section – beautiful are they not? There are four red letters on this page, see?' He pointed to a 'C' 'D', 'H' and 'M'. 'This is his code. He divided the letters into 1.1 equals "C", 1.2 equals "D" and so on through the missal. He got most of the letters of the alphabet this way, though for "X"s and "Z"s, he invents the not very original numbers of 24 and 26 being their ranking in the alphabet. Simple once you have the relevant book.' Fr Jeronimo smiled cherubically and sat back.

Fr Charles said, 'It's cracked the code for us. Our part is a moving description of de Witte disguised, witnessing the martyrdom of Robert Southwell. He was Bishop of Melbury at the time. I think that could be very significant if he did progress towards becoming a Catholic at the end of his life. Anyway, we have had the code typed out, so you can take it away to work on your bits. There is a small comment after St Robert Southwell's death which uses a different code and we can't crack that yet – we need to find another book; but it may be more subtle, we can't make it out, it's very clever. So we'll leave you to it. Fr Jeronimo is here tomorrow if you need him. Please feel free to use the library on the coded parts of your diary.'

Luke took the code and the diary to a table in the library and began to decipher the hidden parts of the diary. He started on the part relating to the treasure. It was tedious work, but eventually its secret was revealed to read, *God's treasure is known in his house, St Peter has the keys. Master Philip has made safe the treasure – it took much work at night, now St Peter keeps it safe.*

At first Luke thought it was only revealing another puzzle and could not solve it. He went on to try the passage where de Witte went into code to describe some important events connected with the squire's wife and leading to his becoming an Anglican. Here the code would not reveal its secret. It had to be the same as the one part confounding them in the English College and was as yet cryptic.

Luke had more luck with a piece at the end of the diary. It seemed to be a reverie on the death of Robert Southwell; it was obviously deeply troubling to de Witte. It all took longer than he expected and by six o'clock he was exhausted by the work and by the effects of his early flight from Heathrow to Rome.

Luke returned to his hotel and found a message waiting for him. The receptionist had given him an envelope on his arrival. At first he thought it was an interim statement of his bill. It read, *Your sister hopes to arrive around seven o'clock, but her boss is causing problems about absence. She will join you as before in the bar. In case mother can come too, a double room has been reserved.*

Luke had a bath and went downstairs to await Francesca's arrival. He went into the bar and savoured the message by reading it several times. He had known she would come, though on past performances it was difficult to predict the outcome with certainty. Her reference to Boscannon made him uneasy. He persuaded himself that knowing she loved him enough to come to Rome was in itself a heady prospect, but he feared her domestic problems would in the end prove insuperable and prevent their love progressing.

While Luke was reading the message, Francesca was in a taxi coming from the airport. Her acceptance of his invitation had been instinctive. Her whole being ached for Luke, yet she was plagued with the knowledge that to abandon her husband would be wrong. It irked her to think that the world would brand her as a Lady Chatterley, seeking pleasure and sensual fulfilment away from a crippled spouse. Somehow she hoped she could find strength from Luke's love to continue to stay at Boscannon. She knew it was specious justification, but without Luke she was convinced that Boscannon Manor was a nightmare she could no longer endure.

She'd had to escape the poisonous atmosphere that had existed after her telephone exchange with Nancy, and invented further important Italian family reasons for visiting Rome again. Boscannon had been furious and she had been subdued into agreeing to be away for only three nights.

Luke had seated himself in a corner of the bar to await her arrival. It was definitely off season and he had the place to himself. He had taken a photocopy of the new pages of the diary he had seen in the English College and was quietly trying to translate an obscure passage when two hands came from behind his face, and Francesca, covering his eyes, said, 'Guess who?' She had just arrived and come straight to the bar. It was raining hard outside and she was wearing the black Armani cashmere coat she had bought on the previous visit to Rome.

Beads of rain glistened on its surface and her cheeks glowed with pleasure. She nuzzled his neck and then shook the rain off her hair as she broke away. 'A large vodka and orange, please, as before. I'll pop up to my room and have a quick bath. I'm afraid Mummy can't come.'

Luke took out a handkerchief and dabbed his eyes. 'Oh, dear, I suppose it's her gout again?'

Francesca returned later, wearing a white silk shirt and a long leather skirt, covering a matching pair of Victorian-style lace-up boots. She looked stunning.

They drank their vodkas and then, hand in hand, went into the dining room to enjoy another excellent meal. This time they shared only one bottle of wine, a Soave, accompanying two *sogliole alla griglia*. They finished with coffee and sat in the candlelight holding hands while Luke told her about the breaking of most of the code and his discussions at the English College. When he told her about the reference to the treasure, Francesca wrinkled her nose in a most attractive way and sat silently for a moment while she considered the clue of St Peter and his keys. After a while she spoke slowly.

'I have a hunch, but I must check it first. The answer may be in the chapel.'

Luke sat back. 'Problem is, when can we find out? We can't just walk in. I suppose we shall have to wait until *they* are out again.'

Francesca stroked his cheek. 'Don't worry, my darling. Now, I want to know more about you before we go to bed. I think that's not unreasonable. How many girls have you known, in the biblical sense?'

Luke was put out by the change of subject. For a moment he was silent. 'Okay, if you tell me about your love life one day.'

Francesca laughed lightly. 'That won't take long. I had a boyfriend just after leaving school. Heavy petting, that sort of thing. Then Charles, a naval lieutenant, came into my life – glamorous in his mess kit and took me to a ball at Greenwich when it was still a naval college. He was teaching there at the time, so he had a room. We got tiddly on too much flowing champagne and he seduced me there and it lasted a month or two. He was selfish and in love with himself. I drifted and then, as I told you before, met Boscannon. That's all there has been, though I wish I had met you first. You are the only man I've loved so hopelessly, even though I hardly know you. One of those cosmic loves, I hope, that only a few are privileged to possess.'

They leant across the table and kissed. By then they were alone in the dining room.

Luke did not know how to start: he felt inhibited in this even though relaxed in every other area of their relationship.

Francesca patted his hand in a maternal manner, then, curiosity overwhelming her, asked, 'Are you a virginal chaste priest, my darling?'

Luke shook his head slowly. 'Don't worry, I know what to do. I had a fling during my last year at Cambridge. Sister of one of my fellow members of the varsity cricket team. She had a thing about blues. We had an affair lasting six months, but we were just satisfying our young animal urges – no love – so it was very unsatisfactory. Then I had my priestly vocation and became chaste. That is until I fell in love with you, and my dream life has been a riot of nightly desire...'

A look passed over Francesca's face that he had never seen before: it was almost as if she was in pain. She had closed her eyes, and her hands were beneath the table. She breathed quickly for a moment, her mouth set hard, then she stood up quickly. 'I'm in room 33 again. Come as soon as you've signed the bill.'

Luke went to his room and put on just his bathrobe. When he reached Francesca's room, he tapped lightly three times on the door and immediately it opened. The room was in darkness and Francesca took his hand and led him to her bed. They both slipped off their robes and kissed sitting naked on the side of the bed, before slipping between the sheets.

They were overwhelmed by the sensation of their bodies coming together. Later, neither could have recalled what followed – they seemed at times to be fighting violently to express their pent-up desire – but at the conclusion of their ecstasy they were conscious of the strangeness of their cries as they experienced something utterly new in their lives. Afterwards, cradling each other, they drifted into a state between sleep and slumber, though waking several times and pouring out the need for each other in words slipping from meaning into just sounds of desire.

When dawn came, Luke left Francesca sleeping and returned to his room and ordered coffee for himself. Later he lay in his bath. He kept repeating a prayer of contrition, but it was only words – he felt nothing but elation. He would go to the last part of his life knowing human passion at its fullest. He knew later the consequences would be demanding and intellectually he would condemn himself for loving another man's wife, but at that moment it felt entirely natural and part of life's plan for him and Francesca. Certainly, he reasoned, she was not truly married to such a husband.

The next two days were spent mostly in Francesca's room, interrupted by gentle sightseeing and light feasting.

It was agreed that Luke would join her in Cornwall when they both left Rome for England. Luke would stay in Alastair's cottage. Francesca felt she could not visit him there, as a friend of Nancy's lived in the same lane, but he would come to her at Dove Cottage, her friend's holiday home. Luke would get the little ferry across the river at Helford Passage and she would meet him outside the Shipwright's Arms in Helford. The boat left on the hour from his side at the Ferryboat Inn and he promised he would get the one leaving at midday. She had told him that her welcome would have to be formal, as she was known there. She would then drive him to the cottage. Francesca had added, 'This time I'll give you a simple lunch, but there's no plunge pool, only a large bed.'

Luke replied that he was happy to settle for the simple life.

Chapter Fourteen

Luke arrived in Cornwall just as it was getting dark. His departure from Melbury had been delayed as he had had a call from Alastair telling him that a circular had been sent from the head to both staff and pupils saying that attendance at Sunday chapel was to be optional, providing they went to Emmanuel Church for matins. It also said that this would enable them to worship with the local community and that, with increasing numbers, the college chapel was getting uncomfortably crowded. The head finished by saying that he felt that the college High Mass, although impressive, had become too exclusive and rarefied and not a good preparation for religious observance in the real world. A roll-call would be taken of those attending both the college chapel and Emmanuel Church. He wanted the college to be more closely linked with the life of the town. An additional note had been sent to all housemasters saying that they should forward to him the names of those attending the Emmanuel service and that he expected them to encourage it. He would be looking closely to see a rising attendance there and he certainly would make sure those who were college prefects, or wished to be in future, should set an example. Alastair had been apoplectic with fury and said this was another signal that he would have to be received into the Roman Catholic Church – all was anarchy in the Church of England.

Luke had gone to Alastair to discuss how they should react. Alastair believed half the staff would discourage attendance at the Emmanuel Church in the town but that certainly the rest would toady to the head, thinking they would be gaining favour with the winning side. It would divide the school, but they had to admit it was a cunning tactic to get round the grip of the chapel council on college worship.

'What is happening in the school,' said Alastair, 'is an

143

intensified picture of what is happening in the outside world. The evangelicals are getting stronger – Holy Trinity, Brompton is its most popular manifestation – and the Anglo-Catholics are talking about setting up their own province or deserting to Rome. Those in the middle are fading away or else just accept whatever changes are visited on them.'

Afterwards, Luke immediately rang Archbishop Humphries and asked him to write a letter to the provost protesting in the strongest terms. The Archbishop's skill in avoiding controversy led him to prevaricate by saying, 'Let's see how many pupils abstain from chapel. If only a few, it will be proved a futile manoeuvre.'

Luke was in despair. He told Alastair that as he was still senior chaplain, albeit on sabbatical, he had a duty to intervene. He would write to the provost and all the college council to protest against this outrage. If that failed, he would send a circular himself, appealing to the college members to be loyal to their traditional faith. The brazenness of the headmaster overwhelmed him as he drove down to Cornwall. His depression only lifted when he arrived. The sun was setting over the Helford, from which rose a light mist. It was the beginning of an unusual spell of warm September weather. As he went towards the front door of the cottage, he looked over the river and stopped to gaze at Boscannon. His whole being yearned to be with Francesca. When he got into the cottage, he lit the stove in the gazebo and swung the telescope towards the manor, hoping to see Francesca. The telephone rang. A voice said, 'Fr Jeronimo, English College, Rome. You remember me?'

Luke laughed. 'Of course. How can I help?'

'I am ringing from St Alban's College, Valladolid, Spain. Fr Charles asked me to ring you. We think it most important that you come here. I have found something very serious regarding your work on Fr de Witte. You must come before you finish your task.'

Luke explained that it would be difficult to go immediately, but that he could possibly leave in a week's time.

'Good,' came the answer. 'I'll tell Fr Charles. There is a flight to Valladolid from Paris every day except Saturday. Fr Charles will come from Rome via Barcelona. Tell me the day you can come.'

'Can you tell me something about your discovery that makes it so important?'

'No, Fr Luke. I must tell you both at the same time.'

Luke presumed he must have cracked the rest of the code, revealing de Witte's reason for converting to the Church of England and the whereabouts of the treasure.

'I'll come next Friday,' replied Luke, and put the phone down. For a moment he stood in a state of shock. The kettle beside him had boiled and was gently steaming.

The telephone rang again. It was Francesca. She spoke in hushed tones.

'I've been ringing every half-hour to check your arrival. I'm speaking from my room but can't say more in case the others pick up another extension. You know my thoughts – till midday tomorrow.'

When that time came both Francesca and Luke were standing on either side of the Helford river, waiting for the boat to leave the Ferryboat Inn. They were tense and almost sick with excitement and when they saw each other as they met outside the Shipwright's Arms on the other side, it took superhuman control not to race into each other's arms.

Once in the car they gripped hands and, as they moved off, Francesca said, 'Just a little drive to the cottage.' They both could hardly speak. The cottage was only a mile away across fields from Helford village, but it was a tortuous drive down narrow Cornish lanes until they came to a gate in the side of the road. Francesca nodded towards it. 'Nearly there, darling.' Luke jumped out and opened it and then got back in the car as it proceeded along a track and through a farmyard. 'Over there!' Francesca pointed. Luke could see the top of a whitewashed cottage with dark blue window frames. It lay across the fields behind a small copse of trees on land sloping towards the river. 'This track goes on, even rougher, down the hill to Frenchman's Creek – all woods and a bit gloomy – and there's another holiday cottage down there, a bit dark and dismal. My friend's cottage here is a delight – two-up two-down plus bath.'

It was a delight. Outside, a view over corn fields to the river, inside, bleached wood, cheerful chintz and light and airy rooms. A fire was burning in a stove. Francesca had prepared this welcome. She opened the door of the stove and flames sprang up. She turned and they embraced, their passion rising. She broke away and pointed to the small kitchen on the other side of the stairway.

'Kitchen plus wine and cold rare beef. Upstairs a large double bed.' They had only to look into each other's eyes for a short moment for Francesca to announce, 'Lunch may be late.' She took his hand and led him upstairs. They loved, they slept, at four o'clock had champagne and food, and then they talked and talked about themselves. Rasputin had been left at Boscannon, so could not interrupt them. Luke had not had the heart or the strength to tell her that they only had a week because of Fr Jeronimo's call, summoning him to Valladolid. He would return immediately to Cornwall after that visit.

During the next few days, a pattern established itself. Luke worked on the diary in the morning and then would take the ferry or use Alastair's boat to get to the other side of the Helford.

One morning while editing the diary he found there were still several pages in code; decoding them was a time-consuming activity. He began a long entry. It dealt with de Witte being sent to try and convert St Robert Southwell, the Elizabethan poet and Jesuit martyr, while he was incarcerated in the Tower of London prior to his farcical trial. De Witte was obviously captivated by this famous but youthful priest, and described him standing up in his cell at the Tower as he entered.

He had been tortured for days by the dreaded Topcliffe, now my Sovereign's personal servant, a man possessed by a terrible devil. I had heard much of Master Southwell and his fine poesy. He was of slim, straight build, auburn hair, fine-cut lips set in a slight smile, mild and courteous, and his eyes, what eyes, God looked from them. Yet he was deadly pale and bowed slightly when I entered, asking leave to sink to the floor, which he did with piteous pain, having been stretched, hung from the wall, his feet to swing above the ground. Dear God, the sight gave me nightmares of what might have been my lot, yet Master Robert was so serene, and in such grace, I felt in envy of his soul. I had no stomach for dispute and I fear he bested me with such learning and quickness of spirit that I feared our Church is man's creation, not Christ's.

146

Master Southwell asked me for a pen and parchment and gave me this poem.

Christ! Health of fevered souls, heaven of the mind,
Force of the feeble, nurse of infant loves,
Guide to the wandering foot, light to the blind,
Whom weeping wins, repentant sorrow moves,
Father in care, mother in tender heart,
Revive and save me, slain with sinful dart.

Luke moved on a year to another long piece in code.

Robert Southwell, Jesuit, is taken to the King's Bench for trial to be judged on the Statute of Anno 27 by which to be a priest is treason. Found guilty, of course, the Lord Chief Justice given judgement that he be carried to Newgate, and from thence to be drawn to Tyburn upon an hurdle; to be hanged and cut down alive; his bowels burnt before his face; his head to be stricken off and his body to be quartered...

Luke had to stop and get a drink. It became apparent that Bishop de Witte later went secretly to the execution at Marble Arch and recorded Southwell's arrival from Holborn along the Oxford Street of today, having been dragged over the rough streets by horse. Then upon the scaffold after that ordeal, he somehow spoke sweetly to the crowd. De Witte did not record the words save the last moments:

The hangman came forward: Southwell lifted his chin for the noose to settle. I heard him softly pray, 'Blessed Mary, ever virgin, and all you Angels and Saints, assist me. In manus tuas, Domine, commendo spiritum meum.' The hangman gave the rope a tug, but it slipped and Southwell opened his eyes, looking at us all with great love, a countenance most lovely. Then methinks I heard him reciting the psalm 'Misere' – 'Comfort me with a perfect spirit' – and for the third time he made the sign of the cross, saying again, 'In manus tuas, Domine...' The cart lurched forward. I left London for Melbury with heavy heart. I have many burdens. Master Robert has fled and the treasure moved. Now that the Spanish threat is passed, my soul tells me it should return whence it came. Only my hearth and books give me comfort. A decision must be made.

Luke left aside several pages covering a further two years, describing de Witte's episcopal life in Melbury – including references to the failure of crops and an outbreak of plague in Bristol – and turned to the last page. It was a tattered piece of parchment, but it had the last date on it.

My decision is made. I told in great secrecy my Dean in the Chapter House this morning. He was thrown into a great rage, trembling with apoplexy, but nothing will change my mind. He says he will come with his Canons on the morrow. I told him to come midday for a collation and some posset. By then my visitor will be gone.

Luke suddenly realised that the date was that of de Witte's death. Was he about to return the treasure, and who was the visitor? Luke would have to research the cathedral archives, though he remembered tradition had it that de Witte died in his sleep, as this was confirmed by the dean of the time in his funeral oration, who described de Witte as 'slipping into a holy sleep as he justly deserveth'.

Luke sat puzzling over his work. He could do no more to the diary than collate all his editing and translations. He would write a short introduction, pointing out some of the unanswered questions and trying to comment fairly on the Elizabethan Church and how its cruelties and persecutions were directed against Puritans as well as Catholics, and noting that the Catholic Church had also behaved hideously under Queen Mary. He concluded that de Witte was a man doing his best in a violent age.

Francesca only had one day off a week from looking after her husband; they agreed it should be spent at her friend's cottage. On every other day they managed to meet for an hour or two while Francesca shopped in Helston or walked Rasputin by the river. During these walks they would end by lying together on the small cliff next to the beach which supported the Boscannon private slipway. The cliff top had a hollow surrounded my gorse and bracken, and there, in the intoxication of their passion, they made love. Their privacy was guarded by Rasputin, who was attached to a nearby tree my his lead.

They spent the day of Luke's departure together at the cottage. He was due to go to Heathrow that night, prior to flying to Spain. It was a repeat of their first meeting, though they were less tense. They had nearly the whole day together, but, even so, lunch was again delayed. They talked of marriage and the possibility of Francesca getting an annulment.

When the day began, it had been beautiful, and Francesca had decided to walk to greet Luke when he got off the ferry. Every moment was precious to them, with Luke due to leave at teatime. They walked together, holding hands, along the lush lanes and paths leading to Dove Cottage, and as they walked through the farmyard they were too absorbed to see their progress noted my two women within the farmhouse. One was the farmer's wife, the other was a Mrs Tregorran, a crabby widow who went to clean three mornings a week at Boscannon and also cleaned the cottage at the end of lettings. The farmer's wife put a finger to the side of her nose, saying, 'Well now, that Mrs Boscannon's been coming and going to her friend's cottage an awful lot in the last week – perhaps we know why now! Handsome sort of a young fellow.'

Mrs Tregorran just sniffed. 'After our coffee I'll just slip down and see if she needs help with any cleaning.'

The farmer's wife let out a loud guffaw. 'Cleaning what, may I enquire?'

Mrs Tregorran sniffed again and took a sip of coffee and a fourth chocolate digestive biscuit. 'I'll give them another ten minutes and then I'll be off. I'll take the cottage key you keep for me when I do cleaning there.'

Twelve minutes later, Mrs Tregorran was banging on the cottage door. There was no answer. She tried to open the door with her key, but Francesca's key was on the inside of the lock. She had secured the door as they immediately made for the bedroom after arriving there. Mrs Tregorran began to bang more insistently on the door. Luke and Francesca were already locked in passion and lay frozen in horror. The banging on the door continued.

'Hell, hell,' whispered Francesca. 'I'll look to see.' She wrapped the bedspread around her shoulders and peered out of the window. 'My God, it's our cleaning lady – I'll have to speak to

149

her.' She flung on her shirt and opened the bedroom window. 'Oh, Mrs Tregorran, hello!'

A voice floated up, oozing curiosity and excitement in equal measure.

'Saw you passing when I was up at the farm and wondered if you wanted any help with further cleaning. I think I left it okay after the last lot left.'

'Oh, thank you, Mrs Tregorran, everything was lovely, there's no need for any more cleaning. My friend is so grateful for your help.'

'Oh good. How are you keeping then? You've been out every time I've been up at Boscannon.'

'I'm keeping fine, thank you so much, though just at this moment I've got a bit of a headache. A friend that is visiting me has just left to walk round the creek. Perhaps you'll excuse me not coming down...'

'Of course, of course,' replied Mrs Tregorran. 'I'll be off, then, if I'm not needed.' She walked back to the farm hugging herself with glee. She would pass on her news to the farmer's wife and then go to Boscannon with some eggs as a gift from the farm. She had no doubt Nancy would be fascinated by her news.

When she got to Boscannon, both Nancy and her brother had gone out for a drive, so she waited. She gave Nancy the eggs and her gossip as soon as they returned at teatime. Nancy received the news impassively, but her lips tightened.

'Thank you for the eggs. Could you look after Commander Boscannon for an hour. I'll just go and see our mutual friend at the farm. I'd like to thank her personally.'

Nancy collected a pair of binoculars and ran to her car. She drove at breakneck speed until she reached the farm. She parked off the lane behind one of the barns, so that Francesca would not see her car. She knew she would get a clear view of the cottage if she walked on down the lane towards the river. There was a high bank to the lane, covered with wild roses and blackberries. This gave excellent cover for viewing the cottage. Nancy had just placed herself in position when she saw Luke and Francesca appear and start walking along a footpath that joined the lane fifty yards away, before crossing it to carry on to Helford and its ferry. They were holding

150

hands and just before the lane stopped under an old oak tree they looked around them, causing Nancy to slide down in a hurry so that she cut her hand on a rose briar. After a moment she looked again; she could just see them. They were joined in a long parting kiss. She focused her binoculars, and, as if only ten feet away, she could see their bodies swaying in one last sensual embrace.

'Disgusting!' she exploded. 'The bitch! The bitch!'

In her distraction she had not heard the farmer walking down the lane, and as he drew near he greeted her. Much to his amusement she leaped back and, catching her foot in a bramble, stumbled into the lane so that he had to put out a hand to stop her falling. She couldn't speak at first because of her rage and embarrassment at being caught spying.

'Are you all right, Miss Boscannon?'

'Yes, just seeing if the geese had arrived for the winter. Please thank your wife for the eggs. I'm afraid I must go now.' She glanced back at the field and saw Francesca standing alone by the tree, obviously sobbing into a handkerchief. Luke had gone.

The farmer went on down the lane to bring up his cows for milking and Nancy ran back to her car. Her emotions were a mixture of outrage at the infidelity; of fear that Francesca would leave and that she would have to look after Boss alone; but above all she was shaking with exultation. She would inflict such suffering on Francesca and assuage years of pent-up hatred and jealousy stemming from a repressed love for her cousin. She had a plan to humiliate Francesca and subject her to a horrendous revenge. Nancy had no doubt she would have Boss's utmost support: they both had a cruel streak. It helped that they were also jealous of Francesca's devotion to Rasputin, and in her twisted mind the dog was to play a tragic role. Again Nancy drove at great speed. She had preparations to see to before Francesca returned to Boscannon.

Luke returned to Alastair's cottage to change for his drive to London. He was going to try and stay near the airport, at the Concorde Hotel, which had a long-stay car park next to it. This would enable him to get his early flight to Valladolid.

Before he left the cottage, he rang Alastair to tell him that he would be away. Alastair told him that he had continued to be concerned about the statue of Our Lady of Walsingham and asked Luke whether he would mind if he applied a very strong glue to its wooden base, to foil a quick snatch. Luke thought that was a splendid idea. Alastair told him that the statue had become a focal point for the religious Russian boys in the school. He had therefore taken the liberty of talking to the Orthodox priest from Oxford of the threat to the statue. The priest had been horrified and had organised a constant vigil during the hours the chapel was open, shared amongst all the Russians in the school. Two boys at a time were in the Lady chapel for an hour each. Access to the chapel had been made the responsibility of the Gethsemane community in the absence of Luke and Fr Peter. This news comforted Luke. Alastair wished him success.

finally he rang Francesca at Dove Cottage and told her not to worry about Mrs Tregorran. They had agreed that Francesca would give her a large tip, ostensibly for her cleaning, but at the same time appeal to her not to pass on the information about him being at the cottage.

Francesca visited her on her way back to Boscannon. Mrs Tregorran was delighted with the tip and agreed such information about her visitor might he misconstrued, though of course not by her. Francesca was relieved at this and, thinking of the happiness of her time with Luke, was humming gently to herself when she opened the front door to the manor house. The door was slammed behind her as she stood amazed at the sight that greeted her. Nancy had been standing behind it awaiting her return.

In front of her, in the middle of the stone floor, sat Boscannon in his wheelchair. His expression brutal and lustful. He was pointing his pistol at her. He had smuggled it out of the navy years before. A heavy oak table was to one side of the hall and Rasputin was chained to one of its legs. The dog leapt forward, wagging its tail and squealing with relief at her return. Francesca stood transfixed. Nancy was dressed in her riding clothes and holding a riding crop. She kicked Francesca forwards towards Boscannon.

'Kneel in front of Boscannon and beg his forgiveness, you whore, you little bit of dirt! You and your fancy heretic clergyman. We know. I saw your parting with my own eyes – you're

152

filth!' Her voice was rising hysterically. 'Kneel and then I'm going to flog the life out of you.'

Francesca stood still. She was in a state of shock – surely this was a dream – but fear overwhelmed her and she began to tremble. She dreaded losing control of her body, but her bowels seemed to be dissolving inside her. She felt Nancy's hand trying to push her down to her knees, and this physical contact saved her from breaking down. Her adrenaline rushed and she turned and punched Nancy in the face so that she staggered back swearing, 'You bitch, bitch! Boss, show her what's coming to her.'

Boscannon pointed the pistol at Rasputin. Although the sight of Rasputin made Francesca want to rush to him and cradle him in her arms, she knew her husband was capable of crippling or killing them both.

'If you don't kneel, he dies, but not at once. Little by little, a paw here, a tail, an ear – it will take time. You've been an evil little girl and you must take your medicine.' A trickle of saliva began to seep from the corner of his mouth as he gave his wife a wry smile. He looked so horrible, Francesca felt sick. Still she could not speak. Boscannon moved the gun and took aim at Rasputin's tail. The firing pin moved back, straining to be released so that a bullet would fly towards its victim. He increased the pressure on the trigger. Rasputin was straining on the chain round his neck and began to howl. He knew his world was disintegrating, he smelt Francesca's fear, she was sweating profusely. The dog's howl broke her trance.

'If I kneel, will you let Rasputin go?'

Boscannon turned his face towards her and leered. 'I give the orders. Remember your wedding oath, a solemn promise to obey? Kneel and take your shirt off.'

Nancy, in her fury, could not wait and started slashing at Francesca's back.

Francesca's tear turned to outrage. 'You're both mad. Never! Never!'

Boscannon turned to aim his pistol. There was a staggering explosion, the acoustics of the hall magnifying it. Francesca and the dog screamed. The bullet had grazed its tail and hit the floor, sending up a cloud of shattered stone before ricocheting into the wooden wainscot.

Nancy laughed shrilly. 'Good shot, Boss.' She stepped forward. Francesca was down beside a whimpering Rasputin. Nancy tore the shirt off Francesca's back and began to thrash her with her riding crop. Boss was rocking in his chair, leering with delight.

There was a loud knocking on the front door; the nightmare was disturbed. The door burst open and Joseph the gardener almost fell into the scene before standing stock still in the middle of them all. He had been alerted by what he was convinced was the sound of a gunshot inside the house. He took off his cap and gasped at the mayhem in front of him and tried to make sense of it. He saw the wounded dog, the weals on Francesca's back and the pistol, now in a limp hand hanging by the side of Boscannon's chair. He decided the pistol was the most important object and stepped forward and took it. No one said a word.

Francesca stood up. 'Thank you, Jo. I'll get some more suitable clothes so that I can take Rasputin to the vet. Would you be so kind as to see that he comes to no further harm?' She looked at the pistol meaningfully, as if to say, 'use it if necessary'. She returned five minutes later with a small suitcase. Only Joseph and the dog were in the hall, and the gardener was comforting Rasputin, who was trembling all over. Fortunately it appeared that his tail had only been grazed by the bullet.

'Oh dear, Francesca maiden! What has been happening? Miss Nancy says I'm to say nothing to anyone and that she will give me a five-hundred-pound bonus at Christmas.'

'For the time being I think that's for the best, so enjoy the bonus.' Francesca smiled for the first time since returning to the house. 'I shall be at Dove Cottage. I think I should appreciate having the pistol.' She went to the car, tying a bandage around Rasputin's tail as he lay quivering on the back seat. 'Goodbye Boscannon and good riddance,' she muttered as they went down the drive.

Chapter Fifteen

Luke arrived at the Concorde Hotel near Heathrow some time after eleven-thirty, but the lobby was filled with people. An international conference of sanitary-ware manufacturers had just begun, and the delegates were checking in. When he eventually reached the desk he was told by a fat receptionist that his reservation had expired at six o'clock and his room had been taken. In fact the hotel was overbooked and they were using this excuse where it suited them. They assumed a late-arriving cleric would not raid the minibar in his room or order food to the value consumed by a Philadelphian sanitary-ware manufacturer. Luke was sent to a depressing motel nearby and thus did not receive messages and calls from Francesca. He had tried to contact Francesca to tell her of his change of hotel, but at the time she had not returned to Dove Cottage.

The following day Luke arrived in Valladolid, having changed planes in Paris. Valladolid, a city famed for the fervour of its Easter processions, was, however, an unprepossessing industrial town north of Madrid. High-rise apartment blocks rose out of barren fields, without the preparatory suburb of bungalows or bourgeois houses common to English cities.

Luke's taxi from the airport deposited him in an area of bleak tower blocks, surrounding a red-brick ecclesiastical building of uncertain age. Luke later learnt that endowments from successive Spanish Catholic kings had supported it as an outpost of English Catholicism, and, like its sister colleges, all now closed, in Lisbon, Seville and Douai, it had also sent missionary priests to serve and die in England. Recent property developments on the surrounding land had added to its wealth, and it continued to train priests at little cost to English dioceses.

Next day Luke assumed Francesca had returned to Boscannon and rang her there to leave a message that her dress had

155

arrived safely. Mrs Tregorran took the message and did not tell him that Francesca had left.

Luke was expected and, having been shown to his room, was taken to meet the rector of the college. He was led to a small sitting room and found Frs Charles and Jeronimo already there. The rector, a Fr Formby, was a friendly Lancashireman. He suggested that they go and take a glass of sherry in the library, and led the way. They followed him through a cloister, along a passage and up some stairs into a low-ceilinged seventeenth-century library. Its shelves were lined with vellum and tooled-leather books.

'Over to you, Jeronimo,' said the rector as he gave them the sherry. They all sat down on well-worn chairs.

'Well, our order, the Jesuits, used to run this college. I've come here to do research on some of the Fathers who were here in the sixteenth century. The other day, I was reading the journal of a well-known recusant Jesuit, Fr Boniface, and I came across a reference to Bishop de Witte. I was interested, particularly because of our discussions in Rome. Here, I will get it for you.' He went to a bookshelf and returned with a pale grey, vellum-covered book. A piece of red paper marked a page. It was dated the day of de Witte's death. Its entry was brief.

I went to Melbury in some fear, suspecting a trap, but had received a sealed message from one de Witte, schismatic Bishop of Melbury. It said he had trained in Rome, but circumstances weakened him and he had left our Faith to become an heretic and now the Queen's Bishop. He urgently needed me to reconcile him, as he feared for his life.

Fr Charles gasped and stood up; he seemed to be struggling for breath.

Fr Jeronimo put down the book. 'Are you all right, Father?'

Fr Charles nodded vigorously and smiled. 'I knew it, I knew it.' He sat down, crossing his arms, and hugged himself.

Fr Jeronimo continued by repeating the last sentence.

I arrived at Melbury in my guise as a tutor, seeking work in his Diocese, and, going to his palace, was presented to de Witte.

156

He, in grievous state of penance and having seen the martyrdom
of our brother, Fr Robert Southwell, said he was prepared to
share that fate. No sooner had I heard his confession in his
bedchamber and reconciled him, than came the noise of many
upon the stairs. De Witte motioned me to hide under his bed.
He was dressed in a simple shift and held a crucifix in a hand,
trembling a little. A stampede of men's feet upon the floor, from
where I saw and heard de Witte cry out, 'How now Master
Dean and my Canons.' There was no answer, save, 'Drink this
for thine apostasy.' Then they left and de Witte sank to the
floor, muttering, 'Jesu, Mary ... hemlock, hemlock.' He died a
martyr, God rest his soul.

They all looked at each other. The journal entry was conclusive.
De Witte had been reconciled to his original faith.

More sherry was poured. Fr Charles got up again and walked
to the end of the room and did a little jig. Luke told the
others about the printing of the journal by the college council
and asked for their advice. They advised him to wait until the
end of the Queen's visit. There was no point in publicising
their find. It would smack of triumphalism, and it would be
far better to leak the discovery later in the following year.

'Perhaps intercession to de Witte might yield a miracle?' said
Fr Jeronimo with a chuckle.

Fr Charles looked pensive and Luke felt embarrassed for
him, as he knew how passionately Fr Charles longed for divine
signs.

Luke stayed the weekend in the college and talked to the
staff and small number of students. Somehow, in this historical
backwater, they were an inspiring spiritual centre, not buffeted
by Roman gossip or swirling ecclesiastical conspiracy. Luke was
impressed by the directness of the rector, conveyed in a slight
Lancashire hint of speech, and decided to set out his life and
its problems to the rector and ask his advice. He saw Fr Charles
more as a fellow seeker after de Witte, not an adviser.

Fr Formby gave his advice. It was simple in essence. first he
must pray that God send him a sign. Second he should only
leave his vocation in the Church of England if his conscience
consistently told him his position was wrong. The rector thought
he could do more for God in his present situation than acting

as an assistant Catholic priest in some less influential area. Maybe, he had mused, the Anglican Church could be a blueprint for a united Christendom, but in the meanwhile any increase in its numbers leading a sacramental, Catholic type of life should be welcomed, and Luke was promoting this.

Luke knew he had received definite advice, but it left the situation still for him to sort out. He left for Melbury still trying to absorb the proof of de Witte's death. He took the rector's advice, however, and prayed for a sign to guide him. His mind was in turmoil. The revelations about de Witte's martyrdom not only blew apart the idea of the diary being a favourable picture of a firm conversion to the Church of England, but also in a curious way they had the same effect on Luke's feeling that he must remain an Anglican.

As he was in Valladolid that afternoon, life was proceeding in its calm routine at Melbury College. The playing fields there were surrounded by trees, golden-leaved in the autumn sunshine. The air rang with the sounds of half a dozen rugby games, the occasional successful thwack of hockey balls being propelled hither and thither, and shrill cries from two lacrosse pitches. The provost, General Phillipson, was giving a tour of the school to the American Ambassador and his wife. The ambassador was later to give a lecture to the sixth formers, entitled, 'After the Cold War – What Next?'

Beside the chapel, in which an organ scholar was practising and two Russians were keeping vigil before the statue of Our Lady, the school army cadet corps was gathering to go in buses to enjoy an evening manoeuvre as darkness fell. Each boy was carrying a rifle and twelve rounds of blank ammunition. In addition, the Russians were carrying concealed flasks of vodka. The college hummed with organised corporate activity. As numbers were being counted of boys in the buses, Brigadier Henshaw and the sergeant major entered the chapel in full uniform. They intended to remove the statue before joining the army exercise.

The headmaster marched up to the Lady chapel with the sergeant major behind him. Their studded boots rang over the chapel floor gratings, from which hot air rose languorously from an ancient heating system. The head took a firm grip on the statue, having glanced disparagingly at the two small Russian

158

boys praying. Out of the corner of his mouth Henshaw muttered to the sergeant, 'Some clever Dick has fixed it. Down to the woodworking shop – at the double sergeant major! Get hacksaws and any other bit of equipment – if necessary, a small crowbar to lever it away from its recess.'

The two Russian boys had stopped praying, and their eyes were wide with horror. The sacrilege of which they had been warned was happening before them. They exchanged agitated whispers and one ran from the chapel. The other went up to the headmaster, who was pacing up and down. The boy wagged his finger.

'You not priest. No touch!'

'Mind your own business and get back to your knitting.'

The boy crossed himself in the Orthodox fashion. 'Not knitting – praying.'

'Watch it, lad, or you'll be going back to Mother Russia on a tramp steamer.'

At that moment the chapel door opened and thirty Russian boys, sons of rich mafia families, entered in their CCF uniforms, carrying rifles. They doubled over to the Lady chapel, crossed themselves and knelt down. Instead of praying, they stared threateningly at the headmaster. Henshaw walked to the back of the nave and stood underneath the organ to await the return of the sergeant major. five minutes later the sergeant major returned carrying a large canvas holdall. Henshaw joined him at the altar. He waved at the boys.

'Out! Join your transport at once.'

The throat-grabbing Russian who had throttled Luke stood up. 'We pray.' They all stood up and moved towards the altar.

'Ignore them, sergeant major. Give me the hacksaw.'

The Russians began to talk amongst themselves as Henshaw began to saw at the base of the statue. Just before he succeeded in his task, the Russians removed themselves to the door leading out of the chapel and lined up on either side, standing at ease in a military manner with their rifle butts resting by their right feet.

Having released the statue, Henshaw gestured to the sergeant major to open the canvas holdall they had brought to convey it to his house and the awaiting bonfire. The statue was heavy, having been carved out of some dense wood, and Henshaw and the sergeant major had to take a handle each as they carried it down the chapel to the main door.

As they approached the Russians, one of them gave a whispered order and they presented arms, and then, as the statue passed between them down the line, each boy knelt on one knee, still holding his rifle in front of him.

As they left the chapel, Henshaw said out of the corner of his mouth, 'Move to quick march, sergeant major.'

The Russians had left the chapel, taken up the formation of a platoon and, having sloped arms, followed the headmaster and the sergeant major. They marched with precision, doing a quick goose step redolent of the Russian sentries outside Lenin's tomb in Moscow.

The master in charge of the platoon stood outside the bus with a look of total incomprehension. He had been about to enter the chapel to order them into their bus, so as to transport them to where the army manoeuvres were taking place, but had for a while thought they had gone into the chapel to recite some Orthodox prayers before battle, as bullfighters pray in an adjoining chapel before entering the bullring. Certainly they were prepared for battle, but not the one planned by the school.

The platoon, quickstepping behind Henshaw, began to unnerve him; the sergeant major was already close to panic.

'At the double now,' Henshaw commanded as the front gate of his house came into view across the first eleven's cricket pitch.

A Russian command rang out behind them. The boys dropped their rifles to the double-march position and kept up with the head. As they were approaching the headmaster's house, they failed to see, in the evening gloom, the provost and the Americans walking towards the house from another direction.

The provost and his guests were duly impressed by this display of military precision. General Phillipson beamed with pleasure.

'I suspect they are carrying ammunition in that holdall, and the head has taken the precaution of having a guard. Can't be too careful, even if it's blank bullets, with the murdering IRA around every corner, pinching explosives.' His voice trailed away as he remembered the name of the ambassador was

160

O'Reilly, who in the past had had some connection with Noraid in America.

The ambassador made no comment, but the remark confirmed the report he had requested on General Phillipson from the CIA records at the embassy. Its general conclusion was that a bumbling, indecisive character lay behind his stiff military persona. He had distinguished himself once by getting an army patrol stuck on the heath at Lüneburg in Germany during BAOR manoeuvres by failing to locate supporting fuel supplies. After that he had been known as General 'fill up soon', as that had been the order to his support group before most of them ground to a halt with empty petrol tanks. Otherwise he had been lucky in that his habit of taking the last advice given to him in any critical situation had been mitigated by having good advisers.

To break the slightly frosty atmosphere after his IRA remark, the provost suggested they popped into the nearby cricket pavilion to see the college's collection of nineteenth-century pictures of past cricket teams. He remembered that in 1880 an American in the school had been in the first eleven. They examined this sepia photo of an unattractive specimen of Yankee youth – a bearded giant leaning on a bat and looking about forty-five. The ambassador's wife said, 'Gee, he was neat,' and the ambassador said, 'Humph', and the provost indicated they should move on to meet the headmaster's wife. At that moment Henshaw reached his house, with the Russians on his heels.

As Henshaw galloped through the gates to the house, he gave the order to put down the statue, and they both turned to try and close the six-foot-high solid oak gates behind them. Henshaw hoped that if they could do this and bolt them, the situation could be brought under control. They were too late: the leading Russians stuck their rifles between the closing gates. Henshaw shouted orders to them to return to their bus at once, but further Russians leant on the gates. Henshaw began shouting obscenities at them as the gates sprung open, knocking both men to the ground.

The provost and his guests had walked up behind this melee. The Americans looked astonished. The provost was struck silent before feebly saying, 'I can only assume this is part of a cadet-force exercise.'

The ambassador's wife had her hands over her ears as Henshaw's words echoed around. 'Well, looks like their playing it for real, O'Reilly.'

The ambassador was shaking his head. 'Provost, that language is a bit rich for Mrs O'Reilly – worse than a bar brawl in the Bronx.'

The provost was ringing his hands in agitation. Four boys had lifted a struggling Henshaw to his feet. The whole platoon had loaded their rifles, and two of them were keeping the sergeant major on the ground with a rifle held to each ear. The sergeant major knew the force of a blank cartridge and lay supine – he was so afraid he had just wet himself.

Ivan, who had nearly throttled Luke in the Black Swan, seemed to be in charge. He walked up to Henshaw and put his rifle under the headmaster's chin. Henshaw had continued to swear and blaspheme, but fell silent as he felt the cold metal. His arms were now twisted savagely behind his back and he could no longer move.

The rifle was moved slowly up his face, paused at the bridge of his nose and then poked under his brigadier's cap, which had fallen forward over his forehead. The rifle was then slipped inside the cap, which was lifted a foot above Henshaw's head. A deep roar of encouragement came from the platoon, then the crack of a rifle being fired, sending the cap spinning into the air. The peak was detached in the explosion and, like a boomerang, sailed into a group standing by a bonfire. Waiting there were Mrs Henshaw and Mr and Mrs Jones, who had hoped to greet Henshaw's arrival with a cheer and then consign the statue to the bonfire.

Now, the arrival of the peak among them galvanised Mr Jones into action. He led a panic-stricken Mrs Henshaw and his wife in a hundred-metre race to the house. They bolted the door behind them and rang for the police. Looking out of the window, Mrs Henshaw saw the sergeant major being lifted by four boys, each taking an arm and a leg, and chucked into the fish pond in the middle of the lawn. The rest of the platoon were following the frog-marched figure of her husband being taken behind the beech hedge at the end of the lawn. His red-epauletted jacket was the first article of his clothing to sail onto the lawn, followed by shirt, vest and trousers. finally his two army boots, thrown with such vigour, that one reached the fish pond, hitting the sergeant major, who was being kept in the pond by two of the boys with rifles pointed at his crutch.

The provost and his party had entered the drive. The ambassador said, 'I'm gonna have to alter my lecture to "After the Cold War – the Hot War"! Russian detachments seizing the private schools of old England – sound first move, I'd say!'

They had to jump aside as two police cars screamed up. At the same time, one of the boys who had been keeping vigil in the chapel had opened the holdall to see if the statue was all right. He was crossing himself as he gave a prayer of thanks. The Russians quickly formed into their platoon and, taking the statue with them, doubled back to the chapel, singing a rousing Orthodox hymn to Our Lady.

A bemused and battered Henshaw appeared on the lawn in his underpants and khaki socks. The police sergeant went to help him into his house. Henshaw did not make eye contact with the provost. A dripping sergeant major followed.

The provost handed the Americans over to a passing Alastair Galbraith to finish their tour. As he did so, he asked Alastair if he knew where Luke was. Fortunately Luke had told Alastair of his impending visit to Valladolid, and Alastair was happy to tell the provost of his whereabouts.

Following the extraordinary goings-on at the headmaster's house, the provost had to work harder than at any other time in his dealings with the school. His first task was to prevent the events turning into a media explosion. As the truth became known and circulated to members of the council, it was obvious that Henshaw should be sacked immediately. He was persuaded not to bring charges against the Russians in exchange for a generous pay-off. The housemasters were told of the incident and instructed to tell their charges that any contact with the press would lead to instant expulsion.

The Russian boys were given a free weekend and a 125-gram tin of beluga caviar each, paid for out of a charitable trust set up in the nineteenth century by an old boy to provide sustaining food for any young scholars suffering from illness or mental stress.

By some miracle a public scandal was avoided: the only record was a watered-down report in the local Melbury police station, and a laconic one from the American Ambassador filed at the embassy in Grosvenor Square.

An emergency meeting of the college council was called for the next day. The provost managed to get a quorum together, including the last headmaster, Canon Frobisher. They started their meeting with a buffet lunch and then, pleasantly full of food and drink, sat in the Tudor council room to discuss the problem of a successor to Henshaw.

The provost reported that he had contacted Luke in Spain and asked if he would return as second master to give them time to select a new head. Somewhat to his chagrin, he was forced to tell them that Luke had said he would only return as the new headmaster.

Luke had received the call in Valladolid just after receiving the information about the manner of de Witte's death and his final return to the Catholic Church. He was feeling a certain anger towards the college and the constraints it had placed on the publication of the diary. He had decided he would only return on his own terms.

The provost asked the members of the council present if they knew of any available candidates of high calibre to succeed Henshaw.

Canon Frobisher put forward the name of a John Bridges, the senior tutor at his college in Cambridge, who had been a housemaster at Eton at one time in his career, after starting out teaching at Melbury. His churchmanship was sound and he was a fine classicist.

Sir John Williams, a member of the council who had been knighted as chairman of a large chemical company, made a strong case for Luke, saying that they had considered him before and his record in the school had been excellent. This speech brought a murmur of approval from half the members – the other half asked Canon Frobisher for a fuller description of his candidate. This was given, and General Phillipson asked for a break of a quarter of an hour for general discussion before they would vote. This positive move was prompted by a quiet discussion with Canon Frobisher at the end of the council table.

The vote was taken – the result was a tie. The provost could have the casting vote. This put him into an agony of indecision and he asked for a further break of half an hour so that he could take further advice.

Canon Frobisher told the meeting that he had told his candidate to stand by in his room at Michaelhouse, and with the speakerphone in the council room he would immediately set up a conference call so that the council members could question him and hear his views as to how he would run the college. Could they have this call first? The pro-Luke faction thought this was a bit Machiavellian, but they knew only one vote had to move.

Contact was made. The senior tutor came over as someone who considered he was probably too good for the job. He indicated the remuneration package would have to be improved.

The vote was taken again. Once more it was a tie. General Phillipson asked to be excused. He would go to the headmaster's study to consider his decision. When he got there, he immediately rang Luke again at the English College. Luke told him he was happy to co-operate by meeting the council and that he hoped to marry within the year. Luke realised that if he was to become head he would have to regularise his position with Francesca.

The provost said, 'Thank you Luke, you will have my casting vote.' As he put the phone down, the door opened and Canon Frobisher strode in without knocking.

'General, I think you will agree that I have the most knowledge of both candidates. I have to tell you my senior tutor at Michaelhouse is the best. An excellent scholar, and – this is important in the present climate of public fear of paedophilia – he is married with two children. You really must choose him. He knows the school well. I know before your time as provost he was teaching here successfully and we were sorry to lose him to Eton. In my view absolutely the right candidate. I'm sure I can rely on you to cast your vote for him – absolutely safe pair of hands for the school.'

The provost sighed. He knew he would now have to break his promise to Luke made only minutes earlier. 'Of course, Canon, I'll be with you all in a few minutes.' He sat at the desk. He really did not know what to decide. He had liked Luke, who had been a good housemaster to his boys; and he had disliked Henshaw. But now the decision of the moment was his alone. As he sat there staring at the telephone, the door opened and in walked Parker, carrying his clock instruments.

'So sorry, General. I understood no one would be occupying this room until we have a new head. I'll come back later. I just need to look at the Tompion grandfather...'

'No, no. I'm just going. I've always admired that clock. How much do you think it's worth – I was told it was valuable?'

'Certainly very rare, marked as 67th of the master's grandfathers. Over £100,000 at least.'

The General looked suitably impressed. 'Well I never! What a staggering amount. My pensionable view of life can't take in such figures; obscene prices for houses that years ago I could have afforded, now going for millions. It'll destroy society.' Parker nodded sympathetically. The provost continued, 'By the way, did you ever meet a Mr John Bridges when he taught here as classics master? Was he a good man?'

Parker wrinkled his nose disapprovingly. 'Certainly not very nice, I'd say. Used to come into the Black Swan frequently. He was carrying on with one of the barmaids, and I mean carrying on. He drank too much – pity, because he had a nice wife and two kids. Anyway, the barmaid – Susan Kidd she was, now respectable Mrs Fred Brown – anyway, her Dad heard she was being mucked about with by a married man, so he and her uncle came into the Black Swan and duffed him up proper. They said if he didn't leave town they'd do him again and again. So he left and went to Eton where they are more tolerant of such behaviour.' Parker chuckled at this last observation.

'Heavens!' exclaimed the provost. He was extremely grateful for such reliable inside information about Canon Frobisher's candidate Mr John Bridges. 'What's your opinion of Luke Howard, our second master on sabbatical?'

'A fine man, sir, of good and honest judgement, who always said you was an absolutely first-class provost.' General Phillipson tried to smile modestly, but was deeply impressed by this second-hand praise, not knowing it was a complete fabrication on Parker's part. 'Anyway, sir, our Fr Howard is a Christian gentleman. A real gentleman, not like Mr Bridges. I believe he had a very dodgy social background.'

The provost sat up. That decided it for him. He thanked

166

Parker profusely and strode back into the council room. He stood at the end of the table, put his hand up for silence and said, 'I have had time to make further enquiries, and I'm afraid, Canon, they have revealed some disturbing facts about your candidate – past improprieties in the town during his time here that would make his return impossible. My casting vote is unreservedly for Fr Luke Howard.'

Canon Frobisher rose to his feet, his face flushed with rage. 'Whatever are you talking about? What improprieties?'

The provost waved him to sit down. 'I'm sorry, John, I cannot repeat them here. I shall tell you at another time. Therefore, I announce the appointment of our new head to be Luke Howard, subject to the usual exchange of contracts of employment.'

Outside, Parker had been hovering by the door pretending to look at the simple wall clock that had survived Henshaw's horological iconoclasm. He heard the news and went off to tell the town. Parker enjoyed reading fiction and concluded at the end of that afternoon he was quite good at creating it.

Chapter Sixteen

When Luke got back to his home in Melbury, he telephoned the provost to make an appointment to discuss his return to the school and to obtain a signed contract of employment as soon as possible. He did not want the college council to have a period in which they might change their mind and appoint another outsider. Luke felt vulnerable in his relationship with Francesca; if it was made public in some way, or, horrifically, if he was cited as co-respondent in a divorce case brought by Boscannon, then once again the prize of the headship would be taken from him. A meeting was arranged for the following afternoon.

Luke then rang Boscannon Manor. He'd had no success when ringing from Rome. His attempts to make contact had always led to the phone being answered by Mrs Tregorran or Nancy, and his 'dressmaker' persona seemed no longer believable, even though by now he had perfected a decidedly camp voice. A suspicious Nancy had asked for his telephone number and told him that Francesca was away with her husband enjoying a holiday on the Riviera. This message, he deduced, was calculated to upset him. Somehow he would have to find her whereabouts when he went down to Cornwall. In the meanwhile he rang Dove Cottage. He had been unable to do so in Rome, having left that number at his house in England. He got no answer and so resigned himself to getting in touch with Mrs Tregorran after arriving in Cornwall. He was desperate to find a time when Boscannon Manor would be free for them to try and find the treasure.

Luke unpacked and then rang his father. Margery answered and told him he should come to dinner, as an old admirer of his father had that very day given them a plump Gressingham duck. Luke said he would be delighted to accept the invitation.

As he walked into the cathedral close, he felt a surge of happiness and he stood for a moment to admire the sun setting in a red, misty sky. The cathedral clock began to strike seven, causing an explosion of pigeons from the tower; the deep tones of the hour bell, named 'Great Michael' since the Middle Ages, hung in the air as lesser bells in the town echoed and followed its message of the hour. A long trail of fragrant bonfire smoke was drifting over the grass towards Luke. Its origin must have contained some herbs; it was incense-laden and Luke was overwhelmed with the joy that he would once again be celebrating the college High Mass and that incense would still be offered up, even had he only been reinstated as senior chaplain. But it was not only returning to Melbury in this way that was important. He felt it was his destiny to be head and to restore the college to former glories.

While Luke was in this moment of elation, the telephone was ringing at his house. Francesca had managed to get hold of Fr Jeronimo at the English College in Valladolid and been told that Luke had just left for England. She had left Dove Cottage that afternoon for the first time since going there immediately after the horror at Boscannon. Only the need for food had given her the nerve to go out. She had suffered a severe reaction and desperately needed Luke's support. She was frightened that the madness exhibited by her husband and his cousin might pursue her to the cottage, and if this madness subsided, what would take its place? Certainly vengeance of some sort: cutting off any money for her or starting separation proceedings, or even a divorce citing Luke. She reckoned they would try and damn him, destroy his reputation in his Church by complaining to his bishop and to Melbury College Council. Her mind was in confusion. Why did their love – an experience so perfect that Luke had himself persuaded her was a gift from God – why had it led to this horror? Was the guilt theirs entirely? Was her Church going to tell her to return once more to nurse her husband, however diabolical? These speculations and the aftermath of the confrontation at Boscannon left her in a state of near collapse. Even Rasputin was no comfort to her; the painfulness of his injured tail militated against any animal expression of love. It seemed her constant sobbing and bouts of crying out loud were deepening the dog's own depression. She had a desperate need for Luke; he was her only salvation. She had to speak to him, and her failure to reach him by telephone had fuelled a rising hysteria.

At last the inspiration came to her that his father might know where she could find him. She would ring directory enquiries to get his father's number.

By this time the plump duck had been consumed, a duck anointed with garlic and herbs and accompanied by a 1982 Chateau Latour kept for such a special occasion – the 'return of the prodigal son' was how his father described it. They had moved on to cheese and grapes when the telephone rang. It was Francesca.

Margery was in the kitchen and picked up the phone in there. She called Luke from the dining room and said she would hold the fort with his father until he had finished.

It was a quarter of an hour later when Luke rejoined them. He had promised Francesca he would drive to Cornwall immediately his future was secured – within the next two days – and persuaded her to stay with friends in St Mawes until he came down. His father and Margery looked questioningly at him on his return to the table and Luke asked them to forgive him, explaining that it was a call from someone in a severe crisis. Knowing that Luke was in England and hearing his news had had a calming effect on Francesca. Even Rasputin wagged his tail as she arranged with her friends in St Mawes to go to them that night.

Francesca's call made it imperative that Luke was appointed as head immediately. This gave his meeting with the provost an added impetus. He told the provost that the college could get back to normal only if he had the authority of being the new headmaster, which was why he had rejected being reinstated as second master. If not, some of the difficult decisions to be made might not be properly acted upon if the staff suspected he was merely a caretaker until another head was appointed. The provost said the council had seen the sense of this and realised that this was the only way they could secure his badly needed presence. Luke explained that he needed another two weeks to finish the editing of the diary, now that most of the coded parts could be deciphered. The provost and Luke parted warmly and it was agreed that written confirmation and his contract would be sent to his address in Cornwall.

The Francesca situation was a time bomb threatening a scandal that could wrest his life's ambition away from him. Luke decided that it would be best for him to leave for Cornwall immediately after his meeting with the provost. He did not wish to get involved with college politics and tittle-tattle until his appointment was known. It was teatime when he had managed to repack for Cornwall and rang Francesca to tell her he was on his way. They estimated he would not arrive until near midnight, so they arranged to meet the next day. He had suggested driving straight to Dove Cottage, but she had demurred, saying they could be trapped at the cottage, at the end of its track and without any other escape routes. Francesca was still in a state of paranoia, suggesting that if his arrival was spotted, Boscannon could set up an ambush. She knew he had a licence for a .22 rifle as well as a twelve-bore, and he was a crack shot. Shooting rabbits and pigeons was his favourite pastime. She expressed similar fears about moving to Alastair's cottage in case her presence was noted by Nancy's friend. She settled for a meeting on the cliff top near the Boscannon beach at eleven the next morning – she knew the path was too rough for her husband to get there. To save time Luke would come by boat.

Luke had told Francesca that all would be well, but as he considered the situation while driving in his Rover down to Cornwall, he had to admit that it was a mess. He also thought about the sudden turn of events in his own life: the realisation that he had accepted the offer to be head without the slightest prayerful reflection. Was it, for instance, right that he should allow naked ambition to rule him and would his nemesis be the humiliation of losing his prize even if appointed head? The situation with Francesca would have to be regularised, or else it would have to end. He realised that the first priority would be to get Francesca away from Cornwall, to a safe place where she could calmly consider her future.

Luke awoke next day to see the sun breaking through a light mist over the Helford river. The warm sunny weather was set to continue. At the appointed time Luke came alongside the slipway leading to the beach and tied up the pram in which he had rowed from Alastair's motor boat, which was now secured to a buoy in deep water. The tide was low and the slipway was covered in green weed so that when he stood on it his feet slid from under him and he fell heavily onto his bottom. A peal of laughter and the sound of barking came from the low cliff overlooking the beach. He looked up and saw Francesca.

'Now you know why it's called a slipway, my darling!' Francesca had laughed for the first time since they had parted. Luke picked himself up and, on gaining dry ground, ran to meet her. Rasputin began to jump about, barking and wagging his bandaged tail as Luke reached her. Francesca took his hand. 'Come to our hollow darling. I'll secure Rasputin.'

When they reached it, Luke saw a rug spread there. Francesca lay down and for a while they lay cradled together while she retold all that had passed and her fears for the future. The recounting was too much and she began to cry silently. Luke rocked her in his arms and began to kiss away her tears, telling her all would be well and that she should move home and be nearer to him at Melbury. At that moment, the spell was broken by the sound of a vehicle coming slowly down the track from Boscannon and crunching onto the pebbles at the top of the beach. A door opened and they heard the voice of Boscannon, shouting, 'Get that back open and push the button, Joseph. For God's sake, you're like a slug in tar this morning!' There was a murmured reply and a whirl of machinery as the back flap turned into a lift to lower Boscannon in his wheelchair. He shouted again, 'Get the boat out!'

Luke and Francesca stayed frozen for a moment until she sat up and whispered that she would have to get Rasputin in case he started barking. She stood up, rearranged her dress and moved quickly to collect the dog. She returned with a delighted Rasputin.

Luke had sat up, his face grim-set. He had looked like that when at the wicket awaiting a delivery from a dangerously fast bowler in his first varsity match.

'I think this unwelcome arrival gives me a chance to sort out one or two things with your husband. I'm going to tell him we are not going to the police, provided he lays off you, but that we shall be swearing an affidavit with a lawyer setting out the facts of his assault on you and Rasputin, so that if anything happens it will he passed on pronto.'

Francesca took his wrist. 'Luke, be careful. He usually brings his gun down with him to blast away at the wildlife.'

Luke stood up. 'Don't worry,' he said, and walked back to the path leading down to the beach. He could see Boscannon on the side of the slipway by the small crane that lowered his chair into the boat. He was unlocking a panel in the side of the crane and taking out a long black cable to which were attached hand-held electric controls.

Luke saw at the top to the beach that Joseph had opened the boathouse doors. A gleaming white motor boat decorated with a broad red stripe around it, sat on a large metal cradle with three wheels on either side. Gravity would take it down the slipway into the water, like the launch of a lifeboat; at the same time it was restrained by a wire from a motorised winch in the boathouse which would also haul it back on return.

He saw Boscannon testing the crane when, to his horror, Luke saw that his own boat had come into view on the flooding tide. He realised that Boscannon was also looking in that direction and he watched anxiously as the rear admiral began a difficult manoeuvre in his chair, mumbling over the green weed with the obvious intention of untying Luke's small boat.

Luke shouted at him, 'Hey, stop that!' Boscannon was beginning to undo the painter attached to the boat. Boscannon looked up, but, because Luke had the sun behind him, he did not at first recognise who it was; as he did so, he snarled, 'By God! It's our adulterous cleric!'

Boscannon decided to make for the Range Rover and his gun on the back seat. He accelerated to the full power of his chair, but to his fury it began to skid on the weed. It slithered in a crab-like movement into the middle of the slipway. At the same time, Joe had taken the brake off the winch to which the motor boat was attached. Unknown to both of them, Joe had not slipped it into a restraining gear, so it was free to unravel at speed like a hurrying lifeboat.

Joe was at the stern of the boat and gave it his usual heave to get it started down the slipway, shouting, 'Boat away!' Because he was bent behind the boat, he had not witnessed Boscannon's uncontrolled slide to the middle of the pier, but assumed he was still at the side by the crane as was usual when the boat rolled down to the water. Joe gave the boat a final push as it reached the top of the slipway, where it became steeper in its descent. To his horror, it shot away with the wire behind hissing over the stones, creating a shower of sparks. Boscannon was still trying to get his chair to move, but it was slithering around the middle in weed. He looked up just as the boat began its rapid run. He let out a cry of rage, which rose several octaves as panic gripped him, and then turned into a short terrible cry of agony as the boat, weighing a ton, hit him sideways with its bow.

At the first cry, Joe had looked up with amazement. As he could see no sign of his master, he assumed he might have fallen over the side of the slipway. Then he caught sight of Luke running down the cliff path, pointing to the boat as he saw Joe turn to him.

Joe could see only the motor boat in the water, floating just above the submerged cradle. The terrible truth struck him: the boat was wedged on something below its bow and was not rising on the gentle sea lapping at the end of the slipway.

Francesca, hearing the cries, had caught up with Luke who, overcome with horror, was standing thunderstruck on the edge of the beach. He had seen the impact of the boat and the flow of blood as the bow had sliced into Boscannon's skull. Francesca had not seen the accident, but stood behind Luke, grasping his wrist, holding him back, saying, 'It's for the best.'

Suddenly Luke felt he was in a nightmare. Perhaps translating the de Witte diary had released its curse. Here was he, a twentieth-century priest being restrained by his lover, just as de Witte had been four hundred years before. Not only restrained, but with the very same words. He shook himself free and ran down the slipway towards the boat, falling over again on the weed before reaching Boscannon, trapped under the water by the bow of the boat.

Francesca came sliding down behind him, sobbing, 'Oh Christ, Oh Christ', and as she caught up with him, 'Please don't ask me to give him mouth-to-mouth resuscitation!'

Luke had already seen the split skull and pushed Francesca back. 'There will be no need for that.'

She looked over Luke's shoulder and saw her husband's split skull, his long hair floating outwards like the green weed below his head; green weed being rapidly covered in eddies of blood and brain. She struggled back up the slipway, crying hysterically, and collapsed vomiting at the top.

Luke had tried to move the boat, but it was still held in its cradle. Joe joined him. Luke turned to him. 'Get the winch going and get the boat back up, then we'll have to get Boscannon up to the top of the beach and cover him.'

The boat was dragged back up the slipway. Joe returned to help Luke get the chair and its dead load up the slipway. It was a struggle over the weed. It also presented a terrible sight, with Boscannon's body slumped forward to one side, revealing the hideous gash in his skull.

Luke shouted to Francesca, who was sitting with her face buried in her hands. 'Get the rug and then take the jeep back to Dove Cottage and ring your doctor and the police. We'll stay here until they come.'

Francesca didn't move. She began to tremble uncontrollably.

Luke went over to her and pulled her to her feet. 'Please do as I say and do it now!' He pushed her in the direction of the path where Rasputin sat grizzling. When she returned, she gave Luke the rug and looked away. She was ashen and still trembling.

'Our being here killed him.'

Luke shook her. 'Don't be silly – his vicious desire to get his gun and destroy us was what killed him. Joe, take Mrs Boscannon home to Dove Cottage and phone the doctor and police. I'll stay here.' He put the rug over the body.

When they had left, he sat nearby and tried to pray for all involved in this terrible accident. He was overwhelmed and sat stunned in shock. Soon after, he heard the sound of children walking along the path through the woods from Helford Passage. They saw the beach through the trees and began shouting and whooping with joy as they broke into a run.

This unexpected manifestation of life and innocence was a contrast to the recent horror and broke through the numbness of shock that had gripped Luke after the accident. He got up and stood in front of the rug-covered chair, shouting, 'Please go away. There has been a terrible accident. The police are coming and...' his voice died away as one of the children screamed, pointing at the chair. The rug was slowly slipping off the body, revealing the nightmarish head of Boscannon. Luke ran to the chair and put back the blood-sodden rug. The children stood, horror-struck, and began to cry, the younger running to the older. Eventually a quivering voice said, 'Let's go back,' and like a flock of sheep they all turned and ran through the wood.

Half an hour later, the police arrived in a Range Rover, and then the doctor and two ambulance men with a stretcher. The doctor and the police Range Rover made a slow procession back to the manor. Boscannon's body was taken away in the ambulance for an autopsy. The doctor was needed to help Nancy, who was in the kitchen clutching a glass of whisky with both hands. Her usual bun of hair was undone and the hair in front of her face was sodden with tears. When she saw Luke she pointed a finger at him,

'You and the bitch killed him. I'll see the truth is told!'

The doctor motioned everyone to leave and closed the door, so that he could get Nancy to bed with a strong sedative.

Francesca needed to collect some clothes before leaving Boscannon. She and Luke went to her room, where she packed the clothes she wanted with the speed of a shoplifter. Luke stood in the doorway of her bedroom remembering his first farcical visit.

From the manor they took the clothes to Dove Cottage. Now that her husband was no longer a threat, Francesca would make it her base to come back from Melbury. At the cottage they found on the kitchen table a note of condolence from Mrs Tregorran and a letter from Nancy. Francesca made them a pot of tea and poured a cup for Luke. She picked up the letter.

'I'll read it outside. I have no doubt it needs to be read in the fresh air.'

Luke sat in the kitchen and concentrated his mind on the hours of happiness they had enjoyed in the cottage.

Francesca came back into the kitchen looking deathly white again and put the letter in front of Luke. 'I'm afraid she's sick, through and through.' She left Luke to go upstairs.

Luke began to read the letter. It was a page of obscenities

directed at Francesca. It ended with a PS. 'Thank God Boss made a new will before he died – you get nothing. May you rot.' Luke sighed. He heard Francesca sobbing and went upstairs to comfort her.

Later he decided she should stay with him at Alastair's house. After dinner they sat in the gazebo watching a dramatic sunset. It was a yellow then red Technicolor show of clouds, broken to reveal pools of the brightest aquamarine sky.

'He's getting a good send-off,' murmured Luke.

This released Francesca's pent-up emotion and she began to sob and cry out loud. 'I loved him once, before his accident. I did love him.' And so it poured out, her life with Boscannon before the injury destroyed his character. Luke just hugged her to him to let her grieve. When her sobbing ceased, they went to bed and Luke held her close until she slept. When he heard her breathing steadily, he got out of bed and telephoned Alastair. Charlotte answered the phone. Luke told her everything and then asked if she could have Francesca to stay after the funeral, until they found somewhere for her to live near Melbury.

Luke went outside and sat on a seat facing the Helford river. He could see a single light shining from Boscannon Manor and wondered whether Nancy was there, alone in her misery. He knew that indirectly he had to take some responsibility for the tragedy that had occurred. If he had not entered the garden of Boscannon at the start of the summer holidays and fallen in love with Francesca, then Boscannon would not have become enraged at seeing him from the quay. Yet he reasoned again that it was Boscannon's viciousness that led to his wheelchair becoming stuck as he tried to reach his shotgun in the Range Rover. Luke sighed and prayed for God's mercy, not only in respect of the tragedy, but also in his loving Francesca in the first place.

His mind was in turmoil. Images of the dead Boscannon battled with theological concerns which had been awakened by an article he had just read in the *Tablet*, the Catholic weekly magazine that Alastair had left in his cottage. In the article by one Michael Novak, an American writer on the Church in the modern world, he read the words, *Is our sexuality a joke perpetuated by our creator? Does it mock us? Was it intended to humble us? It does seem at times like an implacable fate. Utterly baffling. Why do we so often experience ourselves as divided, separated, at times inwardly at war, nearly always alienated part from part, strangers to ourselves, brooding mysteries?*

From this article it appeared these questions had been studied by the Pope in public weekly audiences over five years. 'Hell's teeth,' thought Luke. 'five years, and with what result that could transform the overwhelming need generated between a man and a woman when in love. No doubt the cynical answer was that God was determined that early mankind should go forth and multiply, but if one was a believer it was fair to ask what God had intended when he put Eros into our embodied selves.

From this concern his mind jumped to the chaos in the Church of England. He had just read an article in *The Times*, headed, *Riven by ugly squabbles, ashamed of its past and uncertain of its future, the Church is a thoroughly mediocre product.* This was in reference to a bizarre advertising campaign with such proposed punchlines as *Body Piercing? Jesus had his done 2000 years ago?*

Such crassness made Luke want to weep. He knew, though, that the Church contained a solid core of those who shared his vision of a Church that could still communicate holiness. It had had a liturgy in austere language that could in its rituals and buildings convey the mystery of holiness, yet the fight to preserve that mystery was being lost. That evening Luke felt a lack of strength to continue. He knew to keep that message at Melbury would be a continuous struggle. Into his tiredness intruded the constant nagging question of whether his vocation now called him to become a Roman Catholic priest, added to which was a sneaking touch of pride that maybe such a vocation could bring him a position of leadership in that Church – shades of Cardinal Manning. He put away that siren voice but the question remained: and therefore what of his relationship with Francesca? Luke dragged himself to bed and slept fitfully, while Francesca, having released her sorrow, slept peacefully beside him.

* * *

The inquest meant that the funeral would he delayed. Francesca continued to stay with Luke at Alastair's cottage, and they agreed to wait until after the funeral before looking for the treasure. She contacted Mrs Tregorran, who told her Nancy had gone away; that a solicitor wished to speak to her, for which she gave her the telephone number; and also that she had a letter for her from Nancy which she would leave at Dove Cottage. first, though, they had to go to Boscannon so that Francesca could collect some suitable clothes for her meeting and for the funeral. Francesca's face was drawn and white as they entered the hall of the manor. Luke put his arm around her shoulders, which were trembling under the stress of revisiting the scene of her humiliation there.

Francesca had made an appointment for that afternoon to visit the solicitor who had left the message with Mrs Tregorran. He was a Mr Brentford from a firm of lawyers in Falmouth. Francesca asked Luke to come with her to Falmouth, but said she would see the solicitor alone if only Luke could be nearby. Mr Brentford had said the purpose of the meeting was to read Boscannon's will to her. In view of Nancy's letter – with its postscript – they agreed the will would probably be another load of insults couched in legal terms.

The lawyer's offices were in the old part of Falmouth and near the parish church of King Charles the Martyr. It was agreed Luke would wait there for her. He would read his daily prayers – the Order of Gethsemane imposed the prayer routines of the monastic services on its members – and enjoy the idiosyncratic Anglican dedication of the church to its martyred supreme governor, Charles the first.

An hour later Francesca joined Luke in the church. There was no one else in there. She sat beside him and smiled. Luke took her hand.

'Before you tell me your news, I made a phone call while you were with your Mr Brentford. It was to the provost. He confirmed that the council agreed I should be head – a contract for ten years...'

Francesca took his face in her hands and kissed him. 'Wonderful boy! And I have surprising news. Boscannon had a new will drafted last week, but it was never witnessed or signed. The lawyer wouldn't tell me the details, save to say that I had been cut out. Then he gave me a look as if to say I had arranged this timely death!' Francesca smiled again. She went on. 'His existing will left me some shares worth about £500,000 and the use of Boscannon for my lifetime. Some use that will be to me, except to let it, and then it goes to the nearest male relative. The rest of his money is to be invested to maintain Boscannon. Nancy is left a tea service and five hundred pounds! Obviously, in the past, when he drew up this will before his accident, she must have got on his wick. Of course I have no intention of staying in that ghastly house and I'll give Nancy some of my money – it's too ungrateful to the old bitch not to.'

A few days later, a crowded funeral was held at the Catholic church on the outskirts of Helston. Representatives of yachting clubs, the navy and the Conservative Association for Cornwall sent a good number. They had all heard that caterers had been appointed for the funeral feast at Boscannon. Nancy swayed drunkenly during the Requiem Mass, while Francesca was as still as marble, surrounded by distant relatives of Boscannon. His last bitter years had left him no friends, only acquaintances, and even Nancy did not cry, bitter at her treatment in his will.

After the last guest had left, including Nancy, Francesca went to her room to pack more of her belongings. She opened her cupboard door to find her beautiful Italian clothes slashed. Her pity for Nancy evaporated, but the vicious message of her action reduced her to the first tears of that day.

Chapter Seventeen

The next day they returned to Boscannon to see whether their theory about the treasure being hidden in the chapel was correct. They took with them a holdall with rough clothes and a toolbox and a can of WD40 to penetrate rusty mechanisms. They went straight to Francesca's bedroom to change.

'At least your jeans fit this time,' murmured Francesca as she moved to Luke and fastened his belt, at the same time giving him a lingering kiss. Rasputin had come with them to join in the hunt, but had been shut in the bathroom while they changed. While they were kissing he started whining and scratching at the door.

'I think that jealous beast of yours wants us to get on with our work.'

They went to the chapel, Francesca carrying the toolbox and oil, Luke, a crowbar and large hammer, and Rasputin, Luke's underpants, which he had purloined as they left Francesca's room. They agreed that Rasputin was certainly consistent when Luke changed clothes in the manor.

When they got to the chapel Francesca turned on the spotlights that illuminated the altar and the reredos. For a moment they looked at the statue of St Peter to the right of the altar holding two crossed keys made of iron. The reredos was known to be sixteenth-century, so it would have been new in de Witte's day. Luke got a chair so that he could stand level with the statue. He looked at the keys and his heart quickened; they were like the hands of a clock attached to a spike of iron set in the stone behind. Luke took both keys in his hand and tried to turn them to the right, but they did not move. He asked Francesca to pass him the hammer and he began to tap the keys in an attempt to move them. At first there was no give, but then, to his joy, they began to turn. A pile of rust was released from the casing in the stone holding the iron spike. Luke hit the keys harder and, although they moved a little, they began to bend. He feared they might break, so he got the penetrating oil and squirted its contents into the spike casing. A red oily mass began to flow back, and Francesca went off to get a cloth and a pile of newspapers to absorb it. They agreed they would try again next day. There was obviously some mechanism behind the keys.

'Oh Luke, I can't stand the excitement!' She kissed him again.

As they drove the next morning to Boscannon Manor, it would be true to say they were convinced they were on the brink of discovering the treasure. Again they had taken Rasputin to share in their search. If the keys of St Peter would not reveal an opening because they were rusted against movement, then they could get the builder who occasionally worked at the manor to help them by cutting through the wall. It was not necessary. Luke repositioned himself and began again to tap the keys with the hammer. At first nothing happened, but then they gave and turned, releasing further rusty fluid from the wall. Luke was able to move them slowly by hand and they heard a rattle and a creaking of wood from below the reredos. They looked in astonishment behind the altar cloth and saw, behind the marble pillars supporting the top of the altar, a carved wooden panel sinking into the floor. They looked at each other in triumph and embraced. Francesca had brought a large torch which she handed to Luke, nodding to him to go first. He crawled under the altar and through the opening. Francesca followed. As she stood up, Rasputin came pushing past her so that she stumbled against Luke, who dropped the torch. It went out. The only light came dimly from the opening under the altar. The air was stale and dank. Francesca held on tightly to Luke. He was distracted by her scent and the softness of her body. In the dim light it appeared they were in a small room about twelve foot long and eight foot wide. It seemed empty save for dust and spiders' webs, though they could hear Rasputin sniffing at something in a corner. Francesca felt her way to him.

'Luke, there's a chest or something here.' They decided they must get another torch and crawled back into the chapel. There was a box of candles and some matches in front of a statue of St Thomas More. 'I'm sure Henry VIII's chancellor will be glad to help!'

Francesca gave the candles to Luke, and they crawled back into the room and each lit a candle and placed it on the floor. Rasputin came panting back to join in and knocked over one of the candles with his tail, before cocking his leg on a corner of the chest and then being pushed back into the chapel by Francesca.

They stood for a moment looking at the solitary chest as they lit more candles. It was about four feet long with metal bands around it. They sighed in disappointment, having expected the room to be crammed with treasure. The chest was locked and covered in thick dust. Luke told Francesca to wait and crawled back into the chapel to pick up the crowbar. He returned and wrenched open the chest, the top cracking into pieces as he did so. There was certainly treasure there, but of a heavenly sort. The chest contained several large sixteenth-century Mass books and breviary, and a tattered vestment.

Luke's dreams of fame and fortune turned to dust like that covering the chest He slowly slid to the floor and hugged his knees. 'Dust to dust, ashes to ashes.'

Francesca put her candle on the floor and hugged him. 'My sweet, we found each other, and perhaps that's treasure enough in a lifetime.'

Luke could not reply but just shook his head. That might have been true, but it was not enough to assuage bitter disappointment. They dragged out the chest, and as they did so revealed a gold coin in the dust. Luke examined it.

'A ducat, I think, used in most of Europe from the end of the twelfth century, named probably, they say, after the Duke of Apulia, a nob in Italy at the time.'

Franccsca burst out laughing. 'Santa Maria! Is there no end to your knowledge?'

Her laughter broke the tension. Luke got out the missals.

'Good condition, some dated early 1500s, so maybe there is some value. Obviously hidden away from the persecutors.'

He looked at the bottom of the chest and tapped it. It

sounded hollow, so he got the crowbar and eased up the wood. They gasped with delight and removed a rotting bag made of leather. Inside were three gold chalices and three patens. They placed them carefully on the altar and examined them. Luke whistled softly.

'See the Melbury coat of arms – so the treasure *was* here. These are valuable, but where did the rest go? These were left here to be used. We must pack them up and then we'll take advice as to our position regarding them, but we'll have to report the Melbury chalices. I have got some information about recent legislation concerning treasure finds.'

They went off to get a suitcase to pack them in and then, with the rest of their luggage, set off for Melbury: Luke to take possession of the headmaster's house and Francesca to be warmly welcomed by Charlotte and her family.

Luke and Francesca had agreed between them that he had to make his task of establishing himself as an effective headmaster the first priority, but that he must decide his religious future by the time of the Queen's visit for the quincentenary celebration, even if it was not announced until afterwards.

Luke and Francesca had decided that their relationship would have to be conducted discreetly in Melbury. Their priority was to try and find a small house, or flat, in the area for Francesca to rent, and then they could make up their minds about their future together. Luke knew discovery would cause a scandal. The headmaster's house, which was a pleasant Georgian house to one side of the college cricket grounds, but with a live-in housekeeper, meant that any intimacy with Francesca was impossible. Luke gave her a set of keys to his old house and they met there, arriving separately; but their lovemaking was furtive, as he could easily be seen entering his house, and then callers would arrive or his telephone would ring.

One evening when they met there, Francesca was full of suppressed excitement.

'I have a surprise. Take me for a drive.' She had seen a holiday cottage that day and the estate agent had allowed her to keep the keys. When she opened the front door, it was warm and cosy as the central heating was on. They got as far as the main bedroom, then, lying on the reverse side of the bedspread, they made love. Apart from embracing when they had entered the bedroom, they had not spoken at all except to say, 'I love you' several times.

They decided they would take the cottage until the future was clearer.

Luke had been open with Francesca about his conviction that the Anglican Church was theologically imploding and that he felt strongly drawn to becoming a Roman Catholic; but this might lead to him concluding that he should become a priest as well, and he could see that celibacy left one unencumbered to devote oneself utterly to that calling. Yet he also knew he was being fulfilled in his role as headmaster, and that to witness to Catholic Christianity in its Anglican setting could be necessary at this time of crisis.

Francesca's faith had been modest in its practice under the strains of Boscannon. She accepted Luke's difficulties and began to pray again and attend the Catholic church in Melbury. As for themselves, they had agreed that their secret affair would have to end soon. It was against both their beliefs, apart from the danger it posed to Luke's reputation. If Mr Jones got wind of it, his career could be smashed again.

In the meanwhile, other events distracted them. Christie's sent down experts to examine the Boscannon find. They estimated the prayer books to be worth three to five hundred pounds each, and these were obviously property belonging to the Boscannon estate. The chalices and patens were in a different league and could be worth at auction anything from forty to a hundred thousand pounds. However, these were obviously treasure trove, and Melbury Cathedral and the Crown had first claim, though some sort of reward would result for Luke and Francesca.

Before the Treasure Act of 1996 altered the benefit to be gained by finding treasure, valuables were normally deemed to have been left by someone who planned to recover them later – if the original owners were long dead, the ownership passed to the state. Since the 1996 Act, provided everything is done by the book, such as getting permission from the owner of the land or buildings, and notifying archaeologists, finders stand to receive the full value of any discovery, although the money resulting is usually split fifty-fifty with the owner of the site.

Chapter Eighteen

In spite of the excitement of finding the chest and its contents in the chapel, Luke found tremendous satisfaction as he returned to the school and established his regime as headmaster. He gave a series of informal Sunday lunch parties for all the masters and their wives, so that he could get to know them better, plus the visiting preacher at the day's High Mass. Not all the preachers were clerics, but Luke made sure they were all in agreement with his view of the Church and hoped that the view would be absorbed by his lunch guests. He also held more formal dinner parties when important visitors came to the school, sometimes to address meetings of the political society or other college bodies, such as the literary or historical societies.

Soon after Francesca arrived, he held a dinner party for a previous Conservative foreign secretary who had come to address the political society. Francesca, Charlotte and Alastair were also invited. Before dinner, these three stood together in the drawing room. After the lecture they had been given drinks while they awaited Luke's arrival with the ex-foreign secretary.

Charlotte put a hand on Francesca's arm. 'Although Luke can be a pompous old thing for his years, we all love him as head and as a friend. He is proving a great success even with those who were weak enough to have given way to Henshaw. It was grand having you stay before you found your cottage – getting to know you better. You're right for each other, Luke and you, and Al and I are praying things work out for you both. I know Luke, Alastair and I – we three – have this Rome bug, but I think Luke should stay put here doing his bit for the truth. I must say the Masses and the doctrine preached in the college and cathedral are more Catholic than what we find when we go to the Roman Catholic church in town. We have a charismatic guitar-strumming priest.'

Their conversation was cut short as Luke came over and kissed Charlotte and Francesca before introducing the guest of honour. Before going into dinner, he took Francesca's hand and squeezed it hard, then led her into the dining room. For a moment, she found herself standing by Charlotte.

'God, I love him and need him.'

Charlotte replied, 'Don't worry, he can't live without you, I can see.'

The dinner was a success for Francesca. The ex-foreign secretary had talked to her about his love of Italy, and she was enchanted by the evening and stayed with Alastair and Charlotte after all the other guests had left. Snuggled connubially against Luke on a sofa in front of the drawing-room fire, Francesca imagined a life together there. Luke and Alastair exchanged opinions about those boys who had gained a record number of Oxbridge places and speculated about the college soccer eleven, which had won every match it had played that term. It was among a select number of public schools which played soccer instead of rugby, and had matches against Repton, Shrewsbury, Malvern and Winchester. While they talked shop, Charlotte gave Francesca inside information about staff at the college and the cathedral. In her happiness, the horrors of Boscannon seemed distant to Francesca. Later Luke persuaded her to stay the night, in spite of her determination not to compromise him.

'We shall start the night in the guest room,' was Luke's dismissal of her concern, 'and the housekeeper will bring you a chaste cup of tea in the morning.'

Unfortunately, this serene period of their lives was about to be disturbed by a threatening storm on their horizon.

Luke had appointed a new chaplain to replace Fr Peter. It was this appointment which introduced the cloud. The day after the dinner party he had a telephone call from Mr Jones congratulating him on his achieving the headship and asking if he could meet him and his new chaplain. Luke had put the Emmanuel Sunday services out of bounds to boys at the school, and Mr Jones wanted an explanation.

'Perhaps,' Jones had suggested, 'your new young secretary could call me with an agreed time for me to visit to discuss your dictatorial prohibition of pupils from visiting my church.'

Luke had hesitated before replying. 'I have kept on Henshaw's assistant secretary, Mrs Chalmers – very efficient, though I wouldn't call her young. I am also afraid I believe in keeping the college complete as a community centred on our college worship, so I do not want members of the school wandering about the town as religious dilettantes I don't think there is any point in Mrs Chalmers making an appointment.'

Mr Jones gave a snort. 'No, no, not her. I understood you now have a social secretary. She's taken one of my parishioners' holiday cottages. Posh of you, we thought, to have a social secretary.'

Luke tried to give a light laugh, but he knew that by trying to explain he made it sound a feeble explanation.

'I think there must be some confusion. She's just a mutual friend of Alastair and Charlotte, just here to recover from the tragic death of her husband. With them she helps out in official entertaining. In fact only last night she was here with the bishop and our last foreign secretary.'

Mr Jones gave an insulting, low whistle. 'A widow is she?' he said, and put the phone down.

Luke thought of the diary and its malediction. Was his life about to unravel again. He rang Francesca at the cottage and told her; he suggested they met at his house at teatime. Francesca merely said, 'Oh God, we seem to be bad karma for each other.'

Luke was late arriving at his house that afternoon. He'd had a visit from an official from the Russian Embassy. He had brought news that some of the parents of the expelled Russian boys were talking of suing the college for unfair dismissals that could blight their future careers. University courses might be blocked and jobs difficult to come by. Luke had lost his temper and told the official that in most schools pupils who debagged their headmasters would be expelled, and that anyway he understood the Russian mafia was a growth industry and they could follow in their fathers' footsteps. The official had taken this as an extreme insult to his country and stormed off, leaving Luke knowing that he had gone too far.

There was no sign of Francesca when he got to his house. There was just a hand-delivered note on the floor of the hall. It was from Francesca.

Darling boy. It is breaking my heart to see your turmoil of mind and now I've put you in danger here. You need to be on your own to sort things out. I am going to some of my family in Italy and when I know where I'm settled, I'll send my telephone number. Call me only when you've decided our future. In the meanwhile, I have to go – if I saw you I know you would make me stay, I'm so weak as far as you're concerned. All the love in the world. Francesca.
PS Remember we discussed my willingness to marry you as an Anglican priest, but you could still become a Catholic priest in the future and that would allow me still to be your wife. Only celibacy will finish us, but I do not think your nature could survive the strain of that.

Luke was devastated at her leaving, yet he knew that she had acted wisely. If only he could know what God wished him to do.

Chapter Nineteen

In order to ease the pain of Francesca's absence and to get the diary edited in time, Luke devoted himself to the final pages. He worked in the college library, where he had first seen the diary. It was quiet in the half-term absence of pupils and staff, and he felt an inner satisfaction in working at the desk the librarian had told him was de Witte's. An engraving of de Witte, slightly stained, had been found by the librarian and placed behind the desk. It was too stylised to convey much character, but under a mitre the bishop appeared a small neat figure.

He worked until the college clock chimed midnight. Luke sat puzzling over his work. He could do no more to the diary than collate all his editing and translations. He would write a short introduction, pointing out some of the unanswered questions, and try and comment fairly on the Elizabethan Church and how its cruelties and persecutions were also directed against Puritans as well as Catholics, and also that the Catholic Church had behaved equally hideously under Queen Mary. He concluded that de Witte was a man doing his best in a violent age.

Next day he contacted his secretary. 'Mrs Chalmers, I'm sorry to spoil your half-term, but could you help me? I have some further typing I need done to finish my editing of the de Witte diary. Could you give me two days?'

She was used to worse from Henshaw and, as she had come to like and admire Luke, was happy to help.

Luke rang Canon Frobisher, who agreed to receive him and the diary at Michaelhouse, Cambridge. Afterwards he could stay the night and dine at high table. Thus Luke spent the last two days of the half-term.

Luke arrived in Cambridge the day after the last part of the diary had been typed by his secretary. It was a glorious October afternoon, and his heart lifted as he entered Michaelhouse, which was his old college. The medieval building occupied a small site between Trinity Hall and the Great Court of Trinity College. Henry VIII had tried to eliminate it to make Trinity even more grandiose, but St John fisher had been able to resist the plans. The college building was a rectangular court, incorporating a hall with a fine hammer-beam roof and a small chapel with a fantailed stone roof similar to King's College. The far end of the rectangle housed the masters' lodge which faced The Backs. Between the lodge and the river was a famous, small topiary garden. Americans described the college as neat. It was, and being small had a good community spirit. Further modern accommodation was provided beyond The Backs, by the side of the university library.

Canon Frobisher greeted Luke with a touch of reserve, feeling himself obliged to treat his guest as an equal, not as second master. He had also heard increasing reports of Luke's success in the role he himself had played with diminishing distinction as head of Melbury, so that he harboured a sense of pique over Luke's reputation.

However, he was correctly hospitable and offered Luke coffee and port in his drawing room overlooking the river while he settled down to read the typed and edited diary. Canon Frobisher began at the introduction that Luke had written and wrinkled his nose disapprovingly when he saw mention of the meeting with the martyr Robert Southwell.

From outside the windows came sounds of laughter from punts passing on the river. They contrasted with much sniffing, the master's sign of anger. This diary was not developing as an unalloyed piece of Anglican propaganda: with considerable disquiet he read Luke's observations about de Witte's possible involvement in the loss of the Melbury treasure; the suggestion of an adulterous relationship; and the uncertainty over the manner of his death. After an hour Canon Frobisher broke the silence.

'I understand you have provided copies for all members of the council committee who are responsible for receiving and examining your work. We have agreed to meet within a week to approve its printing. Obviously, Luke, you have worked long and hard and earned every penny we agreed to pay you. It will enhance your reputation. Thank you. Now, I suspect you would like to stretch your legs – we meet before dinner in the Combination Room at 7pm.

And so Luke was dismissed. At dinner he was placed between a Chinese professor and a dull physics don. He saw Canon Frobisher to talk to only at breakfast, but he was silent behind a copy of the *Church Times*.

Two weeks later one of the diary typescripts was sent to him. Attached was a compliments slip, without comment, from Canon Frobisher. All references to the treasure, to de Witte's time at Boscannon, to his meeting Robert Southwell and the witnessing of his death, had been deleted, as was his final reference to a meeting with the Dean and Canons of Melbury just before his death. This bowdlerisation of his work was utterly depressing. He could not believe they had been historically so corrupt.

Chapter Twenty

Luke had a free afternoon after returning from Cambridge. In the morning the Epistle reading at Mass had reminded him that 'the fruit of the spirit is in good works'. It also reminded him that he had not been to visit Fr Peter since he had become headmaster. He had heard that the former junior chaplain was staying at Gethsemane House and, enjoying a strengthening diet of good food and wine, was much recovered. Luke rang to check that Fr Peter would like to see him; the answer was positive, and he was asked to join the convalescent for coffee and port after lunch in his private room. Luke found him looking better than he remembered. They sat facing each other in comfortable easy chairs. Luke told him of developments at the school, and of the excitements and disappointments over the treasure, and generally prattled on about superficial matters and the defeat of Mr Jones in his attempts to get the school to his services.

Fr Peter seemed to have matured through the crisis of his breakdown. He sat quietly with his hands folded in his lap. 'I'm sorry about the treasure – finding it must have seemed overwhelmingly important when Henshaw sacked you. Still, I seem to remember something about the importance of storing up treasures in heaven and the location of one's heart.' He smiled engagingly. 'As to Mr Jones, one can only feel a certain admiration for his zeal however misapplied.'

Luke was a little peeved at the display of priestly magnanimity and the hinted disapproval at his attempts to use the diary mainly to find the treasure. He succumbed to the desire to hit back.

'I don't know if you realised what happened to the nun's clothing in your house when you went back? I assume you've been home on occasions? Anyway, I thought it best to remove the evidence before the police found it. I burnt it all.'

194

Fr Peter continued to look at his hands. He replied quietly.

'I hoped it was you. Thank you so much. It's funny what human beings get up to under unbearable stress. It's a relief to talk about it at last – although I tried to confess it, I funked it. Would you mind if I confess to you now?' Fr Peter looked up at him. There was no look of embarrassment, just a simple request for a priestly service.

Luke could not banish the thought of his own more complex spiritual situation. He felt weighed down by it. He nodded. 'Of course.'

They both sat quietly, heads bowed, while Fr Peter recounted his sins for absolution. Including the episode of his manifestation as a battling nun, they were all sins of a childish simplicity. Luke knew he was listening to the confession of a man with the burden of a difficult but essentially holy nature.

For a moment Luke was silent, struggling with a sense of his own unworthiness, though he knew the effectiveness of the Sacraments was totally divorced from the spiritual state of the priest. He gave the words of the absolution, adding, 'Your recent suffering has been penance enough. Please pray for the college instead, in the words of the college prayer, and for me.'

The two men continued to sit quietly in their chairs. Luke felt the increasing burden of his own problems. 'Peter, I need your help. Will you hear my confession?'

Fr Peter nodded. 'I knew. I sensed it.'

When Luke finished, Fr Peter said, 'Say the 23rd psalm as your penance. The Lord is My Shepherd – this is true for all of us. As for advice, well, you have just said you are not sure if you should marry the woman you love because you might have to follow a vocation to become a Roman Catholic priest. Of course, we know the score about your loving her now, after the death of her husband – it's a matter of fornication. You may well continue to cohabit with her, though it's hardly wise for a clerical headmaster, but I think you should ask yourself if you are using this possible vocation as an excuse not to commit yourself.'

The two men sat quietly together for another five minutes until Luke stood up. 'Thank you, Peter. We mustn't lose touch. I gather you might be replacing Fr Ignatius here. That'll be good, for you can help us a lot in the school. Also it's good to have one's confessor near at hand, particularly one who can discern things so well.'

They did not say anything more, just clasped hands firmly. From that moment Fr Peter was restored, knowing he still had the ability to be a priest.

Luke went back to his car convinced he had been the one to derive most benefit from the meeting. He was to be given another opportunity that day.

He drove back to his headmaster's house via the new ring road around Melbury. After a dispute lasting several years, a dual carriageway had wound south of the town, then been diverted by several miles, when connections in high places enabled the college to prevent the route going over some distant fields it owned. Nevertheless, this route was quicker than negotiating the series of lights and one-way streets that made Melbury a motorist's nightmare.

The initial sunny start to the day had given way to the arrival of black clouds bringing heavy rain, then turning to sleet as evening set in. Luke was looking forward to enjoying a cup of tea and anchovy toast made by his housekeeper when he got back to his new headmaster's accommodation. He would sit in front of his Georgian fireplace, the room lit by its flickering flames, while he listened to a Mozart concerto on his newly acquired music centre. He had settled in to a steady sixty miles per hour when he noticed ahead in the fading light the figure of Mrs Jones in her warden's uniform standing under an umbrella by a car, regarding a flat tyre. The car was half off the road, but it meant approaching traffic had to veer into the centre lane to avoid it. This traffic had had to plough through heavy deposits of water, as the constructors of the road had unfortunately left a dip at this spot. Luke came up behind a heavy lorry with a trailer, which veered into the centre lane to avoid Mrs Jones. As it went through the pools of water it sent up a wave of muddy slush that would have pleased a surfer on the Severn bore, but was a disaster for Mrs Jones. As Luke sped past her dishevelled figure, scuttling to the other side of her car, he let out a cry of 'Hallelujah', and then said, 'Oh God!'

He had to proceed for another mile before he came to a

roundabout where he could double back on his route and start again to reach Mrs Jones.

He pulled up behind her and put on his warning lights, got out of his car and, seeing Mrs Jones in the driver's seat, walked to the nearside door. He tried the door. It was locked. He could see Mrs Jones slumped forward and resting her head on the steering wheel. She was a picture of utter dejection. Luke tapped on the window with his car keys just as a pantechnicon, sounding a horn like the last trump, passed at speed, sending a wave of water over the car and soaking Luke.

Mrs Jones sat up with a start, opened the passenger door and Luke crawled in. He had recently acquired a dark grey clerical raincoat which was now spattered with filth from the road. Mrs Jones did not seem pleased to see him; there was a strong smell of whisky in the car.

'What do you want?' was all she said.

Luke suggested that the best course of action would be to take her home, leaving her car with its warning lights going, and then Mr Jones and Luke could sort out getting the car. Mrs Jones thawed a little and they both went to Luke's car and drove to the Emmanuel rectory in complete silence. An enquiry after the well-being of Mr Jones was met with a grunt. Just before they reached their destination, Mrs Jones broke the silence.

'When are you getting hitched, Mr Howard? You should – at thirty-nine you're leaving things late. All this celibacy nonsense oozing from Gethsemane House isn't healthy, and if you want kids, you should get started before your potency shrivels.'

Luke coughed in embarrassment. 'Someone else advised me today to marry.'

Mrs Jones continued unabashed. 'That young lady of yours out at Fred Sharp's farm cottage, what happened to her?' She gave a hiccup.

Luke blushed. 'Oh, just a friend of Charlotte Galbraith.'

Mrs Jones belched quietly and muttered, 'Balls. I tell you, we married too late, no kids – Mr Jones had shrivelled potency. "Children are like arrows in the hand," saith the Lord. It makes you bloody bitter, having no kids when you want them. God, what a bloody life! I tell you, being a traffic warden is no joke in any weather, but today, bloody hell!'

197

To Luke's relief they arrived at her home and rushed in through the freezing rain. Mr Jones was staggered to find Luke in the role of good Samaritan and refused to involve him further. He said with some pride that the local AA garage owner worshipped in his Church.

Luke returned with relief to his cosy Georgian official residence. He had missed his tea, but sitting in his house in front of the fire with a whisky in his hand he realised that he had a key to the characters of Mr and Mrs Jones. Their barren marriage explained much.

When he returned to Melbury there was a message from the bishop on his answerphone wondering if it would not be more appropriate for him to present the de Witte diary to the Queen, because he was his modern successor as bishop. Luke snorted with indignation and wished he could reveal the real truth about the manner of de Witte's death.

A little later the bishop rang and asked if Luke could see him, as he had now returned to Melbury. Luke told him firmly that the diary was seen as the record of a famous Melbury old boy, not as that of an ex-bishop. This task of making the presentation was therefore the college's. Also he was sorry that college matters made it impossible for him to see the bishop: there was so much to arrange before the celebrations. The bishop suggested a snack lunch at his palace to discuss the matter. He lived in a decaying Tudor residence with ten bedrooms, outside Melbury, on the way to Gethsemane House. Luke demurred, saying he had promised to visit his father for lunch but that he would be delighted to welcome the bishop in his headmaster's residence after the celebrations. The bishop gave a curt, 'Thank you very much,' and slammed down his phone.

Luke found his father in good form. He enjoyed the prospect of a party and was ecstatic that Luke had arranged that he would be one of a select few to join the formal luncheon for the Queen to be held in the Scholars' House. When Luke arrived his father was already in the dining room, coaching his parrot on its perch. Over lunch, Luke was explaining the arrangements for the celebrations when they were interrupted by a series of loud knocks at the front door. The parrot let out a stream of expletives.

Luke could only say, 'Golly, that's a bit risky.'

His father chortled, 'Don't be a milksop.'

Margery had gone to the front door and now appeared in the dining room with the bishop beaming over her shoulder and giving a little flutter of his hand; his action half way between a wave of welcome and a benediction. Luke quickly covered the parrot's cage with its cloth.

'My dear Canon, I was just passing and realised I had not seen you for ages and so I felt, as I was on my way to see the dean, I really ought to find out how your recovery was going on.'

Luke's father sat glaring at this intruder. He was disgusted to see him wearing a purple polo-neck sweater instead of traditional bishop's garb, and muttered under his breath, 'How I was recovering, not "recovery was going on".' He reluctantly rose to his feet. 'Please sit down and have some of this Chardonnay.'

Luke stood up and indicated an empty chair at the end of the table, at the same time failing to notice his father deftly removing the cover from the cage.

'How kind,' said the bishop as he lowered his portly frame onto the seat. 'It also gives me a chance to talk to your son. He's so busy these days.'

'A glass of wine! How kind,' came a fruity echo from the parrot on its perch in the inglenook fireplace. 'Kind, kind.'

The Bishop swivelled in amazement to regard the bird – he hadn't noticed it before. Luke hastily poured him a glass of wine and prayed the parrot would shut up. He looked in vain for the cage's covering cloth. He was disturbed to see his father had a wicked glint in his eye. His father took a long sip of wine and went over to the parrot with a titbit, which it took gently, before throwing its head back like a Russian vodka drinker. It pecked at its feathers for a moment before squawking, 'We have erred and strayed from our ways like lost parrots!'

The bishop gave a guffaw of false laughter. 'How very droll. What a clever fellow. How droll of you, Canon, to use the general confession to teach your bird a sense of repentance.' He guffawed again.

The parrot bowed its head, hopped along its perch and said conspiratorially, 'Who farted – not me – it's the bishop.'

Luke looked at his plate. Out of the corner of his eye he could see the bishop's face colouring to match his sweater. The bishop knocked back his wine.

'Canon, you should be ashamed of yourself!'

'Not me – it's the bishop – who farted?' interrupted the parrot. It was getting into its stride. The parrot was hopping from claw to claw in mounting self-satisfaction. The Bishop stood up, knocking over his chair. For a moment he seemed incapable of speech, then he nodded curtly and left the house, slamming the front door shut. Luke and his father burst out laughing. They laughed until they cried.

At last Luke said, 'I really think you should send that bird away.'

His father wiped his eyes and said, 'Enjoy life while you can, dear boy.'

'Well, in a way that's what I've come to see you about – I'm thinking of getting married.'

'Excellent. About time. I was not worried about you. We marry late in our family, and I know it's the fashion today, but schools like married headmasters. Anyway, marriage is what we are designed for unless for religious reasons you decide to be celibate. Who is the girl?' His father pronounced the word 'girl' as 'gel' in an old-fashioned country manner.

Luke blushed and felt shy. 'She's called Francesca.'

'Pretty name, tell us some more. I sense a bit of hesitation.'

'Well, she's recently widowed, so we can't marry immediately – mind you, I haven't asked her yet, though I'm pretty confident, having known her since August.'

His father looked at him quizzically. 'Known her in a biblical way?'

'Really, Dad, you have a one-track mind.' Luke slipped away from the question. 'My hesitation is about telling you she is a Roman Catholic – not ideal for an Anglican priest, one would say.'

His father was silent for a minute, saddened by the thought that his grandchildren would probably be brought up as Catholics, perhaps disdaining his Anglican orders.

'It's not uncommon, but it would be difficult in your ministry. I don't need to tell you that you'll be having to agree to allow your children to be educated and to worship as Roman Catholics:

rather confusing to whatever flock you have, whether in a parish or in a school. However, better to be a member of the Italian mission than a happy-clappy evangelical. Anyway, you'll be living in the headmaster's house, which will be lovely for me.'

Luke sat silently for a moment. 'Yes, there is a further problem. My faith and my allegiance to the Church of England. I'm afraid I'm getting close to deciding I must become a Roman Catholic as well, and maybe a Catholic priest. Exit marriage! Exit headmaster!'

Luke saw an expression of pain on his father's face. His father got up and put a hand on Luke's shoulder.

'I am not underestimating the terrible problems you have. At the moment I cannot advise you, as it's come as a shock hearing what you've just said.' He moved over to a picture of Luke's mother above the fireplace. It had been painted when she was in her forties and reflected the vivacity that had remained with her throughout her life. 'I'd like you to have this. It could be a comfort. Now, I think I'll just go upstairs and rest my leg. It's playing up today. See yourself out when you're ready.' As his father started up the stairs, he called back, 'Take the picture with you.'

Luke went straight from his father's house to hang the picture of his mother in his headmaster's room. While he was trying to decide where to hang it, he was interrupted by one of Parker's regular visits. In the course of his usual gossiping, Luke asked him a question. 'Tom, you know everything that happens in this place – I tried to ask Canon Frobisher what occurred when I was elected head by the council. He looked furious and said, "Ask Parker," so I am.'

Parker opened the Tompion clock door and pretended to adjust the pendulum. Luke persisted, 'Come on, Tom, I gather I had tough competition from John Bridges, but someone gave false information about him to the provost that caused him to be dropped.'

Parker backed away from the clock. 'Well, Father, he wasn't a patch on you – far too pleased with himself – so I just helped the provost reach the right decision.

'Told him about Mr Bridge's secret drinking and womanising – that sort of thing.'

He winked at Luke who just gasped. 'Bridges was like that? I never knew. How extraordinary! Anyway, thank you, Tom. Thank you very much.'

'Anytime, Father – could you just pass me the oilcan?'

Chapter Twenty-one

When Luke eventually got to bed he decided to read again P.G. Wodehouse's *Right Ho, Jeeves* to distract himself from his problems. He had just finished the first chapter when the telephone rang. It was Charlotte. She was trying to speak, but she was sobbing at the same time.

'It's Anthony, he's in the cottage hospital. We're afraid he's dying, he's got a ruptured spleen. Some fearful louts beat him up outside the Black Swan. A specialist is coming from Bristol. Two other boys from school are here, but just glass injuries. I thought you ought to know. The police are here, they got the yobs. Still, that won't save Anthony...' She began to cry.

'I'll come down right away.' As he put the phone down Luke looked at the crucifix on the wall facing his bed and prayed that the boy might be saved. He got out of bed and dressed like a man possessed and drove to the hospital. Charlotte and Alastair were in a small room with their son. They looked at him dumbly, like kicked dogs. The boy lay there in the dim blue light like an alabaster figure on an Elizabethan tomb. He had a drip in his arm, his breathing was quick and shallow. The air was heavy with the smell of antiseptic. Charlotte was sitting, twisting a damp handkerchief in her hands.

Alastair got up and took Luke by the arm and led him out of the room. As he did so, a young doctor came to check the situation. five minutes later he came out. He shook his head and said the blood pressure was still falling.

'Dear God,' was Alastair's only comment.

'I'm so sorry...' Luke felt his words were utterly inadequate, but he could not find anything more to say.

'Aye, it's not hopeful, so perhaps it's only prayers left.' Alastair's expression was desperate.

Luke nodded. 'I'll go and see what I can do,' he said, and squeezed Alastair's arm.

The hospital was close to the cathedral and Luke had a master key to a side door. He went in. It was a bright moonlit night and the interior of the cathedral was quite illuminated. A bookstall was by the door and from it Luke picked out a large prayer card which had an ancient prayer to St Michael. Luke made his way to the chapel where the Blessed Sacrament was reserved. Luke knelt by the sacristy lamp set into the side wall. Beneath its light he prayed the St Michael prayer on the card.

> *Michael, Archangel of the King of Kings,*
> *Give ear to our voices.*
> *Thou wast seen in the Temple of God,*
> *A censer of gold in thy hands,*
> *And the smoke of it, fragrant with spices,*
> *Rose up till it came before God.*
> *Thou with strong hand didst smite the cruel dragon*
> *And many souls didst rescue from his jaws.*
> *Then there was a great silence in heaven*
> *And a thousand thousand saying,*
> *'Glory to the Lord King.*
> *Hear us, Michael, Greatest Angel.*
> *Come down a little from thy high seat*
> *To bring us the strength of God*
> *And the lightning of his mercy.'*

Luke repeated this prayer several times, savouring the majesty of its words and the eventual triumph of good over evil.

Clouds scudded across the moon, so that the figures in the great stained-glass window seemed as if they were alive, coming and going before his eyes. Beneath the representation of St Michael and the Angelic Host were smaller figures wearing haloes, the apostles and major saints. He stopped praying and began to name them. St Francis and St Dominic, easily recognisable, and the Fathers of the Church, St Augustine and St Ambrose, dressed as bishops. A cloud covered the moon and when it cleared, he saw another small figure dressed as a bishop, standing behind St Augustine. He didn't remember seeing it before. For a moment he froze. It bore an uncanny resemblance to an etching of Bishop de Witte which hung in the college library. He shook himself – no, surely it must be St Gregory. He sat back in his pew and thought about the problems of his own life and the curious adventure of the de Witte journal. Perhaps in the eyes of Fr Charles they had discovered another English martyr. Luke looked again at the tiny figure and, almost absent-mindedly, said, 'Blessed de Witte, pray for Charlotte, Alastair and their son. May he be saved from death. And pray for me, that God may send me a sign so that I may make the right choice before Him.'

A clock in the cathedral struck eleven. He thought about invocation to the saints and knew the teaching, but doubted that God allowed his saints special powers to help in the world. Then he sat up with a start – he must have gone to sleep.

He went back to the hospital. A policeman was waiting there in case they had a murder on their hands. He was sitting in the reception area on a worn plastic settee, sipping a cup of tea. Luke went over to him.

'Any news?'

The policeman shook his head.

At that moment, the swing door leading to the wards opened. A middle-aged man in a dinner jacket came out looking furious. The young doctor and a nurse were behind him. They stood for a moment by the front door. The man in the dinner jacket paused and with a forefinger poked the chest of the doctor.

'In future, don't call for a surgeon, any surgeon, and especially not me when I'm at a dinner party, to look at boys who've been knocked out by a kick in the tummy after drinking too much! Good night to you.' He was gone with the sound of a fast-revolving door.

The young doctor put up his hands and said to the nurse, 'I swear to God, that boy was dying. A fading pulse, falling blood pressure, every sign of spleen damage. Then the bloody kid perks up just as I was having a cup of tea with his parents. I looked at my watch, but by then it was just after eleven, too late to stop that prick Mr Dobbs in his bloody DJ.'

Luke looked at him in astonishment. He felt real fear of a power behind the veneer of life. He remembered the biblical line, *It is a terrible thing to fall into the hands of the living God.*

It was not that this power was anything malign, just overwhelming. For the first time in his life he felt lifted into another spiritual dimension.

He went back into the cathedral and knelt again in prayer. He found it impossible to concentrate. It was late and his tiredness seemed to be playing tricks on his mind. He could not see the figure of St Gregory, who had reminded him of de Witte, in the great east window. He began to fear for his sanity. Had he been involved in some hallucination? His conscious mind told him it was wish fulfilment, that the end of his work on de Witte's diary had left him with an obsession and that the revelation of the Jesuit journal in Valladolid had prompted his imagination to think that one could invoke de Witte. He got off his knees and, sitting back in the pew, smiled at his own gullibility. It was not an article of faith to invoke the saints. At that moment the cathedral darkened as dense clouds obscured the moon, and a wind began to be heard as it sighed among the flying buttresses outside.

Luke sat bolt upright, his tiredness banished by a feeling of panic. Obsession or not, Anthony had appeared to recover at the time of his invocation of de Witte. He felt caught up in a situation he did not understand or welcome.

Some might say that the Anglican God is a comfortable, benign gentleman. Educated preferably at Trinity College, Cambridge. God was a Trinity man, one might say. Admittedly he had treated his son harshly, and the Holy Spirit was a bit of an unknown quantity, but Anglicans should not be uneasy in their approach. Obviously, Luke's faith was mature, but as Luke became aware of the implications of the night he began to tremble: never had he been touched by this unimaginable power before. God really did exist, did really care, and on rare occasions intervened in the erratic life of the world, seemingly in answer to prayer. Luke remembered a tutor at his theological college saying that these happenings would be explained by the world as coincidences, but he would say they were 'God-instances'. This intellectual conviction was transformed into his soul's consciousness. Evangelicals and charismatics would call it his conversion experience. To Luke it was a sudden and overwhelming feeling of being swamped by divine love. He sank to his knees, repeating the prayer of the Kyrie, 'Lord have mercy, Christ have mercy', his face wet with tears. He did not know his future, but in God's time it would be revealed and he would recognise the way. He left the cathedral and decided to leave his car and walk back home through the town.

The clouds cleared, revealing a bright sky again. An early frost was making the grass in the cathedral close sparkle. He stopped and looked up at the universe around him and felt dizzy at the thought that there were further galaxies in their thousands beyond his vision and comprehension. The perfection of the universe could only be a reflection of a stupendously powerful divinity. Luke began to feel as insignificant as dust, saved only by the conviction that this power had somehow become incarnate in Christ.

Next day, Anthony Galbraith was sitting up in his hospital bed receiving visitors and laughed when he heard that prayers had been offered in the college chapel for his continuing recovery and for repentance in his assailants.

'Whatever for?' was his question. 'I was just knocked out after a bit of "town v gown"!'

Chapter Twenty-two

Luke wanted desperately to share his experience with Francesca and broke his resolve not to ring her in Italy. She was not there, and he was told she'd had to go to England to sort out her property and should be there by the next day. Luke knew she would be at Dove Cottage and decided he would ring her there.

That night he dreamt of Francesca. They were together, walking by the Helford with Rasputin leaping around them in high spirits. In the dream, he had asked Francesca why Rasputin was so happy. She had stopped and looked at him and laughed. 'Silly boy, he's going to have someone to play with – I'm pregnant,' and Luke had laughed as well. 'Of course, and we're to be married.'

It took him a long time to wake up that morning and as he drifted in and out of sleep, he could not be sure whether his dream was only a dream. Eventually, when he was fully awake, he knew it was another sign. He had breakfast and rang Dove Cottage. The answerphone replied, 'I'm sorry I cannot answer the phone now, please leave a message after the tone.'

Luke said, 'The headmaster of Melbury will be in the area tomorrow night to negotiate a contract for a vacancy in the school.'

When he arrived the next evening he stopped the car and the front door opened. Rasputin came bounding out, with Francesca following close behind. Luke got out of the car and they melted into each other's arms. He covered her face with kisses. Francesca responded and then broke away, laughing as she asked, 'What's this vacancy? At the school?'

'I'll tell you tomorrow,' he replied.

The following day they breakfasted late. Francesca explained that she had let Boscannon Manor to a company that ran retirement homes and she had come down to supervise the packing of remaining items of value.

'Talking of value,' said Luke, 'I should like to try and recover my signet ring, so if Joseph is around with a crowbar, could we go to Boscannon and try to move that stone in the gazebo where my signet ring disappeared on that horrendous day?'

'It wasn't all horrendous.' Francesca pouted in an exaggerated way, worthy of a Georgian actress in a Sheridan play.

Joseph was found and together Luke and the gardener levered up the stone and slipped it to one side. They all gasped. A stone spiral staircase was revealed. Luke could see his ring on a step, halfway down, where daylight nearly ended. Covered by the gazebo, the steps were perfectly dry. Luke went down slowly and gently picked up his ring as if it were some glittering beetle that might have scurried away. He could see at the bottom a wooden door in a small paved area. He returned to Francesca and led her into the rose garden. Joseph leant on the crowbar, rolled a cigarette and regarded a couple of robins scrapping together. He took no notice of the unexplained departure of Luke and Francesca.

Luke led her into the middle of the garden. In spite of the time of year, there was a profusion of roses. He picked a Gallica rose and a frond of love-lies-bleeding.

'Will you marry me? If you will, then take the rose and I'll throw away the other.'

Francesca just nodded and took the rose – she could not speak. He slipped his signet ring on to her finger. They kissed, then he said, 'We need torches – there's another door to be opened at the bottom of the steps.'

The door was locked in four places and it needed the combined weight of the three of them to prise it open with the crowbar. There was a sound of wrenching metal as each lock burst and the door eventually sprang inwards. Inside was a domed vault containing stone shelves. On these were rows of chests, wooden boxes and rotted leather cases. Inside the largest chest, which they went to open first, was a discoloured silver casket. Francesca opened its catch to reveal inside a simple golden crown.

'Dear God,' said Luke. 'Could this be the missing crown of Wessex?' They looked at each other in amazement and began to prise open the other chests like people possessed. Bejewelled chalices, rotted vestments, silver plate and cases of golden coins and jewels revealed themselves. In the last case they opened they found the golden processional cross and the bejewelled bishop's mitre of medieval Melbury.

Luke said, 'This is more than we can handle. Francesca, could you call the local police? If they can guard it for a while, I'll contact the security company who look after the cathedral to send down a posse. After that I presume we contact the Treasury, and the Church Commissioners or whoever will take over.'

Francesca looked at Luke lovingly. 'Clever old thing.' She embraced him. 'By the way, what's the vacancy at the college you told me about?'

'Headmaster's wife,' smiled Luke.

'How boring. I've had lots of offers to be a contessa.' She ran up the steps to call the police and, turning back at the top, blew him a kiss and called back, 'I'll take the job.'

The next few days saw them besieged by the media as security vans arrived from the Tower of London. It had been decided that this was the best place to lay on a safe display of the treasure. Reporters flew in from the Far East as well as the Americas. Profiles of the tragic widow of Boscannon were written. Historical societies praised Luke's editing of the diary, noting the part it played in alerting him to the missing treasure. It was all the greatest fun, added to which were heady estimates of the amount of the treasure trove they would receive for its discovery. Even Joseph would have a small share, and he bought a new tweed jacket in anticipation of this sudden good fortune.

Eventually, Luke's responsibilities as headmaster necessitated his return to Melbury. It was agreed that they would get married on Boxing Day. Francesca had to remain in Cornwall to organise Boscannon's letting. Before Luke left she asked why he had been so confident that she would accept his proposal of marriage. Luke prevaricated, but she pressed him to tell her. He shyly told her of his dream and how it resolved his future, in that he knew he was meant to marry her.

Francesca had looked at him quizzically. 'You think it's all a dream?' This remark had exercised his mind all the way from Cornwall to Melbury.

Chapter Twenty-three

The imminent celebrations of the granting of the charter to Melbury College and Abbey 500 years before were exercising the college and cathedral clergy and staff. Rehearsals seemed non-stop for the carol service in the cathedral, and a theatrical celebration telling the history of Melbury and the college, but Luke was most involved in liaisons with Buckingham Palace to agree the details of the Queen's itinerary; what speeches to be made; the fanfares to be trumpeted and the presentation of one of the Melbury chalices: all these had to be timed and calculated. Luke was allotted ten minutes to thank the Royal Family for its support over the centuries. This speech was to be made in the Great Hall of the college.

At the end of the carol service, after he had given a short sermon, Luke was to make the presentation of de Witte's diary to the Queen. The sermon became the axis on which Luke's conscience revolved. How could he present the castrated diary to the Queen without reference to the final conclusion of de Witte's beliefs? He had confided his tortured mind to Francesca. He was daily drawn to conclude that after his marriage he should resign as headmaster, and with his young wife venture into the unknown of a ministry enjoyed by only a few others: become a married Catholic priest ready to go wherever he might be sent. With that conviction, how could he proceed with the royal ceremony? How could he continue to be headmaster, with the task of presenting the diary to the Queen. Perhaps he should plead sickness, or, more honestly, resign and ask his predecessor, Canon Frobisher, to present the journal. In its bowdlerised form it was more Canon Frobisher's creation than de Witte's. As the time drew near, Luke began to panic; nothing was resolved in his mind.

In the middle of this mental crisis he had a call one day

211

from Fr Charles, who announced he was in England and would like to come to see the school and the de Witte diary parchments and translations that gave the full story of his life. Luke had not spoken to Fr Charles since they had met in Valladolid, and a shyness and fear of ridicule had prevented him from admitting to anyone that he had invoked de Witte.

Fr Charles came to stay with Luke for the weekend. Francesca was living chastely with Charlotte and Alastair. Fr Charles had arrived in a hired car and on the Saturday afternoon said to Luke, 'I think you need a break. Come and meet one of my brethren, Fr Edward, at Brockhampton Abbey near Cheltenham – he tells me we are about one and a half hours away. Fr Edward is very interested in the English martyrs, so he is longing to hear the de Witte saga first-hand.'

On the way there, Luke had told Fr Charles of the possible miracle and his own spiritual crisis. Fr Charles stopped the car in a lay-by and got Luke to repeat slowly the experience he'd had and the recovery of Alastair's son. After that they drove in silence to Brockhampton Abbey, save for Fr Charles humming snatches of Italian popular songs. At the Abbey, Luke was introduced to Fr Edward. As they had tea in the guest house, Fr Charles got Luke to repeat the story of de Witte to his friend, Fr Edward. The Benedictine had listened intently, then said, 'This new evidence of de Witte's death is staggering. A new martyr from penal times is a remarkable historical happening. If we can find further evidence about him, his cause for beatification should be promoted. If you wished, we could take on the role of postulator and as such become responsible for drawing up the *posito* containing all the documents for judging de Witte's virtue and *fama sanctitas*. If it is accepted that de Witte died a martyr he will then be accepted as a saint. If not, in the next stages in the process, it is necessary to gather evidence of miracles – usually physical cures – in support of his cause. One is needed for beatification, a second for canonisation. Obviously we need further details of de Witte's life, and while we are gathering information I think we should keep the matter to ourselves. I cannot think it would be wise to add this dimension to your quincentenary celebrations, however convinced we are personally.'

Luke was grateful for Fr Edwards' discretion, but he could

see that Fr Charles was bursting with excitement and wanted to announce it immediately.

'I realise it may cause a problem, but I understand the diary has been censored in a most unscholarly way and I think the truth about de Witte's death should be told. It's a disgrace if the diary is published giving a false historical story. We could get an article in the *Tablet* first and then expand the tale in the national press – it might elicit further facts from other sources.'

Fr Edward smiled sympathetically at Charles. 'I know you feel passionately about de Witte because of your own work on the diary, and most understandably because your mother was descended from him, but I think you must be absolutely sure of all the facts.

Luke gasped. 'Charles, why did you not tell me of your family interest?'

Fr Charles smiled. 'I didn't want you to think my research was not detached historical investigation – and thus suspect.' He got up. 'I need a walk to clear my head before vespers.'

Luke said, 'Do you mind if I don't come. If Fr Edward can spare the time, I'd like to ask his advice.'

Both men nodded and when Fr Charles had left, Fr Edward stood up.

'Do you mind if I light my pipe, it aids my concentration. Please begin.'

'I don't know how much Charles has told you about me?'

Fr Edward chuckled. 'Enough – I have a fair idea of your position, but tell me your most pressing problems as you see them.'

Fr Edward sat down beside Luke in another chair and sending up spirals of pipe smoke, preparing himself to listen. He knew it made speaking of difficult problems easier if the listener was beside one instead of looking at the speaker face on.

Luke leant forward and looked at his hands resting in his lap. 'The problems are not being stated in order of importance. first, I am in love with a widow with whom, while still married, I had an intense and overwhelming relationship. I still do, and we are engaged to be married after Christmas. In every way we seem perfectly matched, but our sensuality is a strong and exquisite component, and illogically it makes me feel guilty, as

213

it has a quality that is ever present in my thoughts and distracts me from my spiritual orientation.'

Fr Edward tapped the tobacco into his pipe. 'It's not illogical, only an age-old conflict born of fear of the body and of losing control, but the answer I believe is to rejoice in it and see it as perhaps God's greatest gift to you – not many are so lucky. There is a Greek prayer where God is saying to his children at the end of their lives, "Why did you not enjoy to the full everything I gave you: food, beauty of the world and friends, family and my gifts of human loving, etc.", but centuries of negative thought leave their mark in our psyche.'

For a moment they sat silently as Luke paused before embarking on his next problem. His mind was full of thoughts of Francesca. Luke began to speak again, his uncertainty reflected in the hesitant way in which he started.

'I am a High Anglican and in my practice of prayers and saying the Mass lead a sacramental life outwardly identical to yours, but I've lost faith in the Church of England as a genuine Catholic part of the universal Church. I can no longer accept its belief system, and outwardly it's imploding under the stress of disputes over the ordination of women and about homosexual priests. I know you have the same problems, but we are dealing with ours in anarchic fashion. I mean recently we had the Archbishop of Rwanda and the Archbishop of Singapore ordain four Episcopal priests in America as bishops to counter what they see as heresy in the Western Church – the acceptance of women priests and homosexuality. There are countless examples of schism and scandal. It makes me feel I must become a Roman Catholic, but this means I cannot be headmaster of a leading Anglican school – and if I am to continue as a priest, can I honestly marry first, hoping to be accepted as an ex-Anglican with a wife, albeit a Roman Catholic one.

'I love my job, I'm good at it, and thus I believe I am exercising a benign influence. I adore my fiancée. To put it plainly, must I give her up and go forward as a celibate priest to exercise my talents in a less satisfactory or indeed comfortable existence? finally I have to preach on de Witte before the Queen and an assembled congregation that is going to pack the cathedral at Melbury. What should I say about de Witte,

214

about his martyrdom? Should I resign before it, issuing a statement as to why, or just remain silent.'

Fr Edward turned to look at Luke. 'The best thing I can do is promise you our prayers, and I shall approach our Benedictine sisters at nearby Stanbrook to pray as well, but as for definite advice, I cannot give it. In the old days it would have been easy. "The Church of Rome has all the truth. Join us and take up your cross if you wish to be a priest." Now I see the world of the Church as grey – no black and white. Our beloved Church is like a family full of stress, with some very black sheep. We, too, are divided by the same problems as the Anglican Church, but at the top we have not the same laissez-faire mindset – if you will excuse my categorising it as such – so our conflicts are more intense, and we fear schism. I suggest – I do not categorically say this is right – but I suggest you stay in your present admirable position in life. 'Rejoice in your headmastership, in your wife and family to be, and with your Catholic sympathies you can be an ecumenical bridge – many of us have terrible misconceptions about the Anglican Church and see it as an aberration springing from Henry VIII's marital problems, which took over all our historic churches.' Fr Edward chuckled and relit his pipe.

Luke looked at him. 'Actually, I had that advice from Fr Formby, rector of the college in Valladolid but, because I have the feeling I must follow the Way of the Cross, I am not sure I can accept it.'

Fr Edward knocked the tobacco out of his pipe as the large bell of the abbey rang for vespers. He stood up. 'I think you're talking nonsense. Come with me and let's start some serious praying. Then we will dine, and after join other guests for coffee.'

Luke was taken into the abbey and led by Fr Edward to a place behind the monks in their choir stalls. As vespers proceeded, Luke envied the monks' air of serenity, though he knew their lives also suffered from doubts and trials. Their singing seemed to reflect life from a divine perspective, and thus enabled him to embrace a future that was unknown, but supported by the enduring love of God.

Afterwards Fr Edward took him to dine in the abbey. Monastic dinners are eaten in silence, save for the reading of an edifying book. On this occasion it was a biography of Cardinal Newman. The excerpt dealt with the agony of his leaving the Church of England. It put salt on Luke's spiritual wounds.

Coffee afterwards was provided for guests in a panelled room. Comfortable chintz chairs were ranged in front of a log stove, from which aromatic smoke leaked from a corner. Fr Edward introduced Luke to another guest.

'This is Timothy Arden, a captain of industry. He supports us and teases us – a regular gadfly!'

Luke liked him immediately. His face was kind and had an amused expression, but he lived up to his description by teasing him about Anglican flying bishops, who were created to minister to priests whose Diocesan bishops ordained women, and who could not accept their authority.

Luke knew this position was absurd but deflected the attack by questioning the logic of having a critically ill Pope in the hands of warring Vatican cardinals.

They parted with good humour and were to meet again in the near future with Luke in the role of headmaster to one of Timothy's sons. A tale yet to be told, but the encounter started by Luke saying, 'You have an intelligent son – he will easily see the advantage of flying bishops in the Anglican Church.'

Chapter Twenty-four

By the morning of the quincentenary celebrations, Luke had received no sign from God in spite of hours of prayer and thought. Luke vacillated between his conflicting desire to stay in the Church of England and marry Francesca and his contrary pull towards becoming a celibate Roman Catholic priest.

Luke and his staff had gathered outside the cathedral to welcome the arrival of the Queen scheduled for midday. The people of Melbury and the members of the college were seated expectantly in the nave. Luke stood at the West Door with the provost and the lord lieutenant of the county. Anthony was standing some ten yards in front, ready to greet the Queen with a Latin invitation issued to previous royal visitors during the previous five centuries.

Luke was white with tension. He knew he had to say in his sermon that de Witte had died a Catholic martyr. He had decided the advice he had received in Valladolid, and from Fr Edward, was the easy way out: the truth had to be told. Should he also announce his own plan to become a Roman Catholic? It had become a psychological imperative.

As he waited, he felt a light tap on his right shoulder and turned in surprise to see Mr Jones, dressed in the full colours of his Welsh university gown. Mr Jones leant forward in a conspiratorial manner and whispered, 'On this great occasion I just wanted to thank you, Luke.'

Luke raised his eyebrows in amazement. Mr Jones moved nearer, so that their shoulders were touching, and continued. 'Yes, Mrs Jones told me all about your rescue when our car had broken down on the bypass last week. Saw her in a mess, went past her and came back, and stopped and sorted it all out. That's Christian for you. We may not praise the Lord in the same way, but I realise now we are in the same team. The world's one great mass of chaotic and broken-down traffic, and we've got to untangle it together. That's true, Luke, isn't it?' Luke felt a prickle of fear again. Was this another of de Witte's miracles, as disturbing in its own way as the recovery of Alastair's son? He suddenly felt a wave of affection for the difficult Mr Jones. Mr Jones continued whispering and nudged Luke in the kidneys. 'You do agree, don't you? Anyway, I want you to give the New Year's sermon at Emmanuel Church. I know the old Church of England is a batty family, but if you're born into it you have to support all the members. Can't leave your family. What do you say, Fr Luke? Will you do it? And for Christ's sake, don't forsake us, you're needed here.'

Luke nodded. He couldn't speak but realised he loved the Anglican Church – its liturgy and its ethos. He knew once again his future was unresolved, any radical decision postponed. He later explained his tears were because of the intense pain from the nudge to his kidneys.

Before Luke could answer Mr Jones, he was called forward to join a line of those dignitaries to be introduced to the Queen before she entered the cathedral.

Unexpectedly, the 'batty' qualities of the Church of England were to surface before the Queen arrived. A master of ceremonies from the Royal Household had arrived to place in order of precedence those who were to meet the Queen. first came the high sheriff of the county, resplendent in black breeches and silk stockings, and the usual elaborate ruffled shirt and black jacket, then next to him the Mayor of Melbury and then the ecclesiastical contingent. This party was led by the bishop, dressed in a purple cassock, followed by Fr Robert, robed as an abbot; a somewhat presumptuous attire based merely on the order's residence in the ancient Abbey of Melbury. He was clothed in a gold-and-white embroidered cope with a matching mitre on his head. Under the cope he wore a white cassock, under which his hot-water bottle was secured by a girdle around his substantial waist. To his right stood the dean and the four canons of the cathedral, and finally Luke and the provost representing the college. Anthony was to stand in front of the line to give his Latin greeting. The royal cortège was to stop on the road passing a hundred yards in front of the cathedral, where a platoon of the school cadet force would present arms as the Queen alighted from her car. The lord lieutenant of the county waited there to escort her to those lined up outside the West Door and to make the necessary introductions.

They were given warning of her arrival by the sound of cheers from the crowds lining the approach road. At that moment, the master of ceremonies decided the line-up was not quite central to the cathedral door and asked everyone in the line to take one step to the right. Before anyone could move a gust of wind caught Fr Robert's mitre, blowing it forward over his brow. He put up his hands to straighten it just as the bishop stepped one step sideways, knocking Fr Robert off balance and causing him to fall against the dean. Seen from the front, the ecclesiastical part of the line looked like a row of staggering drunks as they bumped into each other.

When Fr Robert stood up, he found his girdle had loosened and his hot-water bottle had fallen to his feet. 'Sodom and Gomorrah,' he muttered.

The royal car was by now arriving in front of the cathedral. The Bishop hissed, 'For God's sake, move, Robert.'

The master of ceremonies was waving at them to get in their right place. Fr Robert shrugged his shoulders and moved. For a brief moment a teddy bear-shaped hot-water bottle gazed up at the front of the cathedral, before its face was covered by a size-11 shoe belonging to the bishop. The cheerful grin on its face disintegrated under the pressure of fourteen stones, and it gave up the ghost with a slight plop, followed by a sigh of escaping air and hot water.

The bishop felt its softness as his right foot crushed the teddy bear's face, but could not see what it was as it was covered by his cassock. He looked down and saw to his horror a gathering pool of steaming hot water. He looked up as he heard the command 'Present arms' being barked out and saw the royal party approaching with the lord lieutenant leading the way to make the introductions. Gingerly he raised the front of his cassock to see what he had stepped on. He looked, broke out into an uncontrollable sweat, and swayed slightly. He thought he was going to faint. Dimly he heard a flourish of trumpets followed by the Latin greeting, to which the Queen crisply gave the traditional reply, 'Placet'.

The bishop moved forward to cover the puddle, but the

mayor yanked him back into line just as the royal party were being introduced to the high sheriff. An onlooker would have detected a shaking of the shoulders of the exotically robed Fr Robert.

The royal party then moved down the line. The Queen, unaware of the problem, gave the bishop a sharp look. After the last Lambeth Conference of Bishops in London, the Palace had let it be known that purple was the royal colour and that it disapproved of the vast hoard of purple-robed attendants at Lambeth.

The bishop trembled as she passed him by with a curt nod. He heard the Queen saying to Fr Robert, 'And which is your diocese?'

A few minutes later, the royal party entered the cathedral. The bishop was rooted to the spot, but realised he was being laughed at by Fr Robert and the dean, both of whom were creased up with laughter. The others in the line realised something had gone wrong, but were totally unprepared to see the bishop bend down and throw the collapsed hot-water bottle at Fr Robert. It missed. A lucky photographer caught this act and the picture was published in the local press under the heading, 'Bishop loses his bottle!'

The other members in the line-up had no time for speculation and had to follow the Queen into the cathedral. The Queen and the Duke of Edinburgh were led in procession to the front of the cathedral. The bishop caught up with Fr Robert, kicked his ankle hard and hissed, 'You stupid Beelzebub!'

Further insults were stifled by the start of the service. Before the recessional hymn, Luke was to give his sermon. As he mounted the pulpit, he still had the problem of whether or not to tell the truth about de Witte and his martyrdom. He was silent for a good minute as he faced the congregation in the packed cathedral. The congregation was utterly still, as if sensing some dramatic revelation. Luke's hands gripped the elaborate carved top of the pulpit. He began his sermon by addressing the Queen reverently as Her Gracious Majesty, Supreme Governor of the Church of England, and then spoke of Bishop de Witte, who had been an example of that gentleness of spirit that had always characterised many leaders of the Church of England. He paused for a moment.

'There is more to be revealed about de Witte.' His voice faltered. He caught sight of Canon Frobisher sitting behind the Queen, and saw that he was frowning. The rest of the congregation were fully attentive to his words. Luke was about to speak of de Witte's martyrdom and then, sitting in front of a pillar in a side aisle, he caught sight of Fr Edward, shaking his head slowly. Again Luke lost his nerve and he went on lamely, 'There is more to be revealed about de Witte through further historical research. He was an important figure in his time and very possibly a saint. Today we are fortunate to live in a time when divisions in the Christian Church are fading and we are worshipping together. We are about to instigate sharing evensong in our cathedral, what they call "vespers" in the Catholic Church and "evening services" in other Nonconformist churches. Such united worship will take place once a month. Already this has proved a great bond between Christians where it has taken place. We must fight together the common threat of indifference, spiritual chaos and despair that is gripping the Western world.'

As he stepped down from the pulpit an extraordinary thing happened. Mr Jones and the local Catholic priest stood up and started to clap, followed by the whole congregation. Luke caught sight of Francesca in a delicious mink hat, with tears streaming down her face. It was the happiest and proudest moment of his life. He stood still at the bottom of the pulpit for a moment and then gestured to the choirmaster. With one voice, the cathedral congregation began to sing in thanksgiving as the organ struck up the hymn, 'Now thank we all our God with hearts and hands and voices...'